THE BIG LIE

ALSO BY JULIE MAYHEW
Red Ink

THE BIG LIE

JULIE MAYHEW

CANDLEWICK PRESS

Copyright © 2015 by Julie Mayhew

First U.S. edition 2017

Library of Congress Catalog Card Number pending
ISBN 978-0-7636-9125-7

17 18 19 20 21 22 BVG 10 9 8 7 6 5 4 3 2 1

Printed in Berryville, VA, U.S.A.

This book was typeset in Berling.

Candlewick Press
99 Dover Street
Somerville, Massachusetts 02144

visit us at www.candlewick.com

To Alicia

It was no excuse to be young.
—Traudl Junge

eins

AUGUST 2014

I am a good girl. It is my most defining feature. And that's the truth.

If you'd asked anyone on Lincoln Drive or at the elite school, they'd have told you. *Jessika Keller? Oh, she is a superior girl, upstanding, immaculate.* Then they would have told you how good I was at ice skating, but that's a whole different kind of "good." To land an axel jump you have to transform yourself, become all steely eyed and mad headed and fuck you and . . .

Now you're questioning the whole good girl thing, aren't you?

Because I used a swear word. Because that's what you people do, I'm told. You question EVERYTHING. Just because you can. Because it's right there in the laws of your land. But is there nothing you'd greet with a simple *Yeah, okay, fine?* What if the love of your friends depended upon it? The love of your family?

Would you tell a lie? People who are good don't lie, but a good person might, quite reasonably, leave out something that they didn't realize was really very crucial to everyone else. That isn't a lie. But it can be as bad as telling a lie, I have come to understand.

Anyway, forget the swearing — it means nothing. I said that I was good. I never said that I was soft and sweet; there's a very big distinction.

Let's rephrase. I always did the right thing, didn't consider the alternatives. Before Clementine, I didn't realize there were any other alternatives. I swear on Wolf's life — not something I do lightly, because Wolf is one ancient and arthritic dog and he doesn't need any of my empty promises helping him along. At least, he was about to die the last time I saw him. Maybe he's gone and done it while I've been away.

I know how this should continue. You have questions, and I must answer them. So I suppose I should let you know: when it comes to answering questions, I'm also very good at that.

AUGUST 2013

Straight after it happened, I was taken into a small meeting room along one of the marble-floored corridors at the grand hotel on Trafalgar Square—the hotel we'd been using as a base. The room was carpeted, air-conditioned, air-freshened; out in the lobby it was hot, the atmosphere crackling with static. The boys were starting to smell ripe and muddy. The girls stank too—sour, like fish. We were inside a terrifying balloon—that's what it felt like—a balloon positioned beneath someone's foot.

The meeting room wasn't big enough for all three of us—me, Fisher, and the man I was surprised to see waiting in there already. A tall man—broad, really, really large, and . . .

Okay, he was fat.

There. I've thought it and now I've said it. He was fat—an enormous, pregnant Hausfrau of a man. Herr Five-Sausages-and-All-the-Chips!

That's how you do it, isn't it? You let the thought fly into your mind and then fly right out again, via your mouth. Crazy. Before, I would never even have noticed that he was fat. Or if I had, just for one minute, I would have immediately decided that I was wrong.

The fat man was wearing a beige raincoat, even though it was August. There was a huge brown sweat patch beneath his arm when he saluted, the edges of it salty and white. I wasn't introduced to him by name. He was something to do with the HJ, I told myself; someone we hadn't come across yet since the Great Integration. We knew all the boys in the Kameradschaft, the local colony of HJ boys that had joined our Mädelschaft, our fellowship of girls in the Bund Deutscher Mädel. We knew them from the next-door elite school and from around the neighborhood. And we knew one of the HJ leaders, a short, mustached man called Dirk who was forever picking his shorts out of his small, flat bottom.

And we knew Fisher.

Fisher smiled, put his hand gently in the middle of my back, and guided me toward the table. This was reassuring but startling, because they weren't allowed to touch us. It wasn't proper. Spoiled the milk. Our BDM leader, Fräulein Eberhardt, her hair always piled up like a squashed plum pudding, never touched us. Even if we were sobbing. Not that I would ever have let Fräulein Eberhardt see me sobbing. Maybe if one of us had blood gushing from a severed artery she would have made some sort of physical contact. (*Apply direct pressure to the wound with fingers or a cloth until a sterile dressing becomes available.*) Though I would have done my very best to hide that kind of weakness from Fräulein Eberhardt too.

I sat down. The fat man stared, giving me no clues about the way he felt. Maybe he was lost in thought, dreaming of big, greasy sausages, oozing with gravy, swimming in Fritten . . .

Fisher sat down opposite me. He looked me in the eye.

That was the thing about Fisher—his eyes. I know this

4

isn't something you normally ever notice about a person. If I asked you the color of your best friend's eyes, you'd really have to think about it. (Clementine's? Green. I think.) But with Fisher you couldn't not notice. He put his eyes on you and—*kaboom!*—there they were, bright blue, like colored glass, spokes of navy fireworking through them.

Angelika Baker always believed that I had a crush on Fisher, right from the start. She based this assumption solely on the fact that I had gotten used to the relaxation of our leaders' titles while the others had not. They insisted on calling Fisher *Herr Fisher* when he had expressly told them that the Great Integration called for less formality. I challenged Angelika on this piece of shoddy evidence when the rumors began, and she said it wasn't WHAT I called him but HOW I said it. She claimed that when I spoke to him my voice went "all frothy."

I wouldn't even know how to be frothy. Angelika understood nothing.

"Fräulein Keller, we commend your quick actions at the concert today."

"Thank you, Fisher," I replied, gulping back my relief. There was no wobble in my voice, though, no teardrop on my cheek. I was very proud of myself. Proud of us both, in fact, for putting on this polished performance. I snatched a glance at the fat man to see if he too was thankful for what I'd done. His face gave me nothing.

"And what do you think happened?" This was Fisher's next question.

I began to shake.

"In your own time, Fräulein Keller."

5

I cleared my throat, straightened my back, looked into Fisher's freaky hypno-eyes. The fat man shifted against the wall to make clear my answer was going to be very, *very* important. He nudged the portrait of Herr Dean into a wonky angle.

"What happened was," I began, "that the mixture of polyester and cotton in our uniforms proved to be a volatile combination in the circumstances."

Silence.

Both men wanted more.

"And that's because," I went on, knowing I must try my hardest to whack this ball out of the field, "manmade fibers burn faster than natural fibers, but a combination of the two can be the greater hazard."

My last sentence was word for word what Fisher had taught us from the official papers. It was a reply worthy of a round of applause. I watched Fisher and the man exchange a brief look, a tiny gesture that contained within it all the things in the world I did not know.

What I wouldn't have given to be back in the hotel lobby, with my smelly friends, being drilled on how to manage crowds and break up fights and apply pressure to an open wound until a suitable dressing becomes available. What I wouldn't have given to have taken hold of the hand GG had offered me earlier as comfort. It could have been my last chance.

Fisher put his elbows onto the table and leaned in.

"No, Fräulein Keller," he said calmly. "I mean what do you think about what happened?"

The emphasis was on the words *you* and *think*. Which was unheard of. Terrifying.

"I'm not in any trouble, am I?" I blurted. The word had been flying around above us. *Trouble.* But it was so stupid of me to bring that bird down, lay it on the table. I wanted to shrink to the size of my little sister, Lilli, so I could climb inside the gigantic green vase sitting in the corner. I am the sort of person who does not get into trouble. Just like I am the sort of person who does not lie. Though in recounting this to you, I realize I have already told you a lie. Or at least I have left out something that you might think is really quite crucial: I didn't need to be introduced to the fat man because I knew who he was already.

"No. Fräulein Keller," Fisher went on, "you're not in any trouble. Whatever you say to us is in complete confidence."

And it was only then that I noticed he wasn't calling me Jessika. Or Jess. Or Jessie.

Not, mein kleiner süßer Singvogel. My sweet little Jay-Jay.

I looked at the fat man again. I wanted a clue, just the smallest indication of what I was supposed to say. Because I would say it, I realized, if it would make everything okay.

"Could you repeat the question, please?"

"I want to know what your thoughts are on the incident," Fisher said. "Tell me what you think Fräulein Hart was trying to do."

"My thoughts?" Emphasis on both words. Such a bizarre combination.

"Yes, Fräulein Keller, why did Fräulein Hart do what she did?"

Of course I knew what I was NOT supposed to say — that Fräulein Hart felt this country had been stolen, invaded, way back even before she was born, and that all she was trying to do, in her own extreme, and perhaps misguided, style, was to win it back.

I knew I mustn't say that.

7

2002

So where did it all begin? That's your first, obvious question.

2002. When I was seven. The year I was given Clementine. My new best friend.

This was also the year I was given a little sister, though she arrived with much less fanfare. All of a sudden there was Lilli, crying and stinking and hanging off Mum's apron strap like an overgrown tick. I was far too busy trying to understand exactly where babies came from to even begin to appreciate Lilli's fine qualities.

My big sister, Katrin, meanwhile, was eleven and destined NEVER to recognize my fine qualities. She was too busy trying to prove she was better than me. Bigger, brighter, better. She did this to avoid facing up to the real objects of her fury — our parents. How DARE they bring another child into the world after creating the wondrous and flawless creation that is Katrin Eva Keller! I was nothing but evidence of our parents' betrayal, and I had to be destroyed.

Katrin's means of doing this . . . ? Athletics.

By the age of seven, I had been made to stand in the rain and watch her be better than me FAR too many times to count.

Perhaps she was also trying to kill me slowly with boredom. Off she would go, body scissoring, muscles rippling, her mouth snarling, a perfectly enjoyable hundred-meter sprint turned into a jerky, vomity display of frustration by having all those hurdles in the way. The mental fuel powering Katrin over the finish line—I am absolutely sure of this—was the same words over and over again: *Jess must die! Jess must die!* I didn't care. Better that she tried to outdo me by murdering those hurdles than take me down to the bottom of the garden and shove me into the fast-flowing river beyond the tree swing. But without Katrin as a friend, I admit, I was lost for company. It's hard to be a leader when there is no one there to lead, to be a hero with no one there to do the worshipping. I was desperate to start school and enlist some troops.

So on that day when I helped Dad fix his motorbike in the garage (holding the wrenches, passing him rags, depositing drips of oil where directed—all done under a cloud of gloom, his and mine, because I wasn't really enjoying myself and because he was only enduring my clumsy efforts in the name of my mechanical education), my face lit up when he said, "Good news, Jessie, we have new neighbors moving in soon."

I had been sad when the Andersons and their five sons had gone. Not because I played with the boys—they were all older than me—but when they left, the house next door went from being warm and flowering to wide-eyed and silent overnight. It was spooky.

Then Dad said, "This new family, they have a little girl exactly the same age as you."

More firework celebrations across my face.

"And she is called Clementine."

I tried out the shape of this strange name.

Cle-men-tine.

"Like the fruit?" I asked.

"Yes," said Dad. "Like the fruit."

I immediately dropped my wrenches and headed for the front lawn next door to wait for her. I waited until sunset. Nothing.

Mum wandered over, carrying a sore-faced Lilli.

"What are you doing, Jessa, sweetheart?" she asked.

Lilli glared at me because she, in return, had not yet come to appreciate my fine qualities as a big sister.

"I'm waiting for my new friend," I told her.

I had made a daisy chain that could loop around my neck four times over, a matching bracelet, a headdress, an anklet for each leg . . . I was running out of ideas. I looked up at Mum. I was a flower queen with no parade to attend.

"Oh, lovey." Mum was laugh-talking. "They're not coming until Friday."

I hated this laugh-talking. I wasn't being cute for her benefit.

"Dad said they'd be here *soon*," I corrected.

"Friday *is* soon," she said, smirking, and turned back to the house. Lilli twisted her neck to keep her eyes locked on me. Her head was a blond fuzz back then. And it stayed blond. Both me and Katrin went dark like Mum and Dad as soon as we turned three.

I tried to fathom how "five days away" could equal "soon" in anyone's imagination. I didn't understand then how things appear smaller as you become bigger—objects, rooms, time. Not fears, though. Oddly, they only seem to grow.

I stuck my tongue out at Lilli and, for the first time, I made her smile.

When the Hart family finally arrived, stepping from the back of a large black car, blinking like tortoises waking from hibernation, I was at once on the pavement grabbing Clementine's hand. I expected to welcome a small, round, orange child, perhaps even one of those deranged redheads you only ever hear about in fairy tales, but instead she was a white-haired will-o'-the-wisp in a pale lace dress. She was a ghost girl. I pulled her away from her parents, off into our back garden to throw balls for Wolf.

To begin with she was scared; Wolf's nose and eyes drew level with hers. But when he started galumphing up and down the garden, drooling and smiling, falling for our feigned throws, Clementine began to see that he was harmless. Soon she was giggling and throwing her arms around his neck. And mine. And it was then that I knew we were always, always going to be friends.

"Are you named after a fruit?" I asked her.

"No, silly," she said. "I'm named after a pretty lady."

And I thought she meant the one in the song. *Oh my darling, oh my darling, oh my darling Clementine . . .*

As for Herr und Frau Hart, they were different people at the start. They were polite, smiling, eager to please. They'd invite me to stay for dinner after school. They'd ask me about my skating and congratulate me on my promotions within the ranks of the BDM. I think they liked having another person at the table, to make up the numbers. Just one child—it was very sad. Frau Hart had a little boy after Clementine, Dad said, but it wasn't born right and had to be taken away. Frau Hart wasn't allowed to have any more children. I suppose that was why she went and got herself a job, and why no one gave her too much of a hard time about it. Mum always said that when I left for skate camp she would have another baby, "to fill the nest." To make sure she didn't have to pay off the last quarter of her marriage loan, more like. Or to hold back the moment when Dad moved on to start a new family.

I cannot picture Mum with a big fat belly.

My parents made the Harts feel welcome. They invited them to our regular neighborhood gatherings where we cooked food on the grill in the garden and set up a makeshift bar in the conservatory with a keg of beer, boxes of wine, and jugs of juice. The Harts were grateful. My father worked with Clementine's father. Dad had tipped off Herr Hart—the office's lowly telephone engineer—about the house coming onto the market. We lived in Buckinghamshire, on Lincoln Drive—in a desirable community of gated county roads. Houses changed hands even before the sign had gone up on the porch. The Administration occasionally moved underperforming families into vacant homes in the neighborhood, so they could see how life should be lived. Good behavior breeds good behavior. These subfamilies became like us—and very quickly too—so no one really ever knew who they were. The Harts were lucky to have slipped their way in, and to have snagged the house right next to us. We were Lincoln Drive's—or rather, the whole of the County Roads Estate's—most influential family.

12

The Harts were quiet to begin with, knew their place. At our gatherings, they positioned themselves at a table on the edge of the patio, looking down into their glasses. They always dressed well; they drank moderately. Soon they made friends. In fact, now that I think about it, they went through a transformation of sorts. Miraculous. Quick. Because one moment they were the people on the edge, and the next they were the people in the middle. Yet I can't quite remember how that happened. I suppose it was because they were unusual — different enough to be exciting, but enough like us to be accepted. They seemed younger than all the other parents, thinner and more urgent. Their lack of flesh was down to some kind of inner fire burning it all up. Herr Hart was born in Germany and had lived in Berlin for much of his life. He had the accent, so that made him particularly glamorous.

But still, I can't work it out, how we let them become so popular.

AUGUST 2012

At our final garden gathering of the summer, Herr und Frau Hart were at the peak of their popularity.

There they were, at our back gate, immediately smacking lips and cheeks with our guests, throwing a "Grüß dich!" and a "How are you?" to the folk who couldn't get close.

"Where's Clementine?" I asked Herr Hart, lucky to get a word in sideways. I was desperate to see her. The Harts had just gotten back from their annual holiday, and we had some serious catching up to do.

"She'll be over in a little while," he said, his accent making those *t*'s into delicious *d*'s—*a liddle while*. "She's just finishing some homework."

The Harts settled into a conversation with Herr und Frau Gross. The only thing they wanted to talk about that summer was Herr Dean. The Harts in particular (and perhaps all alone in our neighborhood) were terribly excited about his rise to power after the death of our beloved Herr Erlichmann. *Liberal* was a word they used for our new leader. *Nervous* was the word everyone else decided upon, trying not to make it sound too negative for fear of being reported.

"He seems to stand for broad-mindedness," Herr Hart said.

"Well, as much as a man can. Within the current . . . framework," added Frau Hart, thinking her popularity made her immune to being reported.

Perhaps this was what precipitated the Harts' downfall—their rattling on about politics. Nobody was interested. What in the world did it have to do with us? They even began doing it over the dinner table when I ate at their house. Or at least Frau Hart did. *Don't you think our leaders should be more like this and not do that? What if we changed this law and that law?* As if this was somehow within their control or, more specifically, mine. Frau Hart would push me into a corner with her questions, spearing the air with her fork, while Clementine tried to hide her grin. Eventually Herr Hart would give her a look and a sharp little "Jocelyn!," indicating that he too had had enough of her babbling.

"It's high time there was more integration, don't you think, Peter? Equality, if you like, Helen." This was what Frau Hart was saying to Herr und Frau Gross that August afternoon. "I really applaud Herr Dean for that." She was talking about the restructuring of the HJ and the BDM. "I mean, girls and boys are not different species!"

Herr und Frau Gross were slowly nodding, their old faces confused, too embarrassed to tell Frau Hart that she was talking claptrap, that of course boys and girls were put on this earth for entirely different reasons. She was intimidating, though, Clementine's mum, with her big hair and her bright clothes and her fondness for touching other people's arms. Intimidating also because everyone thought Herr Hart was my father's very best friend.

15

"But mainly we're just so relieved it's no longer compulsory, aren't we, Simon?"

Herr Hart closed his eyes in one slow, deliberate, emphatic nod, happy for his wife to be their mouthpiece.

"Clementine is an artist, not a soldier!" Frau Hart exclaimed. "It was just so ridiculous that she was being made to march in line and shoot to kill."

I nearly spat out my orange juice.

Clementine? An artist? I was thinking. *She's utterly hopeless at drawing.*

But also the Harts had been terribly excited when Herr Erlichmann — when he was still in power before his very sad death — had introduced more military pursuits into the BDM, alongside all of our usual housekeeping tasks. (We still had to do those. The same amount. Our sessions were simply extended so we could fit it all in. I preferred it when we knew what girls were for. Because how were we supposed to do it all, to the same standards as the boys, when they didn't conversely have to worry about perfecting their crocheting or learning how to do laundry?) But now all this marching and shooting wasn't good enough for Frau Hart? What on earth did she actually want?

The way the Harts had made their entrance that afternoon had not escaped the attention of my mother — how they'd gone through a showy display of greeting everyone, then stepped straight up onto their soapbox in praise of Herr Dean without expressing the proper amount of grief for the death of Herr Erlichmann. How they'd not bothered to say hello to their hosts. How they'd just abandoned their gift of cherry wine on a nearby table.

16

Mum made her way to our side of the patio and thrust a platter of her famous mushroom pastry parcels into the middle of the Harts' conversation.

"Hi, Jocelyn," Mum said, all smiles. A turn of the head and then, "Hi, Simon."

It was nothing really, but, oh, the steel fist! All conversations stopped. Mum looked from Frau Hart to Herr Hart, waiting for a greeting in return, waiting for them to take her food.

"Guten Tag, Miriam," said Frau Hart.

"Guten Tag, Miriam," said Herr Hart.

They picked up a mushroom pastry parcel each. Mum watched, waiting for them to take a bite. Everyone watched, waiting for them to take a bite. And once they had, still we waited.

"Mmm," said Frau Hart, eventually understanding what was expected of her.

Those mushroom pastry parcels were renowned among the residents of County Roads Estate. Mum was generous with the recipe, but no one could get them to come out exactly like hers. I think this was because when Mum copied out the ingredients, she always left out something small but really quite crucial.

"Yum! Das ist lecker, Miriam!" said Herr Hart.

Mum nodded, satisfied. Then she went on her way.

Sometimes, when I think back to that moment, I hear my mother whispering, "Be careful" at the Harts as she headed off, but I wonder if I have added that in afterward from my own imagination. Still, I had much to learn from my mother. A steady flow of little knocks and taps—that is how you make a person know who's in charge. Softly, softly catchee monkey.

When Clementine finally arrived at the garden party ("How was your homework?" I asked. "Wasn't doing any," she said), we shook off Ruby Heigl and Erica Warner at the juice table and disappeared down to the end of the garden. We didn't feel too old to climb up onto the log swing tied to the tallest elm, so we took turns, kicking off in the dust, hanging backward, watching the clouds slide behind the branches, letting our hair collect leaves from the garden floor.

That summer, Clementine was also at her peak. She had all of a sudden grown up—a ghost girl no more. I began to feel something very strongly for her. Envy. That's what I thought it was.

I watched as she threw herself back on the swing, her T-shirt riding up, her flat, white belly exposed to the air. She stuck one pointed bare foot out to get more height. She made these little grunts of effort that stirred something strange inside me.

I was devastated that Clementine wasn't going to be at the BDM meetings anymore. If it was no longer compulsory, she wouldn't go. I knew that. She wouldn't be there on the camping trips, the hostel evenings, the rallies at Crystal Palace—all those moments in life when you feel the world is so good your heart might burst, she wouldn't be there. . . . And I couldn't talk to her about it, mostly because Clem was now as outspoken as her mother. She would want to tell me how happy she was to be free of it all. I couldn't bear that. So I let her babble away about other things. I loved to listen. Her voice had grown up too. She drawled a little, like she was half-asleep, but with an end-of-sentence lilt that grabbed you by the collar and pulled you close.

"Soooo, they take this banana, right," she was saying. We were lying in the grass now, in the shade of the elm, the sound of the river washing away the chatter of the party. She was telling me about something she'd eaten while she'd been away on holiday. "And they cut it down the middle . . ."

She began to speak more quietly, so I had to tip my head toward her.

"Then they put chocolate pieces in the gap . . ."

And then what? You couldn't help yourself. It was her voice. *And then what?*

"And then they put it on the grill . . ."

Her eyes went wide, but her voice was still tired.

"And it went all, you know . . ."

No, I don't know. What?

Her voice lowered. "It went all gooey inside . . . but . . ."

She held me there for a minute.

"But it tasted *delicious.*"

No one else could talk about a grilled banana like that.

I rolled forward and without deciding or meaning to, I kissed her on the mouth. It just felt like the most obvious thing to do. Clementine laughed. It bubbled out beneath my lips. She put a hand to my head and shoved me away. It was a playful move, but there I was, feeling devastated all over again.

"What was that?" she cried. She was giggling, but beneath it all, I could hear it—she was sort of appalled.

"I don't know," I said.

I didn't. I only knew how it had felt.

She stopped her laughter, noticing that I wasn't joining in. Her eyes were on me, her green stare. (Her eyes were—are—

19

definitely green.) "Oh, it doesn't matter, Jess," she said. "Seriously, it doesn't but . . . we're friends, yeah?"

It didn't feel like she was saying anything to contradict me. "Best friends," I managed.

"Yes, best friends." She took my hand and squeezed it. "But nothing more."

I was finding it hard to breathe.

I had to say something. *Sorry*, maybe. Or *I promise it will never ever happen again*. Or *Please don't tell anyone*. Instead I said, "So where was it you went on holiday?"

My voice was horribly high, so clumsy and fake compared to her effortless drawl.

"America," she replied, not missing a beat. She was looking at me strangely now, differently. She wasn't appalled; I'd gotten that wrong. She had her eye on something; not me exactly, but something in me.

"Oh," I said, not really registering her answer, distracted by her stare. Then, "What?"

"Joke!" She started tearing the yellow heads from a stalk of cudweed.

I laughed. "Like you'd want to go to America! Wander around enemy territory!"

"We holidayed in the Greater German Reich," she said, putting on that voice we use when learning things by rote in school. "We went to Cornwall. I already told you."

Of course, I did want to ask how she had come to lay her hands on a banana—in *Cornwall* of all the unlikely places— but I didn't. Because something was out of joint. Not the kiss. Something else. At the time, I couldn't have said what it was, or even if there was truly anything at all. It just felt like I had been nudged in my sleep, but instead of waking up, I had incorporated the nudge into my dream.

So I said, "Tell me about the place where you used to live, before."

"I can't really remember it," she replied.

This was a conversation we ran through all the time. Always the same words. It was a joke, sort of. A distraction, maybe. Perhaps it was how we reassured one another that everything was good.

"I bet it wasn't as nice as here, was it?"

"No," she replied. "Nowhere near as nice as here."

Sometimes we'd say these lines to each other in a jumbled Mischmasch of our languages. But when I really needed a guarantee, I began the conversation in German. Because I did always wonder if I had been fooled by her white-blond hair and her so-pale skin and her marvelous way of talking. Perhaps she had been softly, softly knocking and tapping at me all these years. Perhaps she wasn't really my friend.

"Erzähl mir von dem Ort, an dem du vorher gewohnt hast," I said to her that day in August. *Tell me about the place where you used to live, before.*

"Ich kann mich kaum erinnern," she replied.

"Es war bestimmt nicht so schön wie hier oder?"

"Nein, überhaupt nicht so schön wie hier."

No, nowhere near as nice as here.

The answers were the same. And this was proof, I decided.

Because sometimes you have to decide what you're going to believe in and then stick to it, otherwise you can drive yourself mad thinking about all the possibilities.

SEPTEMBER 2012

I trained every morning before school.

Skates on and ready at 6 a.m. Always. Right from when I was seven years old. I liked it like that. Dani Hannah could take the 7:30 a.m. slot if she wanted, if the lazy cow was really that desperate to sleep in.

I liked the emptiness and the echo, the proper coldness before our bodies had warmed up the place, the fog rising toward the Party flags hanging from the rafters. I liked being the first one on the ice — the first to make a mark. It was how they used to judge you, on how neatly you drew your figures. It's where the sport gets its name. It was all about surface. Once upon a time.

Now there are jumps and spins and being daring and being brave. I had begun to prepare my free skate for the World Championships the following year. ("Not the *World* Championships," said Clementine's voice in my head. "Only the championships in this little world.") They needed to see my rhythm, my musicality, my strength. Coach Ingrid believed that none of this was possible without one special ingredient — emotion.

"Pretend like you're in love," she said to me.

"I am!" I told Ingrid. "I am!"

"Then we need to see it," she yelled. "Show that desire in the layback. Make that lutz a declaration!"

Ingrid was very small and delicate — black hair, always in a ponytail, thick bangs that made her eyebrows seem impossible and drawn on. She looked like a pixie, but her instruction was fierce. If she was feeling especially passionate, she'd dish it out in German. Ingrid didn't hit me, though. I sometimes wished that she would. That was how you got better. Dani Hannah was forever getting a slap from Coach Dorothea and her upright spins were so fast and smart they made me want to cry.

"That's only because of the way her hips are built," Ingrid told me.

My problem was that I enjoyed it too much. I still got a thrill from the simplest moves, a step from forward to backward, the neatness of a 3 turn, the wind on your skin as you built up speed, ready to fly. You weren't supposed to enjoy it if you wanted to get better. You were supposed to take it seriously.

"Show me your heart!" Ingrid called above Bruckner's *Fantasie*. "Zeig mir dein Herz!" So I pushed my chest out — and lost the camel spin, tipping forward, down onto my hands and knees. I became an ACTUAL camel on ice. There was a clunk from the speakers as Ingrid stopped the music. Her skates crunched into view under my nose. I got a faceful of ice shavings. If Ingrid had been Dorothea, she'd have given me a jab in the belly with her toe pick right there. I'd have felt her blade nip across the end of one of my fingers — just a little scar, reminding me never to do it again.

I think Ingrid was the way she was—too soft—because she had also competed when she was young. Coach Dorothea had only ever taught. Ingrid kept putting herself in my skates, and that made her feel maudlin. She'd won so many medals, but dislocated her knee very badly when she was nineteen in a display at one of the Party's Grand Exhibitions. She couldn't land the big jumps anymore. She was told to give up competition and teach. I asked her once if she was sad about this, that she could no longer perform for her country.

"Well, they could have taken me out back and shot me like a lame horse," she said with a sigh. "Can't complain."

Ingrid said things like that all the time, and when she did, there would be an awkward few moments where I didn't realize that she was making a joke.

She helped me back up onto my feet—a wet, clumsy camel.

"I didn't mean show me your heart literally, Fräulein Keller," she said. "Thrusting your ribs out like that will only lead to you breaking one of them. Come on, you know better."

"Sorry," I said.

"I meant for you to show me love."

"Oh," I said.

"Look."

And she took off, building speed, picking up from the spread eagles, throwing her arms up to the heavens, then wide. *I love you, I love you, I love you*, said her arms, *and I don't care who knows!* More speed, a right foot glide, a jump to the left and—into the camel spin. *I love you, I love you, I love you so much.* Her spine curved, melted backward. Then she let herself dissolve into a broken leg spin. This wasn't part of my routine: she was just showing off. Her arms tangled above her, then covered her face. She spiraled down toward the ice. It was as if her knee had never been mangled at all.

When Ingrid came back to join me, she took my gloved hands in hers and slid us together, toe-to-toe.

"Tell me who it is you are in love with," she whispered.

And this is exactly what I was talking about. She should have been taking off one of her leather gloves and cuffing me across the jaw with it to make me see sense.

"I love my country, and the Führer," I told her, like I was supposed to.

She winced at the echo that my voice sent around the arena. "Of course you do." She worked the ends of my gloved fingers between hers for a moment. "What I mean is," she went on, "is there a real person that you . . ."

"The Führer is a real . . ."

"Is there someone you might want to kiss?"

"No," I said. "There's no one."

"Oh, come on!"

"There isn't!"

"When I asked you before to pretend that you were in love, you said, 'I am.'"

"I meant, 'I am pretending.'"

"Oh." A moment's thought. Then Ingrid said, "It is a wonderful thing, to be in love." Her voice sounded the absolute opposite of wonderful — suicidal, even. She studied my face and I studied hers — this woman I had spent every morning with for the last ten years.

I freed my hands. I was getting cold standing still. I wanted to keep supple, get a decent sketch through of the whole piece before I had to leave for school. When I went away to skate camp next year, I wouldn't need to stop at 7:30 a.m. I would have the world's best coaches drilling me all day. (Clementine's voice: "How do you know they're the *world's* best coaches?")

"Oh, come on," Ingrid said again, playful now. "Your head has been so fuzzy lately, there must be someone."

"There isn't!" I could feel my face getting hot.

"Ha!" she cried, pointing to the redness that must have come to the surface. I clamped my hands on my ears and my forearms across my cheeks. "Ha!" she cried again. "You cannot lie to Ingrid!"

Then she pushed off toward the barriers before I had a chance to argue back. She reached over to hit PLAY on the music system.

"Now, you have your lover in your head . . ." she called out. I stood alone in the middle of the rink. "Dann zeig mir dein Herz!" she called, making a fist at her chest. "Zeig mir deine Liebe!" The fist went up in the air.

I found my starting position during the low piano section at the beginning of the *Fantasie* and then, when those first high, hopeful notes started up, I opened like a flower.

Ingrid said it was the best I had ever skated.

OCTOBER 2012

You might say that Clementine's mum was good-looking.

You might. I wouldn't.

She was very thin. So thin that you could see the sinewy workings of her arms and the clavicles around her neck. Which I believe you think is something to be celebrated. Well done, Jocelyn Hart, for not eating enough of our land's plentiful produce to be the most robust version of yourself that you could be.

Frau Hart had a job. She used to work for the *Evening News*. Clementine told me that she was a journalist, but when I mentioned this to Dad, he smirked and repeated my word *journalist* back at me like it was the stupidest thing ever to have fallen out of his mouth. We were in the back garden, pinning up the honeysuckle after putting in the new fences.

"She does a bit of typing," Dad said under his breath before firing up the drill to drive a screw into the panel, "and that is all."

I was standing with my spine against the main branch of the honeysuckle bush, arms out, holding the bulk of it back against the fence. The sugary smell of it was around my neck. Typing was still an impressive job, though, I thought—but I didn't say this to Dad. I would have killed to have had access to one of those machines all day, feel the *click-clack* of it beneath my fingers. It was one of my favorite activities at the BDM—typing practice. Fräulein Eberhardt would unlock the cupboard, and we would queue up to lift out a typewriter each. I loved the weight of the things. I loved the oily shine of the keys and how they fitted the curve of your fingertips so precisely. We had electric ones, but the manuals were my favorite, because you have to strike them hard like a piano.

The honeysuckle was heavy against my back, years and years of gnarled branches twisting together.

"Just a little longer, my strong girl," Dad said. "Hold your ground."

I widened my stance in the flower bed, careful not to squash the last bright heads of Mum's echinacea. Dad went back to his toolbox on the lawn and brought out a reel of wire. He wound one end tightly around the screw before uncoiling it against me. I was a prisoner of war being tied up by a ruthless Commie! (We were studying the *Endsieg* at school—the final days, when we beat back all those people for good.)

"Right, Jess, slip yourself out from under there."

I let my arms drop and the weight of the bush fall against this new support. I lifted the wire away from my chin as I went underneath it, thinking all the time of Mum cutting Tilsit cheese on the wooden board with the levered slicer.

Once I was free, Dad pulled the wire tight and fastened it to a second screw on the other side of the bush. I stood back to watch him work. Pale-blue shirt, thick black hair, a neat brown belt at his solid waist. The honeysuckle was drooping. There was too much of it now that the fences were lower. It needed hacking back. Over Dad's head, in the next-door garden, a last-minute wasp was bobbing around Frau Hart's washing line, drowsy and drunk. Her underwear were nowhere near as white as mine, Mum's, and Lilli's.

"Don't Herr und Frau Hart mind that we can see into their garden now?" I asked as Dad snipped the end of the wire and tucked away its sharp edge.

"Why would they?" he said, stepping back to assess the job. He patted me on the back. Now that Katrin was out of the picture, away at athletics camp, I was on my way to taking her throne. Biggest, brightest, best.

"I have no problem with them seeing into ours," said Dad, and he picked up the shears and started lopping.

A week or so later, Herr Hart planted mature leylandii along the length of the new fence, ten of the things. Enormous they were, almost two meters in height when they went in. Then, only a few days later, I woke one morning to find that these trees had been neatly beheaded to match the exact height of Dad's new fences. But that was Clementine's flaky parents for you, I decided, doing one thing one minute, and the opposite the next.

By comparison, my parents were solid.

Mum was efficient in all she did. Everything put away in the right place, dinner on the table at the exact time, the front step always swept, our underwear white as snow. Dad's efficiency was more of a mental exercise. We talked.

Of course Mum and I spoke, but about everyday things—who will pick Lilli up from school, what to pack in my trunk for when I go away to skate camp, period pains, how to manage them . . . Dad taught me how the world works, the difference between right and wrong. He was the neighborhood's barometer. Mine too.

Over breakfast he read things out from the *People's Mail*. Warnings. That was how I found out about the Jay Acker music cassettes turning up in our schools.

"It appears," my father told me, "that they have laced the cassettes with traces of radiation."

I stopped chewing my jam and bread. "But how can that be if it's our people smuggling them in?"

"Finish your mouthful!"

The unchewed crust scraped down my throat in one breathtaking lump. "Sorry, Dad."

"Excellent reasoning, Jessika!" He was smiling now. I gulped milk to shift the last of the bread. "But that is exactly what they want you to believe!"

"So . . . it's nothing to do with us?" I said slowly, trying to make the picture fit together in my mind.

Dad shook his head. "Nope!"

I allowed myself a small moment of pride, because I did always catch on very quickly to the things that Dad explained to me. Lilli was too young to understand, so without a son to talk to, Dad had to pass all his knowledge on to me.

"Don't get sucked in, Jess," he told me. "Not only will they corrupt your mind, they'll give you a deadly cancer in the bargain."

I was destined to be a great skater for my country, and then, after that, a great mother, so I often wondered if Dad felt his great knowledge was wasted on me.

"They just want us to be diseased," Dad went on, "like they are."

We had learned all about that at school—the filth, the brutality, all those people living alongside each other, corrupting one another. I would try to imagine it sometimes, how it actually looked and felt. I would see teeth—sharp and hungry. And then nakedness. And then after that I'd see beetles and weevils, people in rags, things smeared in excrement. Medieval scenes.

Dad talked me through the amnesty that the newspaper had set up, the rewards on offer. Hand in a cassette and you could get sweets, chocolate, and music from our own bands.

"But how do you pick these cassettes up?" I asked Dad. "Without getting the cancer on your fingers?"

"You use a bag, of course," he said. "Just like you would when picking Wolf's turds up off the lawn."

And from then on I made sure I kept an empty shopping bag in my backpack to handle any enemy music, should I find it.

And I did find it—in Clementine's bedroom, one day after school. But she didn't have a Jay Acker music cassette. Oh no. Clementine Hart had a Jay Acker compact disc.

And, it turned out, a machine to play it on.

"Do you h-have a license for that?" I stammered as she dragged the big black oblong out from under her bed, followed by its pair of speakers on their cable leashes. She shrugged as if my question was nothing. Then I saw the "property of the security police" symbol etched into the player's case and thought I might drop dead right there on the spot.

"Oh hell, Clem!" I hissed.

I was hyperventilating. I was going to pass out.

"Calm down, Jess, will you?" she said. "It's fine!"

"It's not fine," I told her. "It's a million miles away from being *fine*."

She put one of her hands on my back and started rubbing, which did help. She'd been avoiding contact with me since that day by the river. I'd felt the absence as strongly as I would have felt a punch. No casual arm slung across my shoulder, no tipping of her head into the crook of my neck. I suppose she saw it as a kindness, an honesty, but it was painful. I was just grateful that she still wanted to be friends. There was no way I could imagine living without her. "You're not going to get into any trouble," she said. And her words helped me feel even calmer. Because what Clementine said was always true. Well, it felt true. I didn't have to think about what she said to understand it is what I mean, not in the way I did when Dad was talking. There was no jigsaw to do, no challenge to face—the image was already there. "Believe me," she said. "You're not in any trouble."

I watched her plug in the machine and prod at its buttons while I held my fingers against the pulse on my neck, willing it back to a normal speed. I managed to get a sentence together. "Do your parents know you have this?"

"Of course they do, stupid," Clementine said. "Where do you think I got it?"

I shook my head. I didn't know.

"Dad got it for me, didn't he? From work."

Which made no sense. I take it back—this particular picture she'd given me did need fitting together. And there were jigsaw pieces missing. Herr Hart was merely the telephone engineer at Dad's office and would have had absolutely no access to anything like that. I decided it was theft. Terrifying theft. Or more likely, because this was the Harts we were dealing with, terrifying flakiness.

Then Clementine produced the CD in its plastic sleeve.

"Ta-da!" she announced, shoving it right into my face. The name *Jay Acker* was written in marker straight onto the rainbowed silver, and underneath, the song title: "Feeling Free." I jerked backward.

"Oh, Jessie." She laughed. "You're so funny."

I knew what I had to do. I was back in control.

My hand twitched for the shopping bag in the pocket of my backpack, but I was certain that Clementine wouldn't just hand over the contaminated item. This was a hostage situation. I needed to *isolate, contain, evaluate, negotiate.*

I got up from the floor, shaking still, but doing my best not to show it. I closed Clementine's bedroom door. I went back and sat beside her. I had my palms showing—nothing up my sleeve.

"My dad says we must hand those in," I told her in the flattest tone I could manage. (*When in a hostage negotiation keep your voice normal and calm while working toward building a rapport.*)

Clementine wrinkled her nose. "Why are you talking like that, Jessika?"

She slipped the CD out of its sleeve and placed it into the

33

mouth of the player. It sucked it up, licked its lips. I could imagine the radiation traveling across Clementine's hands now, up her arms, making for her brain.

"My dad," I said, slower this time (*repeat your information until you receive verbal confirmation that your message has been understood*), "says we must hand those in."

"Oh yeah?" Clementine whipped her head around at this. A string of her blond hair caught me on the cheek. Stung me. We had seen technicolor images of radiation on the People's Television, and now I was imagining a slick of it across my face, spreading, mutating. She was smiling and angry. "And who is your dad to be saying that?"

"What?" I said.

"Who is your dad to be saying that?" she repeated. "I'm interested. Really. Who is he?"

Silence. Horrible silence.

"What do you mean?" My voice was papery, like someone had their hands on my throat.

"I mean," Clementine went on, "what is it that your dad actually does?"

There was great emphasis on the *actually*. She stood up, put her hands on her hips. I think that she wanted a fight—hands and fists and everything—which was silly of Clementine because we'd been taught how to deliver a swift downward strike to the brachial plexus at the BDM session straight after her parents had stopped her from attending. I didn't want to use my pressure-point attack on Clementine. It really hurt. Erica Warner had been my partner for the exercise, and she had located the agony of that nerve with her first blow.

34

I didn't even want to stand up and face Clementine. But I did.

"My dad is an auditor!" I tried to sound defiant, but it came out sounding stupid.

"And what does that even mean?" Her face was screwed up with fury, her lips quivering.

"It means . . ." I said, trying to make my voice rise above hers, "it means . . . budgets and . . . stuff."

She laughed at my answer, hard, spraying my face with little bits of her spit.

This was not the usual Clementine, the way she was speaking to me. There is a hierarchy in every friendship, and I was always the leader. I had been chosen to represent the Princely State of England as a skater. I did well at school. I had been given responsibilities at the BDM, responsibilities that would never have been offered to Clementine. Not everyone can be a leader. Some people need to follow. Not a criticism. Being a follower is an important job in itself. I didn't think Clementine was completely lacking in qualities. Of course I didn't. I adored her. She was an excellent pianist, something that often made me feel horribly envious. I would thrash away at those BDM typewriters pretending that I was clattering through a Beethoven piano sonata at the Royal Albert Hall, but really, I didn't know a B-flat from my elbow. Clementine could have represented our country as a concert pianist if she had wanted to. Except that was always the problem with Clementine, her fatal flaw. She had the ability, a wonderful talent, but she could never be bothered to apply it. Or she wasn't willing to.

I used to believe that this behavior was somehow criminal. Instead, she sat writing songs in her bedroom.

"My own little *Götterdämmerung*," she told me.

The Wagner opera.

I had nodded, smiled, pretended that I knew what that collection of music sounded like. The meaning of the title had no impact then. The twilight of the gods. A catastrophic end.

We were face-to-face. She was bristling with something—upset, resentment . . . radiation, maybe. I could only imagine that this was a side effect of picking up that CD. Still, I was furious about her questioning of my dad. No one questioned my father.

"And what about your mum . . . ?" I tried to be smiling and angry, just like she'd been with me, though I'm sure I was nowhere near close to achieving it. "Your mum, the *typist*!"

To have a mother that had a job was shameful enough. I expected Clementine to be thoroughly embarrassed that I'd also unearthed her little lie.

"No," she replied. So cool. "She's a journalist. I told you, remember?" Her answer whizzed past me like a ball I couldn't hit back.

"Oh," I said.

"What?" she said, grinning. "Is that not what *Vater* led you to believe?"

Yes, it's true that we slip between our languages. It's just how we talk. It's as easy as sliding a pair of sunglasses up onto your head and then back down onto your nose. We do it without thinking. We mix things up. It means nothing. But that word was chosen.

"My father," I said, indignant for the both of us, "has better things to do than gossip about your family."

DECEMBER 2012

We first heard about it on the People's Radio. I got the real sense that Dad knew already, though I couldn't understand how. Even the *People's Mail* and *Evening News* didn't get to report anything until the day after the announcement was broadcast. Dad had been in the rankest of moods all week, and when the speech came, it was just so obvious that this was the earthquake his tremors had been leading to.

When our leader's voice came on the radio, he refused to sit down. Herr Erlichmann had been everything to us, but Herr Dean . . . ? We just weren't worshipping him in the same way.

"That idiot," Dad spluttered at the radio. "Does he want to send this nation to the dogs?"

He paced, he stomped, he threw things around. It was exactly like having my sister Katrin back in the house.

I could see why Dad was angry. One minute we were being told we mustn't touch that boy's music or risk catching cancer; the next we're offering him a stage in Trafalgar Square. And more than that, with all the world's eyes on us, we would be giving him a welcome our nation could be truly proud of.

The first American on British soil, on any German soil, in over seventy years.

Usually, if there was a U-turn in Party policy, Dad would sit back, calmly assuring us that it was all part of the initial plan, that our leaders always have our best interests at heart, that there is so much information we do not know and cannot know, for our own safety. We must trust in the integrity and higher knowledge of the Führer. This time he stood pounding angrily on the top of the sideboard at the end of every one of Herr Dean's sentences. Wolf slunk off into the kitchen, his tail curled underneath his backside.

"I let all that . . . that . . . shit . . . with the HJs and BDMs ride," Dad fumed. "But this? THIS?"

For me, though, I think Herr Dean had started to make sense. He reminded me of Clementine, the way she called me out if I ever said that I was a "world-class skater." ("How will you ever know? They might have *much* better skaters than you in Russia, or Japan, or America.")

"How can *anyone* call themselves an international music star," our leader decried, "until they have performed to *our* discerning nation?"

"What does *discerning* mean?" Lilli piped up.

"Perspicacious!" Dad spat, consonants like bullets. Lilli had no choice but to nod.

Jay Acker needed us, that was what Herr Dean was saying. He wanted to be accepted by us. It had been established that he was of pure blood—so why shouldn't we let him in? Didn't we have a duty to let him in? Wasn't it our mission to rescue him?

Our Führer directed the end of his speech specifically to

us—to the schoolchildren. ("For god's sake," Dad scoffed as Dean made this change of address. "Bloody poof!")

"I think it's time," Herr Dean said, "that you, our young people, our future, were given the opportunity to enjoy Jay Acker's music on our country's terms, to experience it safely, and to claim it as your own."

I thought this sounded sort of wonderful, but it made Dad kick a chair right across the room. This was when Mum broke her silence, telling Dad to please calm down, thank you very much. But Dad just thrust his finger right in her face and hollered back, "That man has stuck his penis into a wasp's nest!"

What an expression! I wanted to explode with laughter, but I held it back, of course.

"Daniel!" Mum said with a gasp.

Lilli took a great big breath, ready to ask what a penis was, but I gave her the sternest of stares and she closed her mouth, pretending to zip it shut with her fingers.

The way the nation was run was so important to Dad—more important than to most people. He felt each decision personally, believing it would reflect back on him. I assumed this was because he was the most influential person in County Roads Estate and was so accustomed to everyone listening to whatever he had to say. When the radio wouldn't listen back, he just couldn't handle it. How awful for him, I thought, to watch everyone else marching off in the opposite direction.

From then on, the People's Television bulletins were filled with projected images of what it was going to look like when the stage was up and the crowds filled Trafalgar Square. News came locally that our troop of the HJ and BDM had been chosen as one of the brigades to attend the concert, which meant everyone in the neighborhood was suddenly thrilled about Herr Dean's change of plan.

Poor Dad.

They started playing the Jay Acker song on the People's Radio. It is difficult to put into words how strange this was.

That first time I had almost heard it, that afternoon at Clementine's house with the stolen CD player, I left the room, desperate not to let any of it get into my ears. Now I was allowed to listen, supposed to listen. It was my first taste of the enemy's voice. Breathtaking. Like an unexpected prick with a pin.

You have me in your arms
In your prison
Yet I'm feeling free
How can it be
That I'm locked down in your heart
Feeling free-ee-ee?

It was a peculiar sound to get your brain around—an off-key imitation of something familiar that you can't quite name, as if one of our bands' songs had been fed into a machine and turned into something more, well, fizzy. Or perhaps it was the other way around. Our music was this song made more earthy and real.

But of course it wasn't just a song, it wasn't just a boy. It was a movement.

Everything we did from then on, we did to the rhythm

of that song. The walk home, washing up, getting undressed, brushing teeth. We marched to its beat. Or rather we strutted, letting our hips fall from side to side as we went. We couldn't help ourselves. It was such an earworm. Ruby Heigl sang it adoringly to her reflection in the mirror in the BDM bathrooms. Even GG was humming it. (We called her GG—or rather Gee-Gee—because it was short for Gabi Gubbins but also because (a) she liked horses, and (b) she looked like one too.) And GG was usually as cool as a cucumber about everything.

The girls stuck pictures of Jay Acker in their school lockers, even though he was kind of funny-looking, with his big blond "pompadour" and falling-down trousers. The boys, meanwhile, started to copy his style. Uniform inspections at the start of BDM and HJ meetings became stupidly drawn out while one boy or another was made to comb his hair back into a part and cover up the top of his underpants. Those lineups were already chaotic enough. As part of the gradual implementation of the Great Integration, lineups were no longer done in two separate groups. We were mixed up. Boys AND girls. Together. No one could concentrate.

It might have been funny the first few times, watching Dirk foam and splutter through his lecture on how the belt was "a VERY FINE INVENTION INDEED" and should be "EMPLOYED AT ALL TIMES," but after the fifth retelling . . .

"I swear you've all gone giddy," Fräulein Eberhardt muttered at every available opportunity, patting at her pudding hair.

She was right, of course. Everyone had gone giddy. Giddy and giggly and frothy.

And I really didn't get it at all.

I wanted to. I faked it for a while—pretending to find Jay Acker's eyebrows delicious and his tank tops amazing, or whatever it was Angelika and Erica and the rest were all saying. I really wished that I could be carried away on the wave of it all, because it seemed really nice from the outside. But I didn't get it. Why did they love him so much?

My only consolation: I thought this would bring me closer to Clementine again. She may have had one of Jay Acker's CDs back when we'd been told not to, but now that it was okay to have one, I assumed she'd lose interest. She never acted like the other girls. We would be reunited through our shared disgust for how ridiculous everyone else was behaving.

No.

"This is just amazing, Jess!" That was her response to it all. "Just unbelievably *amazing*."

I went to her house most evenings, to escape Dad and his foul temper. Just when I thought he had calmed down from Herr Dean's national address, someone from the neighborhood would ask, "So, what do you make of this upcoming concert, then, Daniel?" and he would plummet again, into the funk. I'd take Lilli with me in the evenings, lifting her, warm and drowsy, from her bed, and I'd click Wolf's leash onto his collar and trail him behind us too.

I sat up in Clementine's room and listened as she used the word *AMAZING* in every sentence and I pretended to find it all AMAZING too, until I was too tired to keep up the act.

"Is it, though? Really? *Amazing*, I mean," I said eventually.

"Yes!" Clementine took hold of my hands. I would have enjoyed this if her eyes hadn't been wet, filled up with something unfathomable. Mad old women used to cry and cross themselves and fall to their knees at the words of arrogant old popes. We learned that at school. False idols. "This is history happening right now!" she gasped.

Lilli was sitting on the floor in her mouse-print nightgown, plinking and plonking her way up the white keys on Clementine's electric piano. I had told Lilli to put the piano onto a table and sit on a chair, away from the floor, but she wouldn't do as I'd asked. Clementine's room was like the rest of the Harts' house: it could have been really, really nice if only they kept it clean and tidy. Herr Hart's garage was the worst. Lift the up-and-over door and you were likely to start an avalanche.

Clementine and I were up on the bed, which was far from crisp and clean, but it was better than the floor. Wolf had found a patch of something long-ago spilled on the blue carpet and was licking away at the memory of it.

"If it's really so *amazing*, why aren't you playing that CD of yours?" I said.

"Can't, can I?" she replied.

"Oh yes," I said. "Forgot."

The men had come to the Harts' house last month and carried the machine away (sealed in plastic, to stop the radiation spreading, I presumed).

She gave me a cool stare.

This was where I was supposed to say sorry.

"It's just a music concert, though, isn't it?" I said to bring an end to the subject. But Clementine hadn't finished. She started smiling, laugh-talking. I was seven years old again, sitting on her front lawn covered in daisy chain, not understanding the concept of "soon."

"No, it's not," she said. "It's a million miles away from being just a music concert."

"Okay . . ."

"This is them," she went on, "doing their hardest to control something that they just can't control."

Them.

"Control what?" I asked.

"People's desires," she replied. "Young people's desires."

I was lost. Even my best friend in the whole world had been swept away on the sea of it. I imagined explaining this out loud to Clementine. *How do you know I'm your best friend in the whole world?* she'd say back. *There might be* much *better friends in Russia, or Japan, or America.* Or worse, like that day under the tree swing, she'd remind me that we were best friends but nothing more.

Then Clementine used the R word. *Revolution.*

What I said in reply was a reflex: "I love my country."

"I love my country too," Clementine replied, but when she said it, it felt like she was talking about an entirely different place. A different planet.

I thought about starting our rescue conversation . . . *Tell me about the place where you used to live, before.* But instead I said, "He needs us, Clem. That's all. We're just doing this boy a favor."

Lilli started traveling down the keyboard again, using only the wonky, eerie sounds of the black keys. Wolf halfheartedly whined an accompaniment.

Clementine's face became very serious.

"No," she said. "That's not how it is at all."

"Oh yeah?" I said. "How is it, then?"

She was straight there with the words — giving them to me in German. She took hold of my hands again. "Wir brauchen ihn," she said. "Wir *brauchen* das."

We need him. We *need* this.

I told Dad. Of course I did. I had to tell him everything. That was the rule. Though in this instance, I didn't think I wasn't obeying his orders. I thought I was doing something else when I told him that Clementine was really very excited about the concert, and that she thought it was going to be history in the making, and she also thought that the Jay Acker U-turn was down to the Reich being in a desperate financial state and millimeters away from a potential war, which it just didn't have the personnel for if another nation were to stick their beak in, so it needed to make friends with America and begin trading, but yet, despite all this, Clementine was still really very excited about the concert, basically because she thought that it might, possibly, maybe, start a revolution.

When I'd finished, Dad looked up from his newspaper. Mum looked up from her toast. Lilli shrank down into her shoulders.

I had effectively tossed a grenade into the middle of our breakfast table. (*Visually assess the distance between you and the enemy, twist free the pin with index finger of nonthrowing hand, stand sideways, throw in an arc with an overhand motion.*) Or, as Dad might have phrased it, I had stuck my penis into a wasp's nest. (If only there were such an excellent metaphor using breasts or a vagina.) Supposedly I wanted Dad to calm down about the Jay Acker U-turn. The last thing I wanted to do was make him angry all over again. Still, I had said it. That word — *revolution* — had infected me somehow. Yet here was the shock: there was no explosion. (*Check you have the pin in your hand, take cover, prepare for the enemy to return the grenade before it detonates.*)

"Does she, indeed?" Dad said, after what felt like the longest and most terrible pause in history. Then he went back to the article he was reading.

That was that.

Mum, though, was clearly still wary of an outburst. The chair that Dad had kicked across the room during the radio broadcast was an heirloom from Oma Davina and was good for nothing now, except possibly barbecue fuel. Oma hadn't noticed its absence during her last visit, but if another chair went . . . Mum was more scared of her own mother than of Dad. She began to jam the silence with words.

"Well, I really have no idea at all why Clementine should be getting so excited," she said, trying to be jolly and cross all at the same time, but only sounding desperate and needy, "because she certainly won't be getting an invitation to any concert. Will she? Not now that she's stopped going to the Bund." Mum always called it that. "Silly girl! I mean, it's not as if they're handing out those tickets to people who . . . To people who have marked themselves out as . . . People who . . ."

Mum had wandered into a Zone. I was sure of it. I could see it in her face, in the way her skin fell slack. She stopped talking.

A Zone was just my name for it. I have no clue what word other people used. It's not as if we went around willy-nilly chatting about the idea. Maybe there never were any Zones, maybe I made it all up. And even if they did exist—Zones—why would that be such a bad thing? The police put tape up sometimes to keep us back for very good reasons. Who wants to stumble down a big gaping hole or tread on a landmine or, I don't know, discover a corpse?

Though I realize I haven't mentioned something you might think is really quite crucial. I do know what one other person called the Zones. Clementine. She called them the truth.

"To 'just anyone,' darling?" Dad offered brightly, as an end to Mum's sentence. He did not lift his gaze from the newspaper.

"Yes, Daniel," Mum said. "They won't give them to just anyone."

And then she let out the huge blimp of air that had wedged itself underneath her ribs and went back to eating her toast.

JANUARY 2013

After Christmas, I found out that I definitely wasn't "just anyone."

At a meeting of the HJ and the BDM they announced that our Mädelschaft and Kameradschaft had not only been chosen to attend the concert but would be performing too. Marching. ONSTAGE.

"Best not to keep going on about it to your dad," Mum whispered at bedtime when she came to take away my empty hot chocolate mug. "I really can't do anything with that dining room chair now that the leg's gone, and that cabinet—well, we'll just have to live with it as it is."

I had watched Mum knock out the remaining shards surrounding the hole in the glass of the cabinet door; she was so skilled at making anything look nice and tidy.

"Oh, okay," I said.

"And best not say anything to Clementine either," she added.

"Because she'll be jealous?"

"Yes. Let's not make it any worse for her than it is."

But how do you keep that kind of information to yourself? I had been chosen to be part of "history happening right now," as Clementine had described it. If anyone should have been up on that stage, it was her. But I did want it to be me. I couldn't have cared less about the boy or his music, but I did care about being chosen. Only five hundred of us in the whole of the Princely State! Fisher must have recommended me, used my actual name, when talking to those higher up in the ranks. And we, the selected few, would go on to shake hands with officers, ministers, and maybe, possibly, OUR FÜHRER. This meant that I really was one of the biggest, the brightest, and the best. I was fit to burst. So every time I saw Clementine it felt like I had the words I HAVE BEEN CHO-SEN TO MARCH AT JAY ACKER'S CONCERT AND YOU HAVEN'T LA LA LA tattooed across my forehead.

So I avoided Clementine completely. It seemed like the only solution.

This left me with a dilemma, of course—whose house could I escape to in the evenings when there was no BDM meeting? I couldn't stay at home. Dad was still angrily licking his wounds. He needed space, I told myself. Though I think it was me who I was really scared of. Sometimes when I was with him, a thought would come into my head—another grenade ready to toss—and I would have to work so hard to stop that thought from getting out via my mouth.

I briefly considered calling on Angelika Baker, but I knew that inviting myself into her house, with her five vain sisters, would have been on par with jumping into a cauldron of cats. An evening of constant lecturing and one-upmanship in the company of Ruby Heigl did not appeal. Ditto, hours of inane chatter and suppressed yawning with Erica Warner. So I slung

Lilli across my shoulder and slid through the last of the January slush to GG's house, my little sister protesting that she was too big to be carried.

"I just want to stay in bed!" she told me, shivering, eyelids drooping, thumb in — another thing she was too big for.

"I'm protecting you, silly," I told her.

"From what, silly?" she replied. And I found I didn't really have the answer. But I did have an image, that chair of Oma Davina's flying across the room, missing Lilli's head by a matter of centimeters.

GG's mother looked worried when she first opened the door to me, Lilli, and Wolf. She looked down at herself, disappointed and sort of surprised by what she found herself wearing.

"Does your mum know you're here?" she said, smoothing out the creases in her apron before adding a strangled little "And your dad?" to the end of her sentence.

"Yes," I said. An almost truth. "They know."

"But it's coming up to curfew . . ."

"That doesn't matter," I said. Then: "Can I come in? Lilli is really very heavy."

After a couple of weeks of our visits, Frau Gubbins seemed to relax, or at least give in.

"Oh, you three again," she'd say, stepping aside as we headed along the hallway and up the stairs. But I did notice that she'd stopped answering the door to me in her apron.

GG was always very welcoming, right from the start. It quickly occurred to me that I had been an idiot to endure all those years of waiting on front lawns and being exposed to contraband music players and dirty carpets when there had been a perfectly adequate friend living opposite us on Lincoln Drive all along. I could have avoided a great deal of heartache.

If I was honest, GG's horse teeth had always put me off. It was so hard to have a conversation and not be completely self-conscious about the fact you were staring, mesmerized, at the horror of her mouth. But somewhere along the line, when I wasn't properly paying attention, GG had grown into those teeth. All of a sudden she was — not pretty, exactly — but handsome. Her forehead was high and strong, her lips very full, her hair honeyed and golden. But more importantly, compared to Clementine, she just seemed safe. GG was high ranking in the BDM, kept her schoolwork in rows of clearly labeled ring binders, her wardrobe organized by clothing type and color. You knew what you were getting with GG. She was like a familiar statue, or a dependable sandwich. There would be — I believed — no surprises. Though not long into our new relationship there came one startling revelation: she too didn't understand the hysteria over Jay Acker.

"Don't you find him attractive?" I asked.

"No!" she shrieked.

"But you told Angelika Baker that you were in love with his rectus abdominis muscle. I heard you."

She put her finger down her throat, pretended to be sick, and then bellowed with laughter. "As if! I just say those things so the other girls don't suspect."

I could have kissed GG right there and then! But I was on the bed and GG was hanging out of her bedroom window having a cigarette and I didn't want to go over and get the

51

smell of smoke on me. (Mum was forever giving me the "you must care for your body so you have healthy children" lecture.)

I realize the contradiction, of course. How could I have seen GG as safe territory if she smoked? But GG had always smoked. Everyone knew. I'm not saying I approved—I fully intended to harangue her into stopping—but GG headed up the HJ and BDM's patrol that enforced the smoking ban in our local cafés. Clementine had no authority to be breaking her rules. GG did.

I sat there grinning, delighting in GG's confession about Jay Acker, stroking the thick, blond hair of Lilli, who had fallen asleep on my lap. Wolf had been snoring and farting all evening, but my resulting irritation had now completely evaporated.

Then it landed. What GG had said.

"So they don't suspect you of what?" I asked.

GG blew her last mouthful of smoke up at the stars. She stubbed out her cigarette in the lid of the box.

"Ah, Jess," she said. "You are just too cute."

Then she jumped down from the windowsill, made her way over to the bed, and planted a big, gutsy kiss on my unsuspecting face.

Clementine caught up with me. It was only a matter of time.

GG got held back after school one day—another cursory telling-off for smoking behind the PE sheds.

"If you really believe you've seen me smoking, then why don't you take that up with Herr Fisher?" GG would say to Fräulein Allis.

Mind games. Despite all her pouting and eye narrowing, Fräulein Allis was too much of a mouse to question the integrity of one of Fisher's senior recruits. A criticism of GG was simply a criticism of Fisher, and Fräulein Allis wanted to keep her job. No one would listen to her outside of the school anyway. She was far from being an excellent German woman with those painted eyelashes and stockinged calves.

So without GG to walk home with, I walked alone. It was either that or fall in with Angelika and Erica and have to think up something new to say about the shape of Jay Acker's chin.

"Hey, you!"

Clementine ran to catch up as I cut across the playing fields.

She didn't seem angry at all about my complete absence from her life, which made me instantly nervous, and more than a little hurt.

"Hey, you," I said back, missing the little spring in my voice that Clementine had managed.

The tattooed words on my forehead turned into a flashing neon sign.

I HAVE BEEN CHOSEN TO ATTEND JAY ACKER'S CONCERT AND YOU HAVEN'T LA LA LA.

"How's it going?" she said, her breath making clouds.

"Good," I said.

EVERY OTHER EVENING, UNBEKNOWNST TO YOU, I AM PRACTICING A FLAG MARCH TO PERFORM AT JAY ACKER'S CONCERT.

"You?" I asked.

"Oh, okay," she said, neither happy nor sad. We watched a man ahead of us throw a ball for his Jack Russell. The dog leaped a meter or so in the air to make the catch and, following each success, ran around in circles, desperate not to return his prize.

"Funny," said Clementine, commenting on the dog but not sounding even slightly amused. Then, "They took away my place at music college."

"What?" I stopped walking. So did she.

I wasn't sure which question to ask first. *Since when did you have a place at music college? Which music college? Where? Why has it been taken away? Who are "they"?* But the question so desperately on the end of my tongue was *Why didn't you tell me?*

When I was awarded my place at skate camp, she was the first person I ran to with my letter. She was the one I wanted to celebrate with, jumping and squealing and dancing.

"Fuck 'em," she said, still watching the dog. I think she might have cried if she'd had to look me in the eye. "I guess this is supposed to be a warning. But they can stick it up their asses."

She began working her tongue over her teeth beneath a tightly shut mouth — fighting back the tears, but one escaped. She brushed it away quickly with the mittens she'd knitted herself the previous winter. "Probably would have been wall-to-wall fucking Wagner anyway. I'd have hated it. They've done me a favor." She pulled her scarf up over her chin, her hat down over her eyebrows.

"I didn't even know you had a place at music college," I said, trying not to sound wounded.

"No?" She turned to examine me for a moment. Then she gave a small shrug and a nod. "Well . . ." she said.

We watched the dog perform a few more of its impossible leaps. The image in my mind: Clementine's illegal music player, wrapped in plastic.

"But I'm not the only one who is good at keeping secrets, am I?" Clementine was smiling now. Her nose was screwed up, ready for mischief.

"What do you mean?"

"It's okay, silly," she said. "I'm really pleased for you." She stood in front of me, demanding that my attention be put onto her. She stroked the length of my arms with her mittened hands, as if she were ironing me back into shape, making me solid. My mind caught up. She knew. About Jay Acker. She knew.

"Oh," I said. "Good."

"You should know by now I don't think like everyone else."

I was confused. "But you do," I said. "You do think like everyone else. You're as excited as the rest of them."

Her turn to look confused. "What?"

"I mean, about the concert," I went on. "I didn't want you to feel bad that I was . . . Or annoyed that I was . . ."

She was shaking her head now. "No, no, no, no, no!" She gripped the tops of my arms, gave them a squeeze. "I was talking about GG," she said.

"About GG?"

"Jess!" she all but boomed, still hanging on to my arms—arms that had gone limp, turned to jelly. "No one's listening! We're in the middle of a field!"

"I don't know what you mean," I said, hushed, instinctively looking around to see if anyone was actually in earshot.

Clementine brought her face very close to mine, lining up our eyes. The ends of our noses were almost touching. Her breath was warm and sweet. "You don't need to sweep everything under the carpet with me." She spoke very carefully and very deliberately. "Because I don't believe that's the right thing to do."

I nodded slowly, only because I thought that if I pretended to understand, then this conversation might be over. Because I didn't understand. How could I, when I didn't have a word for it. You have those words — words that are good. Though you shouldn't congratulate yourselves too much, because I know you have the bad ones as well.

Then the weirdest thing happened — after keeping me at arm's length for all this time, Clementine pulled me tight and kissed me on the cheek.

FEBRUARY 2013

One evening, Fisher asked me to stay behind after the HJ and BDM meeting. His singling me out came as no surprise. I had begun to suspect he valued my skills and intellect above those of the other girls in the Mädelschaft. My bowline knots were continually given the highest praise; my suggestions in tactics sessions were always congratulated. I was hungry for the validation, especially after Clementine had taken such strange pleasure in my friendship with GG. I eagerly accepted Fisher's request. And very loudly.

"Of course!" I cried, carving that jealous scowl just a little deeper into Ruby Heigl's face.

We'd finished that evening's meeting with a tug-of-war as a reward for doing well in our concert march rehearsal. I was to stay back and help put away the ropes.

Once alone, we wound fat loops around our wrists and elbows, fastening tight the bundles with their own tails. We worked in silence. A heavy, AWKWARD silence. My eyes kept wandering to the hairs on Fisher's arms. I hadn't noticed them before, how blond they were—lighter than the sandy hair on his head. I was staring, I suddenly realized, and became convinced that my mouth was about to blurt out something inappropriate — a grenade of a wholly different kind. Perhaps I would do something crazy, like reach over and stroke that soft hairy arm or . . . ENOUGH, I told myself.

"What will we be doing in Thursday's session?" We were outside of our normal meeting hours, so I hoped he wouldn't mind that I had broken the rule of speaking only after I was spoken to. He'd taken off his tieslide and necktie, after all; he'd made a big show of it.

Fisher looked up and smiled, those scary blue eyes latching on to mine. I felt myself flush red.

"Want to get a head start on the others, eh, Jess?"

He knew me well. If I ever got a whiff of what we'd be doing in the knowledge section of a forthcoming session, I'd go to Dad's bookcase and look it up. I would make guesses as to what Fisher's questions would be and memorize the possible answers.

"Yes," I said. "I suppose I do."

"Excellent," he replied. He gestured for me to pick up my pile of tied ropes and follow him behind the curtained storage section at the back of the hall. My eyes took a moment to adjust to the dark.

Either Fisher was making me wait for a response to my question about Thursday's session, or the answer would be somewhere here, hidden in the shadows. I heard him drop his armload of ropes into the plastic barrel, felt him turn around. I could see well enough now to make out the wet flicker of his eyes, the line of his jaw, and the open collar at his neck.

"Let me help you," he said.

I moved forward to tip my pile of ropes into his open arms, but as we made this exchange — DISASTER. The knuckles of one of his hands bumped into one of my breasts.

I shot backward.

"I'm so, so sorry," I said. What if he thought I'd made that happen on purpose? What if the mad, grenade-filled part of my brain *had* made that happen on purpose?

"Sorry for what?" Fisher asked. He was smiling; his teeth flashed in the dark. He wasn't appalled. Not appalled at all. Thank god.

"Nothing," I said. "It's nothing."

Someone of Fisher's standing had much better things to be doing than going around noticing girls' breasts, I told myself, even if he did just poke his fingers right into mine.

I turned to go, but he stopped me.

"What do you know about sexual intercourse, Fräulein Keller?" he said.

I was a little shocked, yes. The question had come from nowhere. Mostly, though, I was terrified that I wouldn't be able to give the right answer.

Then it came to me. Of course! This was going to be the subject of the knowledge section of Thursday's meeting. Sexual intercourse! And it was going to be horribly embarrassing for him, to have to teach boys and girls together. He was looking for reassurance. That was what my staying behind was all about, and the loosening of his tie. He needed my respected opinion.

"Well, my mother has shown me the book," I said.

I meant *Mädel von Heute, Mütter von Morgen — Girls of Today, Mothers of Tomorrow*. On the cover there is a picture of a good deutsches Mädchen about my age, in profile, looking deadly fierce and ever so soft all at the same time. Our copy is a family heirloom. Oma Davina's name is written on the first page next to the date—1955.

I tried to sound breezy and confident. I was not the sort of girl to get giggly and stupid about these things. They were, after all, just a function of nature. I swatted a hand through the air to demonstrate how it would be absolutely no big deal when it came to discussing the ins and outs (so to speak) with us girls. "I'm sure most of our Mädelschaft have seen the book too," I added.

They had, ages ago. We'd all brought our copies into school and had a good snicker over our favorite sections. Well, they had snickered. I, as always, as the continual ambassador for my father, had controlled myself.

Fisher nodded, moving off to another corner of the store where a box of rubber quoits had tipped over and spilled. I went with him. My eyes had adjusted by then. I could see where I was going.

"But it's one thing to read a book, Jessie." He began threading the escaped quoits onto one of his arms. "It's another to have practical expertise."

The knowledge sections of our meetings were usually followed by hands-on experience. We were told how to pitch a tent, then we put up a tent. We were told how to clean out a gun, then we practiced doing just that. So in some way I managed to convince myself that it was entirely normal that Fisher should, once we'd both shed our armload of quoits into the box, take hold of me by the hips.

They weren't allowed to touch us. It wasn't proper. There was a rule. So this had to be some kind of practical demonstration, it just had to be.

He put his lips to mine.

And I let him. Of course I did. How could I have said no? He had chosen me. Also, I did want to know.

He started pushing his tongue into my mouth.

And the first thought that came into my head was *So this is what it feels like, on the other side of things, when one person kisses another, unexpectedly, without asking.*

Or had I asked him? I wondered. Silently, somehow? When Fisher put his face up close to ours during uniform inspection, his hot breath hitting our noses, had I given him some signal that he should, at the first available opportunity, close off that gap? Or maybe it wasn't even as considered as that. I had no conscious thought before leaning in and pushing my lips against Clementine's. *Only men obey commands of the blood. Men and animals.* That's what our schoolbooks told us. Men, animals . . . and me.

I focused on the scent coming off his clothes, tried to work out what brand of washing powder he used, because I thought this would keep me calm.

He pulled away.

"You have to use your tongue too, Jess," he breathed. His eyes were heavy lidded, full of something.

I nodded, cleared my throat. The idea of putting my tongue in his mouth seemed ridiculous, revolting even, but also entirely natural. Hadn't that been my instinct, after all, the instinct that I had held back? I couldn't decide if continuing what we were doing was a terrible sin, word of which would reach my father, or if not doing as Fisher asked was actually the very worst sin, guaranteed to enrage him. The inspirational quotation poster on the wall of the meeting hall that week read: LOYALTY IN FEELING MEANS ABSOLUTE OBEDIENCE. I put my mouth back on his and slotted the tip of my tongue between his lips. He loosened my spine with his hands, fought my tongue back with his, then began kissing his way down my jaw and neck. He went close to my ear.

"You have skin like milk," he whispered. "My sweet little Jay-Jay."

My back became rigid at his words. To be spoken to like this, by a grown man, by my superior. The knowledge we were taught was always general; it applied to everyone. These words were just for me. I think this was the first time I had ever felt truly alone.

I tried to conjure up one of the phrases the girls had used to describe Jay Acker, something I could whisper back into Fisher's ears, something to save me.

"Felix," I managed, feeling an odd thrill to be using his forbidden first name. "Your eyes are . . ."

I didn't get to finish. He made a start on the buttons of my shirt. He left my necktie still fastened around my collar, so we could maintain the pretense that this was still a lesson, that we were still on official business. He slid his hands inside my bra. My breath caught at the sensation — the cold contact creating a loop of energy between us, an electrical circuit. Parts of my brain were lighting up — parts of my body too. He began squeezing at the flesh of me in the same way Fräulein Eberhardt had taught us to knead dough, his breath getting brisker, rasping. He pulled at my skirt with one panicky hand, unzipped his fly with the other. I may have stood there rigid so far, but I understood what was supposed to happen next. Anatomically. It was all in the book.

"We're not going to actually . . . ?"

"Yes," he panted. "Yes, yes, my sweet little Jay-Jay, mein kleiner süßer Singvogel."

"But I'll have a baby," I said.

"And what a fine child it would be," he replied, tugging at my underwear. "We'll get married. Don't worry. I'm a leader, you're the pure-bred daughter of —"

"No!"

"Your father, he —"

"NO!" I shoved him away.

I was wrong. I would never be alone. I would always be my father's daughter. In that moment, all the connotations of that seemed to hit Fisher just as hard.

"I d-didn't do anything that you didn't want me to," he stammered. "You never said that . . ."

It hadn't really occurred to me until then that Fisher was young. He was the one with all the stories on the hostel evenings, of Bismarck and Göring and Norkus and Hitler, so well read that he could recite whole sections of Ernst Jünger's *Storm of Steel* by heart. He was someone I had obeyed unconditionally. But only a couple of years ago, he would have been standing in line just like we were. Wet eared. Wide-eyed. Soaking it all up.

"No," I said again, as a final word on the matter. He stood back, disheveled, and watched me button my shirt and straighten my skirt.

Once I was close to presentable, I marched away from behind that curtain, only letting myself shiver and cry when I was halfway home, dashing between the spilled light of the lampposts so no one would see me and ask why I was out so late after curfew.

I was sure I would be punished at the next meeting, be made to ceremoniously undo the knot in my necktie for some made-up insubordination, be made to clean the floor of the boys' bathroom with a toothbrush. But no. Fisher still praised me above all the others when I gave my answers during the knowledge section—on how to form successful corralling lines. There was no mention of sex, of course.

I reframed that evening for myself, filed it away as some kind of success. It was the best thing to do, the only thing. I had proved that I was attractive to men and my desires worked as they should. I was normal. Or, indeed, still special, and for all the right reasons.

MARCH 2013

My visits to GG's house stopped.

I had proved that I was normal, and special. Staying away from GG, I understood in some fuzzy, indistinct way, would help me maintain this. I mustn't let people get close to me. Only bad came of it.

I decided I should spend more time with my father. I was missing his good influence and excellent warnings. We had grown apart since the Jay Acker announcement, and it was my fault. I intended to fix things.

One day after school I set out my papers and books on the dining room table, like the best bait in the most irresistible trap. There was a copy of *Deutschland: Damals und Heute,* which translates as *Germany: Then and Now,* and Dad's *Pictorial History of the Kampf um Lebensraum 1938–1940,* which is a little more difficult to put into English. *The Battle for Habitat,* shall we say. *The Battle for Space.* Dad immediately got a sniff of something as soon as he came through the front door from work.

"What have you got going on in there, Jessika?" he asked as he hung up his beige raincoat.

"Oh, just this controlled conditions essay to prepare for tomorrow," I said with a sigh.

He came into the doorway. I read aloud the question as if it was the toughest challenge a girl would ever have to face.

"Detail how the Nationalsozialistische Deutsche Arbeiterpartei achieved a successful resolution to the English government's intrusion on Kampf um Lebensraum with Operation Seelöwe."

As if he could have resisted. Off he went to the highest shelf of the bookcase, pulling out his treasured souvenir editions of the *People's Mail*, all yellowing and thin, and the photo albums containing the pictures of Uropa Joachim—Great-Grandpa Joachim. We had a large, staged portrait of him wearing his green belted uniform with the eagle on his chest, and more casual shots too—Joachim lying back on a picnic blanket with a group of other sturdy-looking lads in Bavaria in the 1930s, Joachim standing in the doorway of a small terraced house in shirt and suspenders, his arm around a grinning young woman. This was his new girlfriend, Sally, the British woman who would become my great-grandmother.

My father and I began by discussing the lead-up to the liberation of the British Isles—the outrageous and insulting treaty that had to be avenged, the nine European States already emancipated. Then on to England's systematic, yet indiscriminate, bombing of Germany. Dad opened up his photo history of Berlin. We were quiet as we took in the faces of the families picking through the rubble of their homes looking for their missing babies. We looked at the bodies laid out in the exhibition hall.

"This was the turning point," Dad said. "We had a sacred wrath. We still do."

I wrote that down.

On to the air campaign, where we redoubled our efforts. England relied on a flimsy system called radar—until our intelligence services liquidated those communication stations.

"England was drowning in its own decadence," Dad told me with a disgust so strong it was if he'd actually been there, felt it. Smelled it, even. "They knew they were defeated."

He always used the term *they* for the English, never *we*, unlike Herr Robertson in history class, who often aligned himself as English when describing the events of 1940.

"Why are you doing that, sir?" Ruby Heigl demanded.

"Because my grandparents were English," he replied.

Of course, someone reported him, and he disappeared (back to teacher school for a reminder of our sacred wrath, I imagine), and he was replaced by Herr Manning. Everyone had presumed it was me who had dobbed him in, but it wasn't. The way he talked only made me think of my great-grandmother Sally. Was she, an innocent young woman, responsible for the actions of her country?

We moved on to Winston Churchill—a man who had always seemed so unreal to me. He was someone I knew from the comedies on the People's Television—some actor with cotton balls in his cheeks, a cigar in his mouth, woofing like a bulldog. How did someone as ridiculous as that commit so many horrors? How did he ever even get into power?

"Not 'ridiculous,' Jessika. *Dangerous.*" Dad would always get terribly stern about this. "He was a charming monster. He took England's schoolboys, sent them off on his renegade schemes, and brought about their terrible early deaths. All the while, what was he doing?"

"Drinking champagne, Dad."

"Bingo."

The English troops began to collaborate, self-sabotaging, ignoring orders, desperate to save themselves. They ran from Dunkirk in any small boat they could find. Ground staff put antiaircraft guns on the wobbliest of buildings. They removed barbed wire from the aircraft stations and deliberately went unarmed so German planes could land and refuel.

Then came the flood of all those unwanted people, those Untermenschen, into England, in the thousands. The natives were desperate for order. And it arrived, on September 15, 1940. An end to chaos. Members of the Wehrmacht and Schutzstaffel landed in Kent and Sussex and began the liberation, bringing about order and a system for getting rid of the uninvited. The men cheered, the women covered the faces of the German soldiers with thankful kisses, the children waved flags. Operation Seelöwe set the people free.

Dad loved all those documentaries about the evil of Churchill on the People's Television. This was just what he needed. The color was back in his cheeks, the fight in his belly. I knew it would revive him.

My next task was to revive Clementine.

"She needs your help right now," Dad reminded me. This was true. I had turned in on myself. Self-absorption was a weakness and a total waste of my intellect. A disgusting decadence. I decided I must learn from what my forefathers had achieved over seventy years ago. I must look outward, perform a rescue. I would recharge Clementine's heart. I rang her doorbell before school.

And there were screams coming from inside the house. Frau Hart's screams.

I thought about turning and leaving, walking to school alone, but I made myself stay. *She needs your help right now.* Didn't this only prove that I had returned to Clementine's doorstep at exactly the right moment?

I put my finger on the bell again and held it there, so that a good, long buzz sounded through the house. *Pull yourself together, Frau Hart! Your daughter needs you! Answer the blasted door!*

I heard Herr Hart's voice coming from inside, rising above his wife's wails and pushing them down. Clementine opened the door. Her eyes were puffy and red, the irises dishwater gray, not their usual piercing green. Those eyes stopped me from speaking. We stared at one another. It was this awful moment of reckoning, I realize now, though at the time I couldn't have said what it was we were calculating or making even.

"All ready for the essay today?" I asked brightly, ignoring the strange whimpering sounds coming from farther in the house. They were the sort of noises Wolf made when he wanted you to open a door.

"Yes," Clementine said with no intonation at all.

Then Frau Hart was there, sprinting down the hallway, her hair even wilder than usual, dressed only in a nightshirt, which

69

was soaked through with sweat, maybe snot and tears. The material had gone see-through and you could see the dark outline of her nipples. She grabbed Clementine's arm and tried to pull her back into the house.

"You can't go!" she sobbed. "You don't have to go!"

Then Herr Hart was there, clamping his arms around his wife, trying to pull her away from his daughter, away from me. Because Frau Hart was staring at me as if she wanted to literally rip my face off. I couldn't help but think of those madwomen we'd seen on the school visit to the asylum.

My job at this point should have been to shout out tips to Clementine's father on how best to restrain her (*find a contact point and grasp, move to the side, keeping your head to their chest, then form a choking grip around the neck, jerk backward*), but in the heat of the moment, my knowledge just wasn't there. I said nothing. I watched him clumsily drag Frau Hart back into the house, kicking and yelling, not caring that she was showing the world how she wasn't wearing underwear. It was brutal, what he did, but necessary. And, strangely, it also seemed very loving. It was nowhere near as terrifying as watching a dining room chair fly through the air and rebound off a cabinet with a jaw-aching crack.

Clementine had remained still during the whole performance. Head forward. She hadn't seen her mother flail a leg in the air and expose the dark place between her legs.

"Shall we go?" Clementine said briskly, pushing past me.

Frau Gross watched us from her living room window as we walked out into the cool spring air, up out of the cul-de-sac of Lincoln Drive and down the shortcut that took us to the stream and the ditches. We said nothing. There was just the rustle of our backpacks, the riffing of the birds, a light breeze through the leaves. I could hear Clementine thinking; it was as loud as the whirring of a clock.

"What's up with your mum, then?" I asked lightly, as if Frau Hart had just been a little moody.

"PMS," Clementine replied, not missing a beat.

She picked up her pace and I picked up mine, and then, noticing that I'd done this, Clementine slowed down to a crawl. So did I. Then she jolted into a march again. And I copied her.

Clementine started laughing. "God, Jess, you're just such a sheep!" And she carried on laughing. Harder now. I watched her until it became infectious and I had to join in. There we were, Jessika and Clementine, giggling away, back to how we used to be. But then Clementine's laugh turned, and she was crying. Really crying. Big, heaving sobs. I'd never seen her properly cry before. It wasn't something that Clementine did.

"What's up?" I asked.

Clementine kept walking, a plodding pace now. "Ask your fucking dad," she muttered. "Doesn't he know the answer to everything?"

I managed not to be spiteful back. Envy could be a horrible, corrosive thing. Dad had taught me that. I had good, solid parents, the type of people who guided and protected me; Clementine did not. She was angry. Angry and jealous.

"I'm here for you, Clem," I said. "I can help you."

I put a hand on her shoulder, which she jerked away, as if it had stung her, or would infect her with something.

"It's all different now that we're not kids, isn't it?" Her voice trembled.

"We are still children," I said, in an attempt to reassure her. In an attempt to reassure myself.

We carried on along the path through the woods, the sound of our footsteps changing under the canopy of trees. Then she told me.

"I've got my date," she said. She pressed her teeth together. The pain of something stretched her mouth really wide. The tears were streaming down her face.

I could hear Angelika Baker's righteous braying somewhere behind us. We both turned to see her there, a short distance away, arm in arm with Erica Warner. Michael Baxter and Karl Pfizer were kicking along in their wake.

We snapped our heads back around and Clementine wiped her face dry of tears. They would catch up with us in a moment.

"Your date for what?" I asked.

She took a few deep breaths, sighed them away, trying to get rid of the hiccups that had come with the crying.

"For what, Clem?"

She didn't want to say. Or she was cross that I hadn't worked it out.

"Tell me."

Her features were swollen and quivering. She took her finger and she sliced it, hard, across her belly, the very lowest part, and then she sliced that finger back again in the opposite direction. A terrible X.

I watched Clem write her essay in history. She didn't cry then, but she was twitchy and strange, as if there were a bomb in her pocket, seconds away from detonation. We had been told in English lessons never to say someone is "writing furiously" because that is a cliché, but that was what Clementine did in that hour. I thought she might tear holes in the paper. Clementine didn't usually take exam-condition lessons seriously. She'd look around the room, make faces at the rest of us who actually cared about our education. But that day she wrote from the moment Herr Manning said "Turn over your papers," and she kept on writing. Furiously. She was finished well before everyone else. She scraped her chair back, threw down her pen, walked out.

I did a terrible job. I couldn't get all the information to hold together like it had around the table with Dad the night before. I'd get an A minus at best.

As soon as we had finished our essays, we were to quietly leave the classroom, get changed, and head off on a cross-country run. The route would take us out of the school grounds, around the playing fields, and on through the park. We were meant to come back along the main street, past the lamppost where they hang the traitors, past the other school—which they made us do as an incentive to the children there, I think, so they knew what to aspire to—and then back to our own grounds. But I took a wrong turn.

I'd stayed to the end of the lesson, right up to the moment Herr Manning said "Put down your pens." Almost everyone else had gone. Manda Darby was still there, of course, because she was stupid. We reckoned she only got her place at the elite school because her father was someone terrifying within the secret police. How on earth had he passed the medical exam? And how had she? You didn't need a measuring caliper to know that giant Balto-Slav forehead of hers should have been put in the other school. Or on a fast train to Highpoint.

I was toward the back of the field of runners when I eventually set off. Most of the time there was no one to follow. I was distracted and dithered at the forks in the path. I hadn't paid proper attention to the route when it had been explained. So when I suddenly saw GG ahead of me, her long, horse-rider thighs powering away in those white shorts, I was really very grateful. I did all I could to catch up. It didn't occur to me to wonder why she was so far back in the group. She had finished her essay not long after Clementine and was usually pretty speedy at cross-country, always beating the pants off Ruby Heigl. All I was thinking was how I would like to talk to GG about what had gone on that morning at Clementine's house. GG would know how to blow a raspberry at it all, make my worries seem like nothing. But I was far too embarrassed to speak to her. It would mean explaining why I had stopped going to her house. I purposely hung back a little.

I trailed her to the slope to the right of the bandstand, through the trees that led toward the lake, and then . . . GG was gone. I blasted up the hill, my heart leaping out of my mouth, then I let myself jog for a moment — and that was when someone leaped out of the bushes. They found a contact point — my neck — and grasped. Keeping to my side, they drove their head to my chest and jerked me backward into the undergrowth. The grip only shifted to incorporate a hand over my mouth when I started screaming like a loony.

This was it, I thought — a Commie bastard! Come to rape me! I was dead. But then I realized this Commie bastard smelled familiar, beneath the grassy stink of sweat — like figs when they'd just been split open, the burnt tang of brown sugar.

In the clearing, she let me go.

"Good god, GG. I nearly wet my pants!"

"Sorry," she said, "but I didn't think you'd come willingly."

"Why's that?"

She shrugged, took a moment to find a suitable answer. "Because you'd get into trouble?"

I nodded.

We were quiet for a few moments, except for my gasps of air. I had my hands on my hips and I was looking down at my running shoes, trying not to vomit. She was right, of course. I desperately wanted to be there with her. But I also desperately wanted to get back on the path.

"Are you all right?" GG asked. "I've been worried."

"Yes," I said. But then out of nowhere and for no reason I could put my finger on, I burst into tears. GG took hold of me and squeezed me tight. She was horribly sweaty, but then so was I. It didn't matter one bit. I was just so grateful to be held. It felt safe.

"I'm sorry," I said as I heaved out great gulping breaths. "I'm really sorry. I don't know what's the matter with me."

"It's okay," she said. "It's okay."

She ran a soothing hand over my hair, down the skin of my neck. I could feel my heart thundering against her chest.

And then I kissed her. No, she kissed me.

No — we kissed each other.

APRIL 2013

Clementine got suspended.

Dad told me when I came home for breakfast after skating that I wasn't to knock for her as she wouldn't be going to school.

"Why not?"

"Because the school needs some time to decide on a suitable punishment."

"How do you know?" I asked.

"I'm not sure I like your tone of voice, young lady," he replied.

I hadn't slept.

I'd tripped over my own skates at least three times at the rink that morning. In the buildup to that blasted camel spin, I'd caught my toe pick in the ice and bent both hands backward as I tried to break my fall.

"Verdammt, Jessika!" Ingrid raged from the benches. "Since when do you land like that?" She leaped onto the rink, struck over to me in short, angry thrusts, stopping messily on purpose, spitting ice over my legs. I pulled myself up onto my elbows and tried to move my wrists, but they were numb, fixed like concrete. *Please don't let them be broken,* I was willing. *Please don't let them be broken.*

"Answer me!" Ingrid snapped. "Antworte mir!"

The pain was coursing through the cold now, forcing hot tears onto my cheeks. I hadn't realized there was a question; I couldn't answer her.

"Oh, for goodness' sake!" Ingrid sighed, crouching down and making a grab for one of my hands. But I snatched it away.

"Don't!" I barked.

"I was only going to—"

"Don't touch me!"

Ingrid recoiled. I think I had really upset her. She placed her knees onto the ice and sat back on her heels.

"I just don't want anyone to touch me," I said, trying to make it sound calmer now, more reasoned. It was the truth, though. Nothing good came from physical contact.

She stared at me, her eyelashes batting at her long bangs. Each blink a thought.

"And why's that?" Her voice had lowered like mine. "Why are you crying, Jessika?"

If this had been Coach Dorothea, she would have smacked my ear for speaking to her like that, for showing emotion after a fall. I think I would have appreciated it. *Smack!* That's for how you enjoy being touched, by boys, by girls, fingers, lips, skin . . . For letting your tongue slip so easily into GG's mouth without anyone telling you to put it there. *Smack!* That's for being helpless to stop your best friend from having her insides sliced out.

"Come on, I need to examine your wrists, Jessika." Ingrid offered me her open palms, as if beckoning a toddler. "You know that's not how you save yourself."

I did know. (*Anticipate the fall, bend your legs to get closer to the ice, roll forward and to the side, keep the arms in.*) But what if you can't anticipate the fall? What if you don't see it coming?

I gave in. I put my wrists onto the warmth of Ingrid's gloves. She nodded herself a point won.

"Please don't make the last ten years a total waste of time," she muttered as she slowly rotated my left wrist, her fingers interlocked with mine. "I'm talking about myself, of course." She smirked, though I understood it was no joke. "Please don't make *my* last ten years a total waste of time."

I was Ingrid's first ever student. I was the first girl she had secured a place for at skate camp.

"Will you get a medal when I go?" I asked.

"Bloody deserve one!" she scoffed.

She looked for the smile and I gave it to her. Another nod, another point won. She started work on my other wrist, loosening the joint. I had only jarred them. I would be all right. The worst I'd have would be bruising, some pain when extending my hands for expression.

"I don't care about any medals," she said, shaking her head slowly for emphasis. "I just want you to always have this in your life." Her eyes flickered upward and caught mine. "Because where else can you be truly free," she whispered, "except on the ice?"

I hadn't slept because I had been trying to work out a solution, a way to save Clementine. Inspiration had slunk into the room at 4 a.m.

This was a terrible mistake. An administration error. I would convince the authorities. Use my position. After all, on the surface, didn't it look all wrong? Only the proper idiot girls had this operation. The deaf ones too, the deformed ones, the ones who fell into jerking fits in the middle of the street. The horrible drunks. Basically, the type of girl who was grateful for it, because she didn't have the money or the sense anyway. Clementine was not like that. We would write a persuasive letter of complaint, draw people's attention to the situation, the injustice of it, and then in the face of reason they would have no choice but to reconsider.

In the daylight my plan seemed even more promising. Dangerous, but promising.

I poured myself some milk and tore at a bread roll, scattering the poppy seeds over the striped cloth.

I would take my best writing paper and fountain pen to school with me, then, if my nerve held, I would go straight to Clementine's. Mum would be picking up Lilli and taking her to gymnastics. No one would ever know that I was there.

I could feel Mum's glare on me, because of the mess I was making. I started brushing the table with the side of my hand, aiming for my palm but sending most of the seeds onto the floor.

"Jessika! Come on!"

I let out a massive yawn.

"And hand over mouth!"

I dusted the seeds from my fingers and covered my mouth like she'd asked, though it was too late now.

Dad was watching me during all this. Chewing and thinking. Thinking and chewing. My eyes were jittery with tiredness and the seeds looked like they were moving—little black insects colonizing the table.

"And you're not to go over to Clementine's house at all until this has been resolved," my father added.

A guilty throatful of orange juice came back up into my mouth. I swallowed it back. The idea that he could actually read my mind seemed very real. He knew everything, saw everything.

"Sit straight, Lilli!" Mum snapped, just as my little sister thought all the attention was going my way.

"Your time is better spent across the road with Fräulein Gubbins," my father said.

With GG?

I looked up to see if this was a test, but Dad seemed entirely earnest. He posted the last chunk of his bread and Leberwurst into his mouth as a full stop.

My throat burned with the orange-juice acid of guilt, but there was another sensation beneath it all. A very small victory. I knew something he didn't.

Still, I hid from GG at lunchtime. Because I also knew that my father's permission was misguided. I went into one of the high-sided wooden cubicles in the library and pretended to study. Biology. Humans and Nation. *If the quality population have an average of two children and the inferior population have an average of four children . . .* There were small illustrations of the smiling, upright two-children family and the wonky, bow-legged four-children family, then a bar chart to show the fall in quality population.

Now: 97% quality, 3% inferior.
After 120 years: 67% quality, 33% inferior.
After 300 years: 3% quality, 97% inferior.

I let my head rest on the book, on a page of images of great German nationals who would never have been born under the two-children rule. Schubert, Bismarck, Adolf Hitler . . . My eyes must have closed.

She found me. Her voice was suddenly very close, right inside my ear.

"Come and have a cigarette."

I gasped, shot upright, and butted her in the chin with the back of my head. She yelped. All around us there was a rustle of papers and bodies. Everyone had turned to stare. GG was clutching her face and laughing.

Fräulein Wainwright's head popped up from behind her reference-desk parapet. "Girls!" she hissed.

GG ducked into the cubicle next to mine, but made no show of getting out her books.

I turned the page. There was a chart filled with rows of paper-doll children, and in each row a single doll colored black to show the birth number of some of our nation's greatest men. Bach was the eighth born of twelve children, Wagner was the ninth born of nine . . .

"Come and have a cigarette," she said again, her whisper traveling through the wooden partition.

"I don't smoke," I whispered back. "It makes your babies come out with two mouths."

I was a second child. I would still have been born under the

Zwei Kinder System. Did that mean I would never amount to much? But then I saw, right there in the book, an error, or perhaps just an exception that proved the rule. Ludwig van Beethoven was the second child of six.

GG's head appeared around the edge of my booth. She made herself go cross-eyed.

"Come and watch me smoke, then."

"Girls!" Fräulein Wainwright was heading for us now, with her frumpy shoes and short hair that refused to grow. She was only twenty-five—if that—but she'd clearly already given up. She dressed like my Oma Davina.

I closed my book. It was time to leave—or else get an embarrassing dressing-down from Fräulein Wainwright in the reference section. We got up and made for the exit.

"This is a place of study, ladies, not a coffee shop!" she called after us, trying to be funny. We clattered out of the library doors before I could start to feel sorry for her.

We walked through the gloomy atrium with its rubber floor of raised Lego circles that felt like cobbles beneath flat buckled shoes. I'd often wondered how they might feel under grown-up heels, like the ones Fräulein Allis wore. Precarious, I think.

"Fräulein Wainwright could actually be quite attractive if she made an effort," I said to GG as we pushed out through the second set of swinging doors into the sunshine of the courtyard.

"I dunno about that," said GG. She made for the alleyway between the library and the science blocks. I followed her. Unthinking. Distracted, maybe. Or perhaps a little thrilled by our small—almost—act of rebellion in the library. Thrilled, at least, to be with GG, who could do it with so much more confidence than me.

"If she could get her hair to grow," I said. "Wore something that fit."

We cut a diagonal across the grass square at the back of the science block. I knew where we were going—beyond the hedges and behind the PE equipment sheds. That's where GG went to smoke.

"If she put on a bit of weight," I went on, "maybe she could get a husband."

We hitched up our skirts and stepped over the flower bed that was purple with snake's head fritillaries. We slipped between the sheds.

"Maybe she doesn't want one," GG said, sitting down on an upturned crate.

I dropped my books, only really understanding as I planted myself on the grass beside her that I had broken a promise to myself—to stay away from her. But then I thought about what my father had said that morning. *Your time is better spent with Fräulein Gubbins.* Maybe my dad did know best.

"Of course she wants a husband," I said.

GG blew smoke across the town, laid out below us from our vantage point.

"Everyone does," I added.

GG raised her eyebrows, shrugged.

We let the noise of cars and children drift up to us for a moment.

"You know she failed the physical exam," she said. "Couldn't get her certificate to marry."

"What, Fräulein Wainwright?"

83

"Yep."

"No! What did she get failed for?"

"Dunno. Everyone says one of her uncles was a bit"—GG stuck her tongue behind her bottom lip and brought up a hand, making it twisted and shaky—"you know."

"Oh my gosh!"

GG nodded solemnly. "And you know who she was going to get hitched to, don't you?"

"No."

She sucked on her cigarette and made me wait. "Herr Manning."

"No! That's not true!"

"That's what I heard."

"But he got married to . . ."

"Cyndi Payton . . ."

"What, two weekends after she left school?"

"Manning passed his marriage tests with flying colors; wasn't like he was going to hang about."

"God." I'd always felt a little bit sorry for Fräulein Wainwright. Now I wouldn't be able to look her in the eye. "How many kids has Cyndi got now?" I asked.

"Three."

"Already!"

GG started chuckling. "Bloody hell, Jess, you know fuck-all, considering you're . . ."

A little stab of adrenaline ran through my jaw. GG gave me a tight smile and went quiet. The moment drifted off across the breeze. I followed her gaze, out over the park below us, the river, the steeple of the Party building, our own desirable neighborhood somewhere beyond the trees.

"Those girls at the other school get it easy, don't you think?" she said.

"Do they?" I couldn't see how, in any way. Our boys got the best jobs, we got the best husbands.

"I saw one of them in the supermarket . . ." GG went on.

"Really?"

"Well, outside, walking past. She was our age. I think she works at the cleaner's, ironing or something, out back where no one can see her. Mariel, is it? Anyway, she had her hair dyed. Two different colors. Blond underneath and black on top."

I knew who she meant. I'd done the rounds of her neighborhood with Clementine during the Winter Aid Program the year before last, when Clementine was still in the BDM. We'd taken Mariel's family a bag of secondhand clothes (mostly donated by Angelika Baker and her sisters—those girls couldn't walk past a mail-order catalog without ordering three blouses and a handbag). We also took the family new dishes and bed linen, a rug and some food coupons. Their ground floor apartment was small and filled to the polystyrene ceiling tiles with babies and small children, but it was clean, and her family were good stock who were willing to work. A warmth came out of their home that had made me feel strange. Envious, I suppose. But only because it was cold outside and we couldn't feel our toes. We'd been walking the streets for a good few hours by then, selling little flags as we went, keeping pace with the truck that was still strapped up with the banner from collection week. OPEN YOU'RE PURSES FOR THE WINTERHILFSWERK! Clementine had painted it. She was good at fancy letters.

When we had handed over the stash to Mariel she had said her thank-yous, then: "It's spelled wrong, your banner. It should be Y-O-U-R. No apostrophe. No E at the end."

Which I thought was a bit ungrateful given the circumstances.

If the girls at the other school did get a better deal than us in any way, it was only that their lives weren't as full with charity work and so forth, which meant they had more time to spend on spelling, grammar, and punctuation. That was it.

"Gosh," I said to GG. About the two-tone hair. "Imagine one of us doing that."

"I'd quite like to be able to do that," GG said.

"But I like your hair." My hand went to the curls of her ponytail and gave them a quick stroke. Then I remembered myself and snatched my hand away. GG saw the whole thing, seemed to understand it.

"That's not what I meant." She got up from her crate and came to sit with me on the grass. She offered me her cigarette.

I shook my head. "The tar in that cigarette is turning your eggs black," I told her.

"Probably."

She slotted her arm across my shoulders. I was so conscious of it, of my succumbing to it, that it may as well have been a python draped around my neck.

"Oh, Jess, relax," GG whispered. "What are you so worried about?"

She pressed her forehead close to mine as if trying to connect to my thoughts.

"I'm worried about being a bad person," I whispered into the warm space between us.

"There's no such thing," said GG with complete conviction, whipping her head back to face the town again. "You're only bad if they catch you."

She grinned at me, and I laughed like she wanted, but I was thinking about Clementine. Was that the reason she was being punished, not because she was behaving any worse than anyone else, but because people found out? Because someone had told on her . . .

GG's hand went to the nape of my neck and she started playing with the strands that had come loose from my braids. I tipped my head toward her, grateful for the contact. I watched her lips go tight around the filter of her cigarette and her chest lift to inhale. I actually wished for one ill-informed moment that I could smoke. It looked like it might help somehow.

"And anyway, you and me," GG added, letting the smoke go. "Well, especially you . . . We're untouchable."

I suppose Frau Gross could have gone and told tales to Mum. She was always sitting in the armchair by her front window. Always on surveillance. But Frau Gross had no reason to think that my going to the Harts' house was anything out of the ordinary. And perhaps GG's words had filtered through somehow. Maybe I was beginning to think I was in some way untouchable. If the laws about smoking didn't apply to GG, which laws could I defy?

I expected Clementine to be home alone, but as we headed up the stairs, I saw that Frau Hart was sitting in the kitchen. She didn't turn around to say hello. She stayed very still behind her halo of hair, a mug of steaming tea in front of her. I was grateful that she hadn't spoken. What are you supposed to say to a woman who only the day before was screaming and raving and flashing the place between her legs for all the world to see? *Nice weather for April, isn't it?*

"Why isn't your mother at work?" I asked, once we'd reached the landing.

Clementine didn't answer until we were in her room with the door shut.

"She lost her job."

"Oh," I said.

Clementine sat down on the edge of her bed, sort of perched there, as if it weren't really her room, as if she were waiting to be taken away. I thought she would be excited to have me here—at last, someone to confide in about her suspension! But she just stared up at me, waiting to be disappointed.

We'd had a read-through of *Hamlet* that afternoon in drama. Act 4, the bit where Ophelia goes mad, which is a metaphor for the Weimar Republic or something (or is that Gertrude? I can never get my head around it). Anyway, Claudius says, *When sorrows come they come not single spies but in battalions.* This came into my head then, and I quoted it at Clementine. She gave me this look of disgust and I felt instantly embarrassed for thinking it might be what she wanted to hear. Clementine was in the other drama group, doing *The Merchant of Venice.* That was much easier to get your head around—evil Jews, pounds of flesh.

"So, why did your mum lose her job?" I asked.

"Why do you think?"

"I don't know," I said. "Was she not very good at typing?"

Clementine dropped her head into her hands.

"At being a journalist," I corrected feebly.

Clementine's hair was matted at the crown, like she'd spent too much time lying in bed. I waited for her to lift her head and tell me the actual reason her mum had been fired, but the silence dragged. I'd always assumed Frau Hart's job was hanging by a thread, a thread that would break any day. Saying what you really think all the time wasn't really conducive to the job of journalist.

"So!" I announced. "I've brought this!" I pulled the pad of expensive writing paper out of my bag with a flourish. "And this!" The fountain pen this time. "We're going to write a letter!"

Clementine kept her head buried. "Who to?" she growled through the mask of her hands.

"Um." I pulled the chair out from beneath Clementine's desk. I hadn't thought that bit through. "To your doctor, I guess."

She lifted her face. She'd dug her fingers into the skin; there were white blotches in her cheeks and moon-shaped fingernail dents in her forehead.

"Saying what?" she asked.

"That you shouldn't have the operation." I sat down, started clearing a space among the junk—plates with crumbs, old magazines. "We're going to tell them that they've made a mistake."

Her head went back into her hands.

"I don't want children anyway," she said. I ignored this. She was being difficult on purpose. How could anyone not want children?

"Dear Sir," I said, speaking as I wrote. When I'd imagined this moment, I'd thought that Clementine would sit and do

the writing while I paced the room and did the dictating, like Dad did on those occasional evenings when Fräulein Krause came to the house taking shorthand on some urgent business. *Change in directive. Any person seen in the vicinity of 35a George Park is to be assumed complicit and to be brought in immediately for . . .* But I could be adaptable.

I went on. "*I'm writing to you concerning the sterilization order for Clementine Amelia Hart dated . . .* What was the date on your letter, Clementine?"

I waited. Her head stayed in her hands.

"Never mind. We can put it in later. *I believe there has been some mistake. Clementine Hart is of sane mind and good health with no genetic abnormalities.*"

"George," she said.

"Sorry?" I said.

"George." Her head was up now. "My brother."

"What brother?"

"The one who was killed."

"Oh . . . Yes . . . Put out of his misery," I said, trying to soften the moment. "I didn't realize you'd given him a name."

"Of course he had a fucking name, Jess!" she spat. "He was a person! A real, flesh-and-blood person!"

Her telling me his name stopped me in my tracks. George. With this name came an imagined face. A real baby. I put down my pen.

"Is that the reason they gave you in the letter?" I asked, not looking her in the eye.

"Yes," she replied.

"Oh."

I didn't know what to do. Or what I felt. Because, of course, if there were abnormalities, if there was a good chance her children wouldn't . . . Then she had to . . . Anything that is weak and not strong must die out, because that's for the best, that's how nature is arranged. But this was Clementine, and she was my friend, and I didn't want this for her. I didn't want this to be the last of her.

"Still, it doesn't seem right," I said.

"No," she said. There was a fierceness in her voice, tears dripping down her cheeks. "No. It doesn't."

I had been desperate to talk about Clementine's letter with Ingrid this morning at the rink. I thought she might be the right person to help me. But I knew asking her outright was altogether too bold. Instead I'd asked, "How come you don't have any children?"

"How do you know I don't have any?" she'd said back, trying to be playful.

She worked all day; I knew that she wasn't a mother.

"Because I wasn't able to," she said, the playfulness gone.

"Aren't you married?" I asked. I really did know nothing about her, I realized, this woman I had spent every morning with for the last ten years.

"No, I'm not," she said.

Her voice had an edge to it now. So I shut up. My last question had been pretty silly, after all. If Ingrid couldn't have babies, who would want her?

"I think I should still write the letter," I told Clementine. "What do you think?" One of my own tears splashed onto the page. "I think they'll listen to me. Don't you?"

"And why's that?" she asked. She already knew the answer, but she wanted me to say it out loud, so we could both hold it up to the light. "Why would they listen to you?"

"Because . . ." I tried to wipe away the tear before it would spoil the paper, but this only smeared ink across the page. I was making a mess of things. Of everything. I tore the page from the pad and balled it up, bashed it smaller and smaller in my hands.

Neither of us said anything for a long time. The house was quiet. Frau Hart didn't have the radio on. The People's News would be starting right now. She usually liked to listen to that, butt in every five minutes with her own particular thoughts. There was just the bump and whistle of the central heating system. I looked around Clementine's room for something to talk about, but everything seemed tired and trivial and not really relevant to anything. Relics. Props on a set.

Then Clementine said, "It's hard for you."

"I beg your pardon?"

"I said it's hard for you. Harder than it is for me, I think."

"What do you mean?" I said, gathering my things together. I was ready to go now. I needed to be back in the house before Mum and Lilli returned. "I'm fine," I said, laughing her concern away. "It's you I'm really worried about."

"But at least I know what I am," she said.

"What?"

And there I was, furious with her again. I wanted to help, but she just kept poking me with a stick.

"I know what I am, thank you very much!" I told her. "I know what I am!"

I hated her in that moment, as she nodded at me solemnly, as if my shouting at her was proof of something somehow. I could have actually clouted her one if she hadn't chosen that instant to get up from her bed, lurch across the room, and hug me.

I didn't want her to say anything else. I couldn't bear it.

So I whispered in her ear: "Erzähl mir von dem Ort, an dem du vorher gewohnt hast."

Tell me about the place where you used to live, before.

"Nein," she replied. Then into my ear: "Erzähl mir von deinem Vater."

Tell me about your father.

"Er ist ein guter Mann," I told her.

He is a good man.

"Aber?"

"Aber . . ." I said.

But . . .

We waited, knowing neither of us was going to speak. Why is there no English word for Zwischenraum? The space between things, all the things we say without saying them, the gaps in the jigsaw puzzle. Did the English never need the word before?

"I have to go home now, Clem," I said. "I'm sorry."

And as I went she pulled some sheaves of lined paper from the mess on her desk, folded them up, and pushed them into my bag.

"Ich hab dich lieb," she said as she closed her bedroom door, leaving me to find my own way out. I stood on the landing for a moment.

I love you, she had said. No, actually, a small, gentle step back from that. *I have love for you.*

"Ich liebe dich," I said to her closed door before moving away.

I love you, pure and simple.

The poison was in my ear. It didn't kill me — it did something far more awful than that. It divided me in two. It created another version of me.

GG was wrong. There was Good Jessika and Bad Jessika. Bad Jess was up onstage, doing and thinking all these terrible, crazy things. But that wasn't me. *The devil hath power t'assume a pleasing shape.* Meanwhile, Good Jess was forced to watch and judge and have her conscience caught. Sometimes Good Jess would hide behind a curtain and listen in on other people's conversations, hoping (and dreading) to get a little bit closer to the truth. Or was it the other way around? Was Good Jess up onstage acting — pretending — and was Bad Jess sitting and doing nothing, still a slave to the devil?

I kept the pieces of lined paper that Clementine had slotted into my schoolbag under my mattress. Then I realized that this was the first place that anyone would look, so I found a gap big enough behind the loose baseboard by my desk and pushed them into there. It still wasn't perfect, but it would do.

On the papers were a series of notes, with handwriting just as messy as Clementine's room.

Detail how the Nationalsozialistische Deutsche Arbeiterpartei achieved a successful resolution to the English government's intrusion on Kampf um Lebensraum with Operation Seelöwe.

That was written at the top. That bit was the neatest—clear and underlined twice. Then followed pages of half sentences and phrases and crossings-out, all vomited onto the page.

They were Clementine's notes for the controlled conditions essay.

This question is bullshit.

is how those notes began. Then . . .

Operation sealion was not a resolution.

~~IT WAS NOT THE END.~~ITS NOT THE END!!!

~~1940.~~ Earlier than that . . .

Peeple of britain live in terror as nazis rampage across Europe. Nine countries ~~taken~~ raped! Occuppying, pilaging, banning books, murdering peeple. No mercy. Thousands of Jews, and men who love other men, and disabled people and mentaly ill, sent to their deaths in gas chambers. Mass graves to hide piles of bodys. ~~The british knew~~ Everyone knew, surely??

Pictures of nazi rallys shown in british cinemas. We laugh at them. CRAZY CRAZY FUCKERS.

95

Hitler. Huge ego. Thinks hes the dad of everyone. Thinks hes god.

Treaty of Versailles just an excuse. DICKHEAD.

German peeple charmed by window dressing. Did not see what was going on? Chose not to see? Did not care?

@@@@@Hipnotised@@@@@

~~Desprate after poverty of pre war years.~~ Who gives a shit! No excuse!!

"Look at me in a funny way and I will burn the whole of your village to the ground, eastern SCHWEINEHUND!!!"

So . . . ~~Operation Seelowe~~. BATTLE FOR BRITAIN, MORE LIKE. Churchill - WE SHALL NEVER SURRENDER!

We are underdogs but we scare the hell out of them.

Dunkirk spirit!!!! Fuck yeh.

Lord Halifax pushs for peace but Churchill knows . . .

Peace = Ocupation = murder, murder, MURDER. Death of spirit. DEATH TO THOUGHT.

No comprimise!

France surrenders. Nazis use French air bases to close in.

Londoners pick thro remains of there houses for the dead. Southampton in ruins. Nazis have world-class airplanes, more of them. Hundreds dead at Biggin Hill. We fite fite fite until the end.

But the bastards still come.

September 15th 1940 - THE DAY OF THE BASTARDS!

We spit on their soldiers, sabatage their trucks.

The lucky ones escape. Flee to ~~america, canada~~, ANYWERE BUT HERE.

The Jews that had escaped france and germany are rounded up, shot.

Churchill and his Clementine exicuted in public display.

"Diletants and drunks - let that be a lesson to you!!!"

NO. WE RESIST.

We hide books so they cant be burned. We keep thought alive.

Resistence fighters = arrested. Inprisoned. Shot. Sent to work in factorys in Eastern Europe until they are crippled/blind/ dead.

British sorted like buttons. Valuble blood. Useless blood. Bring up your children to be Good german citizens or we will take them from you and do it ourselves!!!

It comes down to this . . . you have to make a choice. Oh but theres a member of the SS holding a gun to your childs head while you make this choice - dont let that sway you either way!!! Or holding a gun to your richs/your title/your busness/your livlihood. WHATEVER.

Fight or keep your head down and try to make the best of a horible situation?

Do you choose to survive?

We choose survival.

WE WILL SURVIVE.

We keep our mouths shut so we dont sudenly DISAPPEAR.

(Can you smell gas??????)

Children grow up thinking that THINKING LIKE THIS is normal. We cant travel outside the reich. They control our TV and our radio. No way of seeing that this is BULLSHIT. (Shiiiit!!! Don't let the peeple know the real capabilitys of the internet because then your fucked!!!! Ha ha ha ha).

We are prisoners. We keep Churchill alive in our hearts.

WE SHALL NEVER SURRENDER!!!

WE SHALL NEVER SURRENDER!!!

WE SHALL NEVER SURRENDER!!!

WE SHALL NEVER SURRENDER!!!

WE SHALL NEVER SURRENDER!!!

WE SHALL NEVER SURRENDER!!!

WE SHALL NEVER SURRENDER!!!

WE SHALL NEVER SURRENDER!!!

WE SHALL NEVER SURRENDER!!!

We decide that surviving isnt enough. We
want to live. We are waiting for our moment.
And when it comes . . . .

REVOLUTION!!!!! ARSCHLÖCHER!!!!!

Revolution, you assholes.
I understood why she got suspended.

When Dad got home, he told me that Frau Hart had lost her
job and I pretended that I didn't know. She had been fired, he
said, for theft. Not even the Reich Labor Service would trust
her with a broom in a factory after this.

"Oh my gosh, what did she steal?" I gasped.

"No one likes a scandalmonger, Jessika. Control yourself,"
he snapped back.

I wondered if he could feel it too, how we were performing,
playing our parts. Without much enthusiasm. *I have of late—but
wherefore I know not—lost all my mirth.*

Dad told me, "Just let there be a lesson in there for you, Jess."

He never usually spelled things out like that. The moral was always implied and understood. It lived there in the Zwischenraum—that space between. You absorbed it like oil through the skin. Now he was drawing my attention to it, this slick of oil.

There it was, sitting on the surface.

APRIL 20, 2013

I was grateful for the birthday celebrations — a day of song and ceremony. Something to replace that missing mirth. It was just what Clementine needed too. Though she had opted out of the BDM, she couldn't opt out of this. The Hitler birthday celebrations were the highlight of our year.

We boarded the train to London that Saturday with the extra thrill of knowing that the day would be one big dress rehearsal for the show we'd be putting on in Trafalgar Square that summer.

Clementine did not sit with us; she was in a separate car, with the others who had opted out. They were all from the other school, of course. No one else from our school would have dared leave the BDM. I didn't like to think of Clementine being grouped with those other girls. Despite all evidence, I still believed that she was one of the upright, quality people from the illustration in my biology textbook. How could she be wonky or abnormal? Because what would that have said about me if she was my friend? Or rather, what did it say about my dad, choosing her as my friend?

There had been talk of Clementine being moved to the other school, as punishment for the essay.

"How awful," I'd said when Dad told me.

Though I couldn't help thinking about that girl GG had envied — Mariel — with her hair dyed two different colors. Clementine would have actually liked to switch schools, I was sure of it. She would have taken a twisted pride in being considered wonky and abnormal, enjoyed the liberties of it.

"They won't move me, though," she said during one of my secret visits to her house. "They can't. Because that would only demoralize all the 'little people' at the other school, wouldn't it? To say that going to their school was somehow a punishment."

"I suppose so," I said.

Clementine's little knocks and taps — I couldn't deny it — they all made sense. I was hungry for more of them, just to test them out.

"And they have to keep all of those lowly folk on message, don't they?"

I shrugged.

"Yes, they do," she said. "Because they'll be needing them for cannon fodder down in Egypt and Tunisia any day now."

"Nothing's going on in Egypt and Tunisia," I told her.

I was aware of Frau Hart's words coming through in the things that Clementine said. *Demoralize. Lowly. On message. Cannon fodder.* It made me nervous.

"No, you're right," said Clementine. "It would have been on the People's News, wouldn't it? If something was happening. A big deal like that."

She raised an eyebrow and let me do the rest.

Clementine and the girls in the other train car were wearing armbands. I didn't know why. I thought perhaps it was a gesture to remember the fallen. But the day wasn't about that. It was a happy one—marching, dancing, all the ten-year-olds getting sworn into the Jungvolk and Jungmädel, their very first step on the ladder. So it had to be some kind of health and safety measure, I decided. Their teacher in charge needed a way for her group to stand out in the busy crowds of London, as they didn't have a uniform like us. That was why they wore that black triangle.

The train was decorated with strings of tiny little flags. Helium balloons bobbed against our car's ceiling. Ruby Heigl led us all in song. Fräulein Eberhardt had just announced that Ruby would be the new leader of our area's Jungmädel in September. I was doing my very best not to be cross about it. It didn't mean that she was better than me. I had a different calling. And if I hadn't been going off to skate camp, I would have been chosen to lead those girls (including my little sister) and teach them how to use a sewing machine and bake a soufflé and how to tuck and roll their way out of an explosion. I would have signed up for Faith and Beauty too, like Angelika and the others who were all staying local, and become an expert in hairstyles and all those lovely dances. Everyone was gradually being given their opportunities. This would be the last spring and summer that we would all be together like this, in our little Mädelschaft, alongside our Kameradschaft of boys.

Karl Pfizer was joining the air division. Michael Baxter was going out on the boats. Erica Warner was being all secretive, acting like she couldn't tell us what she'd been allocated because it was so absolutely classified. Total shit, we all decided. Something deathly dull in the Reich Labor Service. Her skin would be turning yellow while she stuffed TNT up the backsides of bombs.

The quota place at university for a girl was going to Helen Beider. No one talked to Helen Beider, apart from Greta Askwith, because they were both über-bright to the point of weirdness. Then something happened, because all of a sudden the girl's place was going to Greta and absolutely no one was talking to Helen.

"Greta snitched, didn't she?" GG said.

"For what?" I asked.

"Dunno, but she found something."

GG had gotten what she wanted—she was going to the West Country to help train the horses.

"What's going to happen to you?" I'd asked Clementine.

"I know, right?" she'd exclaimed, as if the question had been rhetorical.

Ruby started us off with "Tanz Rüber, Tanz Nüber"—*"Dance Hither, Dance Thither"*—our favorite song, especially when the boys weren't with us, because we could have fun doing all the voices. We bellowed it back and forth to each other across the train car.

Oi, lend me your sweetheart because mine ain't here!
No, I won't!
No, I won't! You parasite!

Lots of fun. Then we went all hymnlike for a bit of "Kein Schöner Land in Dieser Zeit"—*"No Country More Beautiful in*

This Time"—with Angelika and Ruby competing to see who could make their voices warble on the highest harmonies. Ruby was the victor, of course. She could have joined the opera with lungs like hers. Except if she did, who would she get to boss around then?

We moved on to some marching songs, ready for when we got off the train at Marylebone.

In the east wind, lift those flags!
In the east wind, they stand so well!

We got drunker and drunker on the sound of ourselves. The songs always seemed to unify me with my friends. Just the right combination of notes to swell the heart, the perfect rhythm to match the fall of your feet. I'm not sure I ever paid much attention to the lyrics, only the melody, only the feeling.

We kept up our singing as we took the Tube across town, joining in with the boys, our words bouncing off the curved ceilings.

Clear the streets for the brown battalions!
Clear the roads for the storm troopers!

We joined up with other companies from across the city, from across the Home Counties. By the time we reached Victoria Station there were thousands of us—one big voice, an amazing sight. I was arm in arm with GG and Erica. Women lined the concourse, having come especially to show their little children the sight of us. They lifted them up onto their shoulders for a better view, and the children waved their flags, their faces painted red, white, and black.

Millions look up to the swastika with hope!
A day of bread and freedom is coming!

We transformed that train station into a stadium. The vibrations from the singing went through your belly and into your bones. As we made our way along the platform, I turned to find Clementine in the crowd. I wanted to see if her heart was full too, if this had been some kind of tonic for her. Her group was a short distance behind us, heads down. Most of the girls' mouths were moving along to the words, but none of them were really giving it their guts. There were no smiles.

The female teacher from the other school who was leading the group, a pug-like woman with a decorated hat, saw me craning to see and followed my line of sight. Clementine's mouth wasn't moving at all. The woman looked stung by this, and by me—told off, I suppose, even though I hadn't insinuated anything. She took her elbow and jabbed it sharply in Clementine's ribs.

"Sing!" she instructed.

Clementine swung sideways like a punching bag. She was off somewhere else, in her head.

"Sing!" hollered the woman again, her elbow giving a double stab this time.

I let go of Erica and GG, let them press ahead while I moved against the surge of the crowd to find my way back to Clementine.

I would tell this woman, this subordinate teacher from the subordinate school, to leave Clementine the hell alone. And she would listen to me—that was what I was thinking—she would listen because of who I was.

But before I could get there, Clementine had neared the pair of Wehrmacht men who were keeping order on our side of the platform. They had heard the woman yelling. They were watching, waiting for Clementine to get close.

"Sing, Schlampe!" the nearest man barked as Clementine passed.

Sing, bitch.

"Sing fröhlich, du Hure!"

Sing gladly, whore!

And he poked the end of his rifle into Clementine's cheek, so hard that it nearly knocked her off her feet.

At Crystal Palace, Clementine was herded into a low section of the stadium with lots of other children who weren't in uniform, other children with black-triangle armbands. They were crammed in tight by the running track. We had a high position in one of the stands where we were able to see the formations of the dances. The Faith and Beauty girls spelled out the words WIR GEHÖREN DIR for the Führer. WE BELONG TO YOU.

"You should have seen it from where I was standing," Clementine said later as she lay bundled up in her bed. She was under the duvet, her forehead hot and damp, as if she had a fever. I was on my back next to her, on top of the covers.

"Their tits were jiggling," she sneered, "their little white shorts even shorter than last year . . . SS stiffies all around."

Clementine told me that she had gotten the round, purple bruise on her upper arm (to match the one on her cheek) when she didn't salute at the correct moment and was instructed, "Salutier, Schlampe!" and given another jab with a Wehrmacht gun barrel.

"Oh, they made sure our arms didn't droop too," I said, because they had, and because I was sure that Clementine must be exaggerating. I let myself wonder if she had given herself the second bruise to support her story.

When the rows of chosen HJ boys did their march past, Clementine said that they did an extra eyes-right, after the one for Herr Dean up in his part of the stand, just so they could spit on the black-triangle kids.

She waited for my reaction.

"We should have a day to mark Herr Dean's birthday as well, don't you think?" I said in the perkiest voice I could manage. It had been a day of celebration; I didn't want her to twist it. "It's silly that we don't already, isn't it?"

"It's because we're living in the past, Jess, and a pretty shitty one at that." Her dark boulder of a voice squashed mine flat.

"Oh, come on, Clementine," I said, pleading a little now. I put my hand on the duvet-ed shape of her. "I really must forbid you to think like that."

She shrugged me off. "Well, you can't," she spat. "Because you don't have that kind of power."

I should have given up, walked away, let what she'd said so far settle in my mind. But we were still desperately grappling with each other then, trying to pull one another over some invisible line.

"So, why were you wearing those armbands anyway?" I said. It was supposed to be a way to change the subject. On a conscious level, at least. I thought we could share a joke about the fussy dog-faced lady who'd been leading her group.

"Oh, stop playing innocent," Clementine cried from beneath the covers. "You know why I was wearing one."

"I don't," I said. "I don't know why." *And I am innocent, actually,* I wanted to add.

"Asocials," she said. It was a heading to a familiar list: reasons to wear the black triangle. I knew it. But I hadn't put the two together—Clementine's black triangle and THE black triangle. I hadn't let myself. Because why would they have ever gone together?

"Vagrants," she began. *"Beggars, idiots, workshys*—what a lovely poem this is!—*the diseased, the damaged, the dissolute . . ."*

"Okay," I said. "Okay."

"Alcoholics, prostitutes, pacifists . . ." She said that last word with a little upward inflection of pride. Then she threw another word into the air, a word that wasn't on the list. "Lesbians?"

It fell fast, like a stone.

"It's not a crime," I told her.

She rolled over then to face me properly.

I folded my arms—eyes to the ceiling. "I mean, they said it was okay for you to opt out. That's not a crime," I went on. "There was an announcement."

"Yes, there was," she said. "You're right. And wasn't that just a wonderful, wonderful trap?"

"No, you've got that wrong." *Nonsense,* my brain was screaming. *This is nonsense.*

"You wait until they make changes to Paragraph 175," Clementine said, rolling back over, "without anyone telling you first. Then you'll see how it feels."

Paragraph 175.

I wouldn't give her the satisfaction of asking what that was.

"Anyway," she muttered, "I should have been wearing a red triangle." She curled her fingers into a tight, defiant fist against the pillow. "All of my crimes are political."

Sometimes, I would pick Lilli up from school if Mum was busy with charity work, or sewing club, or extra Frauenschaft responsibilities.

"Where's Mum?" would be Lilli's first words as she handed me her satchel. Not hello.

"Oh, she was really very naughty so they put her on a fast train to Highpoint," I'd say.

And Lilli would tut and roll her eyes.

"No, she wasn't," she'd say. "No, they haven't." Then she'd launch into an epic monologue about her day, as if her life was just the busiest in the whole of dem dritten Reich.

I would take Lilli the short walk across town to the gymnasium, fold her clothes while she changed into her leotard, help her work the lockers. Then I'd go up to the rows of seats in the balcony gallery and watch her practice. She would work on the bars: her killer blow in competition. Her wrists bound, her hands powdered, she mounted the block she used as a launch pad to the highest bar and up she went—a flying monkey.

One of the stern-faced trainers—usually Bettina—stood at the side, shouting instructions. The training made Lilli's muscles visible in her thighs and shoulders. It was hard to take your eyes off her. She was such a different creature from me. Blonder, leaner. The skating never really changed my body like the gymnastics did hers. I stayed soft.

Beneath one of the sets of practice bars was a large pit of broken foam shapes. The girls were expected to fall. It was encouraged. They didn't want anyone developing a fear of the drop that would make them cautious. After a few swings, a few kips and beats, Lilli would throw herself into this foam pit, get swallowed up by it. Then she would swim her way back to the side. She would do this quite urgently, panicky almost.

On the way home after one practice session, Lilli told me: "If you slip down to the bottom of the foam pit, you end up in China."

I laughed.

"What's so funny?" She was furious with me. "Why are you laughing?"

"Because it isn't true," I told her.

"Yes, it is," she spat. "Bettina said."

"Well, Bettina is pulling your leg!"

"No, she isn't!" Lilli was almost breathing fire. "It's true, Jess, I'm telling you!"

And nothing I could say would convince her otherwise. Bettina was a big, solid woman, a woman in charge, whose every word meant the world to Lilli. Bettina would never, ever do anything as terrible as tell a lie.

Did I feel the same way about Ingrid?

Not exactly. I knew she didn't lie to me, but I understood that she left things out. It was like when I marked a routine on the ice for the first time, just to get a feel for the pace and my position on the rink: I left gaps. In here will go the single lutz; in there, a double axel. Ingrid left spaces in her life. She never mentioned where she lived, who with, what she did when she wasn't coaching. I never bumped into Ingrid in the outside world, caught her doing anything as normal as walking down the street. She was a half-made-up person who existed at the rink, a ghost haunting the scene of her death.

But if I'm honest, I didn't really want to see her anywhere else. If I witnessed that, I knew it would be sad. It was exactly like she had said herself: on the ice we are free. She was free. No rules, only wonderful secrets to help you fly. (*For an axel jump, get a good grip on the edge, don't prerotate, then leap out, leap forward.*) The real world, when I left the door ajar, was a dangerous intruder.

I decided to ask Ingrid about Paragraph 175.

I watched her flow through a sequence of single and double axels, biding my time. Ingrid had never landed a triple in competition. Girls didn't really do it when she skated, but it would be expected of me. I had managed it a few times in a pole harness, a giant fishing-rod contraption that Ingrid held to keep me straight in the jump and stop me from having a bone-crunching fall. Soon, like a baby bird jumping from the nest, I'd have to do it all by myself.

I loved watching Ingrid skate. I'd often pretend that I didn't understand what I had to do so that she would huff and sigh and take off in one of those whip-smart demonstrations. All her jumps rotated to the right, whereas mine, like most other skaters', went to the left, so her demonstrations were only useful to a point. We stepped onto opposite feet in everything we did, Ingrid and me. But that wasn't what I was looking for when I watched her skate. I watched to understand her. I could see into all the gaps.

"Your turn," she said, returning to the center of the rink with pink in her cheeks and more air in her lungs. "I need to see that beautiful curve in your body on the landing," she said, taking hold of my arm and stretching it to show exactly what she wanted.

Then I asked what I wanted. "What's Paragraph 175?"

Ingrid let go of me as if I were a red-hot pan handle. The color washed from her face.

I had known this was a question I could not ask my father. It was a question to ask someone as they stood very close to you, in the middle of an expanse of ice.

"Well, off you go, then," she said. She wasn't ignoring my question, just buying herself time to shape her words, to make them land as perfectly as I was about to.

I did as I was told, skated off, built up speed, switched to the backward edge, waited and kicked forward, whipping myself through the air. One and a half turns. I landed that single like a curved arrow shot from a bow. I went back to Ingrid for my answer.

"It's a rule," she said. "It's a law." I felt the heavy placing of each word, like stones onto the ice. Stones that left dents. "It is a law that says men must not love one another."

"As friends?" A genuine question. I was ready for the next jump.

"Go again," she said. "A double now."

Off I went, placed my feet as carefully as Ingrid had placed those words, but lighter, filling my leap with all the necessary desire. Two and a half turns—a double—again with that curve just as she'd wished. I spiraled back, knowing I'd earned my answer.

"No, as lovers," she said, her voice low. "As sexual partners."

"But men can't . . . How would they be able to . . . ?" I stopped. A violin melody was whining from the loudspeaker. It sounded sarcastic somehow.

I saw the sadness in Ingrid's expression. But was it for the men? The law? For the things I didn't know? She kept her eyes on me, so much better at reading my mind than my father.

"Ah, the feeling of a triple axel!" she announced suddenly, her voice loud again, deliberate, as if we had an audience. "The feeling when it's yours. I can't imagine . . . Well, I can. I mean, I came close but . . . I wish I had . . . I wish I'd grabbed that joy with both of my hands, do you know what I mean? Joy in whatever form it comes to you. Whatever the consequences . . ."

Her voice trailed off.

The violin climbed higher in place of her words—a strange, plastic imitation of a violin, making Ingrid sound genuine, crystal sharp.

Consequences.

"Do you mean falling?" I asked.

"What's falling?" Ingrid replied with a silly shrug and a smile—a smile that I knew slotted into one of the gaps in her past.

MAY 2013

We stood between the gap in the curtains in the room shared by GG's three little brothers, hidden behind the lace curtains, and we watched the strange people come and go from the Hart residence.

GG had decided what Frau Hart must be doing and why she was doing it—there was no way she would find another proper job after being sacked, and she had to earn money somehow. Our street wasn't a cheap place to live—the salary of a telephone engineer wouldn't be enough.

"There are women going in there too," I said. "Do you think . . . ?"

GG shrugged and blew noisy air through her lips, steaming up the window behind the lace curtains. "Who knows? But bang go the house prices."

We watched as a man in a beige raincoat walked up to the Harts' door and knocked before casting his gaze along the street. He was a tall man, broad, really large. He was fat.

"Oh good grief, look at the state of that one," I said.

"Poor Frau Hart," said GG.

"Do you think she'll have to . . . ?"

"I really doubt you get to pick and choose in this game," GG said, as if she were an authority on the subject.

Then—PANIC! The fat man had seen us! It was as if our whispers had traveled through the double glazing and across the street. He glanced up, right at our window. We dropped to the floor, our backs against the wall beneath the sill, giggling at our own sudden fear. We huddled together in our underwear and bras.

"Clementine's in there," I said.

"Tell me about it," said GG.

"Do you think she can, you know, hear what's going on?"

GG made a face. "Gross!"

It was GG who had come up with the plan for us to be there.

As we were both moving away after the summer, we wouldn't get the opportunity to join the local Faith and Beauty group, like Angelika Baker and the rest. So GG asked the school if we could have a couple of afternoons a week off to set up our own ad hoc club.

"Just to teach ourselves the essential skills before we go," GG told Fräulein Allis.

Fräulein Allis had questions, of course. "And what will these 'essential skills' be exactly, girls?"

She kept directing her questions to me, even though I wasn't the one doing the talking. I was the one most likely to confess, though, I suppose—to run from the room and tell her not to worry.

"Oh, you know, the usual," GG cut in. There was barbed wire in her voice; I could hear it. "Just a bit of Familie, Kinder, Haus."

Family, children, house.

Fräulein Allis paused, absorbing the words as if they'd been a curse. She wetted her painted lips. "Why do we always end up doing this, Gabi, huh? Doing battle like this."

I looked to GG to understand what was going on. Her jaw was tense, her eyes shining. Was this a hangover from all of their arguments about GG's smoking?

"You know we're fighting for the same side, don't you?" Fräulein Allis continued.

I shifted in the silence, willing GG to speak.

"I don't know what 'side' you're talking about," she said at last, her voice lacking its usual punch. "All we're going to do is some embroidery. Knit socks for the boys in the barracks, write them love poems, that sort of thing."

She gave Fräulein Allis a tight, painful smile. Our teacher sighed. I looked into Fräulein Allis's spidery-lined eyes and wondered why no one had reported her for setting a bad example by wearing mascara. But also I was thinking that she was, just as she'd said, on our side. She had meant that.

Then GG added: "This is all Jessika's father's idea, so . . ." And then the deal was done.

I was furious, of course.

"Why did you say *that*!" I squeaked on the walk home. "What if she goes and discusses this with my dad?"

"She wouldn't dare."

"But what if she just mentions it, in passing, at a parents' evening or something?" A panic attack was centimeters away, I could feel it. "Then what do I say to my dad when he comes and asks me?"

"You tell him that we're setting up an ad hoc Faith and

Beauty group," she said, throwing an arm across my shoulder. "Because that's exactly what we're doing."

I gathered together a stack of Mum's embroidery patterns, some scraps of weaver's cloth, and a box of threads to take to school the following day. Then at GG's oh-so-quiet house after lunch, when our mothers were off making chutney and singing "O, Women with German Hearts" at the meeting hall, I spread the patterns across her dining room table. GG grabbed the box of pins, opened it up, and shook them free. She snapped the paper bands off a couple of bundles of fresh thread and unraveled them, willy-nilly.

"What are you doing?" I asked.

"Making it look convincing," she said.

She opened up the cupboard beneath their People's Radio and dug out some half-finished embroideries still in their frames—one of some flowers, another of what was maybe, possibly, a cat.

"They're Lindy's," she said. "She was into all that."

We stared down at the lopsided eyes of her older sister's awful embroidery, tilting our heads to see if it looked better from another angle.

"I never said she was any good at it." GG laughed. Then: "Come on, let's go."

"Where?" I asked. I had started to thread a needle.

"Upstairs," she said. She was already out the door and into the hallway.

"But I thought you said that we were actually going to do this, sewing and knitting and stuff."

"Oh, come on, Jess," she said. "Don't play innocent."

I am innocent, I thought as I followed her up the stairs. Though I understand now that word can also mean naive. And certainly I was that.

We sat on the floor beneath the window and I told GG, "She's gone a bit mad, you know, Clementine."

The papers she'd given me were burning a hole in my wallpaper from their baseboard hiding place.

GG nodded. "Bet she's gone properly cuckoo at home all day with nothing to do."

"I mean, she's gotten into all these conspiracy theories," I said. I needed to talk to someone. I needed someone to make things straight.

"What, the ones about the Americans?" asked GG. "The ones about them having satellites that watch us?"

I shook my head. "No."

"Because if the Yanks were sitting up there with their binoculars, we would just wipe out New York in a second."

"I *know*!" Repeating other people's theories only made you sound like a believer yourself. "Not that theory!"

"Which one, then?" GG asked.

Deep breath. "The one about the Jews."

Silence.

Then GG started chuckling. She let her cheek fall onto my bare shoulder. She grabbed hold of my knee.

"Oh god! Angelika Baker believes that one too!" GG managed through her laughter.

"Does she?"

"Yeah, her mum is totally neurotic about it. She's convinced Angelika that some of them are still hiding out, that they've all had their noses fixed and are passing themselves off as normal people." GG let the giggles take over for a moment. "She's terrified that Angelika is going to pop her cherry with a piece of dirty Jewry and that'll be it. Spoiled blood. Onto the scrap heap. Kaputt!"

"No, no," I said, shaking my head again. "I meant the other theory."

"What's that, then?"

"The one about them all being killed."

"Oh, right." GG stopped laughing. "I wouldn't know about that."

We were both quiet for a moment. We stared at the half-built train set laid out on the floor of GG's brothers' room.

"Do you think it matters if they were?" I said. "Killed, I mean."

I wanted to have this conversation. But at the same time I wanted to jump up from the floor and shake myself free of it. Why had I gotten myself into this madness? Believing every single silly thing that I heard.

"Maybe if they really were so evil . . ." GG shrugged.

"They stole and lied, didn't they?"

"They killed and ate their own children," GG said.

Quiet again.

"But that's not what happened, is it?" I said. "What Clementine says? That they were all murdered."

"No," said GG. "They all went to America. They all got sent there."

"All of them?"

"Yeah, I guess."

"How did they get there?" I tried to make it sound like a reasonable question, not one from a crazy person. "Because we didn't have planes that could fly that far back then, did we?"

"They put them on boats." GG was using the voice she'd used with Fräulein Allis now. The one that said, *There you go, that's the answer you want, isn't it?*

"Right," I said.

GG was up on her knees. She poked her head over the windowsill again. I joined her. The fat man had gone—inside, we guessed. To get what he'd come for. The street was still. The flags on the poles at the front of both our and the Harts' gardens were hanging as limp as tea towels. I thought that was it, that there would be nothing more to see and we were going to have to face the silence and my questions again. Then a bunched-up coat flew over the Harts' high garden gate at the side of their house. Hands appeared at the top of the gate, arms next, a head, shoulders. A woman with dark curly hair who we'd seen go in through the front door earlier was swinging a leg over the fence. She was dressed really oddly, like a man, like someone from a play, maybe, in tight black trousers and a maroon turtleneck. She jumped onto the path, fell onto her side, and scrambled quickly to her feet. Then a bearded man in a scruffy T-shirt was pulling himself up over the gate, then another woman, and another man. They all waited until the last man was over, though he was urging them to go without him, and then they dashed away, off down the street.

"Oh my god!" we both gasped.

"Do you think . . . ?" I asked, not really knowing what it was that I thought. An image shot through my mind—Clementine's fingers curling into that defiant fist. *All my crimes are political.*

"They're trying to leave without paying Frau Hart for the sex," GG said, utterly convinced.

"What?" I said, realizing I was about to do it again, like I had with my father—say my line, perform my part. "No way!" I gasped.

GG folded her arms and nodded. "Yep."

We waited for more action from the street, but none came. We got to our feet. The show really was over.

"Have you noticed how things get busy there on the afternoons when all the women are at the Frauenschaft meetings?" GG said, rearranging the curtains before we left the room.

"How do you know it isn't like that on the afternoons when our mothers are around?" I asked.

"I don't, I guess," she said. "It's just the vibe I get."

She made for the doorway and I found myself grabbing her hand and pinching it too tight.

"Please don't report it," I said. We both looked back instinctively to the window, to what might be going on in that house across the street. "Any of it," I added.

"I wasn't going to," she said.

"Good," I said.

"Because people in glass houses . . ." said GG. But she didn't finish her sentence.

JUNE 2013

It began with things she would say in conversation. Awkward, stagey things. It was my mother's turn to read a script—and hers sounded like it belonged to one of those awful dramas they put on the People's Television in the afternoon. The ones where it doesn't matter if they're romances, horror, or knockabout comedies, the ending is always the same—the hero is strong and does the right thing.

"You know when you take Wolf for a walk . . ." Mum said as we did the washing up one evening.

"Yes," I said.

She had her rubber-gloved hands in the water. I was drying.

"And you know you sometimes see mushrooms growing . . ."

"Yes."

"Well, you understand that there are good mushrooms and there are bad mushrooms, don't you?"

"I never pick mushrooms," I told her, taking my finished stack of dinner plates to the cabinet. I came back to dry the dessert bowls.

"No, no, I know you would never do that, but if you did . . ."

"But I don't."

"No, and I'm not saying that you would."

"So what are you trying to say?"

She stopped washing, rested her wrists on the edge of the sink, and turned to look at me. We are alike, she and I—the same shape nose, the same color eyes. I think she finds it easier to deal with Lilli, because Lilli is clearly a different person. But I am just a piece of Mum. She closed her eyes and bit her bottom lip. I waited for her to get to the point of this bizarre lecture on woodland foraging.

"Are you talking about when we do the collecting for the health service?"

Mum looked down at her rubber-gloved hands and shook her head.

"Because I'm nearly always on chamomile. Sometimes birch leaves. We don't do mushrooms. And if we do collect mushrooms for the Aid program, then it's the boys who get that job. They've had the better coaching, and no one wants to murder anyone's granny by accidently picking a death cap."

She was still looking down.

"I could tell Fisher to give the girls a class on identifying mushrooms too, if you're really that worried."

"Ask," she muttered.

"What?"

"You wouldn't tell Fisher to do the class, you would request it."

"Yes, I didn't mean . . ."

Then came a horrible wail from the back garden. Mum's eyes sprang upward, to the window.

"Oh *no!*"

I started snorting with laughter.

Lilli had been rolling around on the grass with Wolf. I could get quite jealous of her, all that time she had for mucking around. But then I would remember that she was going to turn eleven that month and the fun would end and the hard work would start, and then I'd feel bad for wanting to rob her of the time she had left.

Lilli was up on her feet, weeping, her shoulders hunched around her ears, looking like she was about to throw up. She'd rolled in one of Wolf's turds, hidden in the grass, and they were getting sloppy in his old age. It was all through her hair and across her cheek.

"Oh, for goodness' sake!" Mum sighed, pulling off her rubber gloves. Out the door she went, focused now on cleaning up a whole other kind of mess.

Then came the book.

I went up to my bedroom after the BDM meeting the following evening and there she was, on my bedside table—the deadly fierce yet deadly soft, good deutsche girl on the cover of *Mädel von Heute, Mütter von Morgen*, nose in the air, thinking she's better than everyone else. The sight of her stopped me like a downward strike to the brachial plexus. I picked up the book. It was definitely our family copy—Oma Davina's name and the date were there on the first page—but it should have been in my little sister's room. She was dutifully working through the section entitled "Examples from the Animal World" and still had a number of excruciating chapters to go. I felt a pang of pity for Lilli. I believe it is entirely possible for a person to die of cringing, and I was very lucky not to meet my early death while finishing that book. It's written as a conversation between a mother and her daughter, but no mother and daughter I have ever met. Every other word is "mein Schätzchen" or "mein Herzchen"—*my sweetie pie* this, *my little heart* that. Our mother always called a spade by the right name, and we certainly never talked to each other about where babies came from. As for love—I'd rather have been struck by lightning than have her try to explain it to me.

There was a bookmark in one of the later sections. Lilli was eager to get things over and done with, it seemed, and was motoring ahead. I opened it up—she'd reached the part where the daughter tells the mother some gossip about Anni, a girl who everyone is talking about because she's only seventeen and has found herself—dun, dun, *dun!*—"with child." The daughter is apparently "trembling like the aspen leaves" about the whole thing. The mother's response is not that her daughter should stop being a wet firework; instead she calmly explains how Anni's child will have to be taken away and given to proper, deserving parents, which any daughter with half a brain would have worked out anyway. And then the mother offers up a moral to the whole sordid episode: "Two people must only indulge in each other if they are married."

Indulge in each other.

I was back there, behind the curtains of the meeting hall, Fisher pushing the hard lump of his crotch into my belly. I was in GG's bedroom, looking at the naked shape of her in the curtained afternoon light. I snapped the book shut.

This was Lilli's doing, I decided. She was so desperate to

avoid any more squirming that she had casually "lost" the book in my room. That was the only possible explanation.

Then the phone trilled unexpectedly through the carpeted quiet of the house one afternoon after school. The phone NEVER rang at that time of day, when everyone knew there would only be me to answer it. My fingers trembled a little as I lifted the handset from its cradle. It could only be bad news.

"Keller 74837?" I said, trying to mimic my mother's telephone voice.

There was a huge sigh on the other end of the line, then, "Jess?" It was a lead-heavy question.

"Yes . . ." I said.

"It's Katrin."

A weird, confusing pause.

Katrin?

My big sister always called on a Sunday evening, with my father taking the handset first, then my mother, speaking until Katrin ran out of coins. I would then be regaled—in parent stereo—with her fantastic achievements until I was nauseous.

"Yeah, I know it's you, you . . . twonk," I grunted, wincing at the uselessness of my insult. I was off guard. I hadn't recognized my big sister's voice at all. I'd never spoken to her on a phone line before, had had no reason to. I was right. There must be something wrong. I was about to ask what that something was, but she spoke first.

"So," she said with another sigh. "What's going on?"

She didn't sound in trouble. She sounded as grumpy as always.

"Nothing much," I said defensively. I buried the *Why do*

you want to know? that was bubbling beneath the surface. Was Katrin trying to be friendly? I couldn't be entirely sure. It was all very peculiar. "How's athletics camp?" I asked, because I felt I had to, though I made it clear in the tone of my voice that I cared not one bit about her answer.

Katrin didn't reply. There was a crackle and a clunk as my sister put a hand over the receiver. I got the muffled swirl of noise you hear when you put a seashell to your ear. She was saying something I couldn't make out to a person there with her. The seashell came away.

"Look, Jess, what do you want?" she demanded. "I need to go."

"But you . . . But you called me," I fumbled.

"Only because Mum told me to."

"Oh." Was Mum trying to get us to become friends? Wasn't it all a bit late? "Right," I said.

"So, what do you need to talk about?" Katrin pressed, getting cross now.

"Nothing," I bit back.

"Well, fine!" she snapped.

"Fine!" I echoed.

"But I really do have to go."

"Well, go, then!" I yelled. "And you can—"

But I was shouting at the pay phone's beeps.

It was all leading up to this.

The following afternoon I walked in from school to find Mum sitting in the hallway, waiting for me. She was wearing her good dress, her good shoes, and her good wool coat. Outside, the needle was knocking seventy-five degrees.

"Did someone die?" I asked.

"We're going to the doctor," she replied. Her face was pale, her voice flat. She looked thin all of a sudden.

"Why?" I dropped my bag. "Are you ill?"

I was going to take her hand, kneel beside her, do something, but she didn't want that. She got up, swerved her hips around me, and stalked off into the kitchen. Her gloves fell off her lap but she didn't notice. They were her best ones too—silvery gray with an embroidery cuff. The ones she wore to look respectable rather than to keep warm.

"Go to your room and rebraid your hair. We need to leave in five minutes," she instructed.

This was awful.

I picked up the gloves, placed them back on the chair, and went upstairs to do as she said.

She was silent in the car, kept her eyes on the road. She wouldn't answer my questions. My first was, "Is it serious?" Followed by, "Does Dad know?" And then, "Maybe we should have him come with us too, don't you think?" After a few moments searching for the right amount of courage, I eventually asked THE question: "Is it cancer?"

The only question she would answer was, "Where's Lilli?"

"She's playing at Suki Franz's house. No need to worry about her."

I couldn't get anything from Mum in the waiting room. Respectable people do not discuss their ailments within the earshot of others. It was talk enough that we were there in the first place. Though logic runs that the other people in the waiting room were there for some weakness too, so if they wanted to go and blabber about it, they'd only be shaming themselves. And anyway, we used a different doctor from most of my friends. A better one.

Mum thrust a copy of *Das Deutsche Mädel* into my hands, one I already had at home. The front cover showed the Faith and Beauty girls from the birthday celebrations in April, an aerial shot of the culmination of their dance — WIR GEHÖREN DIR — which now only made me think of SS stiffies.

I was obedient. I flipped open the magazine and tried to read. There was an article about Jay Acker's upcoming visit that I hadn't bothered to finish in my copy at home.

It would not be a surprise if the boy requests asylum from his own brutal nation after seeing the freedoms of the Greater German Reich, read one enboldened paragraph. Some of the Faith and Beauty girls had been photographed for the piece too, with their opinions printed underneath.

I think that this is his true home, really, said Anneka.

This will be like a homecoming for him, said Frida.

*Blah blah blah blah blah something-something repetition-of-the-word-*home, said robot-eyed Jenny.

I slapped the magazine shut. I was starting to think like Clementine. In the article, Jay Acker had explained, in *German,* how thrilled he was to be visiting our nation. The writer had been very keen to emphasize that there was no interpreter, no translator, yet there was also no explanation of how he came to speak our language so fluently. The inspirational quotation on the wall of the BDM meeting hall that week had been: EVERYTHING IS GERMAN THAT BELONGS TO GERMAN HISTORY, IN WHOM GERMAN BLOOD FLOWS, WHO SPEAKS THE GERMAN LANGUAGE.

Coincidence? asked the voice in my head. Not Clementine's voice anymore, my voice.

Mother had not picked up a copy of *Frauen Warte* for herself. She stared straight ahead. I had pretty much decided she was definitely, certainly going to die. The doctor would break the terrible news to me. He'd explain how I was the woman of the house now and must give up my place at skate camp to become my little sister's new mother. I would have to take on this information without crying, because both my mother and the doctor would be expecting great strength. I would need to be like the good deutsche girl on the cover of *Mädel von Heute, Mütter von Morgen*. Chin up, eyes to the sky.

"Fräulein Keller!"

The sound of my name sent an electric shock through my entire body. We stood, my mother and I, and it was only when the door of Dr. Hardy's room was shut behind us that I realized I still had the office copy of *Das Deutsche Mädel* in my hands—rolled up tightly, as if ready to use as a weapon.

The last time I had been in Dr. Hardy's room was for a damaged tendon in my arm, an injury I'd picked up skating, which Ingrid had initially suspected was a break. That was a couple of years ago. Dr. Hardy had gotten a lot more beardy since then. I wondered how he thought I had changed. Did I seem mature enough to become the new commander in chief of my mother's kitchen?

He gestured for us both to sit. We did. He cleared his throat. "And what can I help you with today?" he asked.

He was staring right at me, wearing just half his smile.

I opened my mouth, closed it. It felt like Katrin's phone call all over again. I slowly shook my head and looked to my mother.

She cleared her throat. "I believe, Doctor—and I'm sure that my husband and I can rely on your complete confidence in this matter . . ."

She paused so Dr. Hardy could give her a nod—his signature on this particular deal. Her voice was strange, like polished metal. "You see, my daughter requires medication of some sort. A cure for . . . Well, she has some misplaced attentions, and I have been reliably informed that a course of hormone injections is all that is required to correct this . . . this . . ." Her eyes went wide as she fished around for the right word, any word except THE word. And I realized I had gotten my mother all wrong. She did not call a spade by the right name after all.

"To correct this blip?" Dr. Hardy offered helpfully.

He made me strip down to my underwear and lie on the bed. He measured my pulse, took my blood pressure, and put an icy stethoscope against the warmth of my chest, only because he needed to make a good show of things for Frau Keller. That's what I believe. The room was cold. A ropy old radiator chugged away beneath the examination table, warming only my left thigh. I lay there desperately trying to work out who had informed on me. This was far too brave an act for Fräulein Allis, too reckless for GG or one of her family. Had Helen Gross seen us? Could my father really read my mind?

Frau Keller stood at the end of the bed examining me as well, her eyes wandering all over my body, searching for clues. Any lasting evidence, maybe. Dr. Hardy lifted each of my arms in turn and twisted my palms this way and that.

He traced the path of my veins with a finger. He was faking it, just filling time. He asked me about the regularity of my periods and whether I experienced pain in my breasts, in my calves, in my chest, in my head. After each of my answers he pooched out his lips — big, fat, pink things buried in the undergrowth of his mustache. He chewed over my words as if deciding what to do. But we all knew — all three of us — that he was only ever going to do what Frau Keller had originally instructed.

And I let him do it. I made no fuss as he stuck the needle in my stomach. I said nothing as he calmly explained how this "blip" was due to an imbalance in my hormones — something he could easily fix. I kept my mouth shut while I put my clothes back on, and I didn't speak on the journey home. No words were needed when we repeated the trip the following week and the week after that. Even when the nausea got so bad I could barely eat and when my hair started to fall out in handfuls, even then I stayed quiet.

Because I was so ashamed.

I kept my silence at school, speaking only when a teacher asked me to.

"What's wrong, Jessika?" asked Ruby, Erica, Angelika, and the rest. "Are you ill? You seem really quiet. Why aren't you eating your lunch?"

They knew, I told myself. Everyone knows.

"Are you not talking to GG anymore?" they probed. "Has she upset you? Shall we have a word with her? Because we will do that if you want us to."

I'd shake my head and off they'd go, to have a giggle and a sneer behind my back, I assumed. "Who would have thought it? Poor Herr Keller! The disgrace!" That's what I imagined them saying. The knife had sliced through the curtain to reveal me hiding there. I was naked in front of everyone. Bleeding to death in front of everyone. It didn't occur to me then that Herr Keller was certain to have made sure that no one knew. And if they did, he would have made them quickly unknow it. To everyone at school it was just two friends falling out, and all they wanted was a little piece of the drama.

In the small moments when I thought I wasn't being watched, I would steal a glance at GG, only to work out if she was getting the same treatment from Dr. Hardy's office. Was she looking puffy and dark in the face? Was she in any kind of pain? It didn't seem so. She still went off behind the PE sheds to blow smoke across the town. At the BDM meetings she kept time in the march. She was fast and strong and took good aim. Her cakes rose. Her hospital corners fell at the perfect angle.

GG seemed to have escaped. Though Herr Keller was certain to have given her parents their instructions. If GG wasn't feeling shame, she was definitely feeling fear.

The side effects, meanwhile, were killing me. My milk-skin broke out in red, headless lumps, my belly ached, and my head swam.

Ingrid said I was a danger to myself on the ice.

In the middle of the rink, I lifted up my training top, just enough for her to see the pink welts and the small blue bruises where Dr. Hardy pinched the skin of my stomach and stuck in his needle.

Ingrid's gloved hands flew up to her face. Somehow I knew I would not need to explain to her what this was. Somehow I knew I could show her and she would not be disgusted.

"Mein Herzchen," she whispered. *My little heart.*

She took the fabric of my top from my hands and pulled it back down, arranging it neatly over my practice skirt, looking over to the door as she did.

"Es tut mir leid," she said. "Für dich, für uns beide."

Two apologies. Both sides. *So sorry for you, so sorry from me.*

"It's not your fault," I said. But I could see how she might feel responsible. She had wanted me to have what she hadn't, not realizing it wasn't there for anyone's taking. Not even mine.

That morning I embraced the freedom of the ice more than ever.

My mother did not call me her "Herzchen" or her "Schätzchen." She came into the bathroom one evening to find me sitting on the edge of the tub, crying. As she spoke to me she pressed against the radiator on the opposite wall. I wanted her to hold me tight, but she wasn't going to do that. She insisted that I tell her the reason for my tears.

"I have this pain," I said. "A burning. Down there."

She nodded calmly; her only words of sympathy were that we must trust in Dr. Hardy. Men grow up prepared to die for what they believe in, she said, and women must grow up willing to suffer. This was normal; this was expected.

That week's inspiring quotation on the wall of the meeting hall: ONLY THE GREATEST SACRIFICE WILL ONE DAY REVEAL THE GREATNESS OF VICTORY. WHAT IS EASILY WON IS EASILY FORGOTTEN.

"The pain," my mother told me in a voice that had an edge of a warning, "is just the evil coming out."

When I was well again, she assured me, the visits to Dr. Hardy would stop. Did I understand?

She waited for my nod of agreement on this particular deal, and I gave it to her.

The strongest piece of truth I took from Clementine's essay notes: you have to make a choice. Do you fight, or do you keep your head down? Do you put your chin up and your eyes to the sky, or do you tremble like the aspen leaves and contemplate throwing yourself in the fast-flowing river at the bottom of the garden? Or is there, I asked myself, a way to do both? Can you be two people—someone to fool them, and also someone who is not a fool to yourself? Can you live like that?

After school the next day, I set out my books and papers on the dining room table—*Ausgewählte Reden aus der Geschichte* (*Selected Speeches from History*); Mum's *Compendium of Celebrations*; the scrapbook of newspaper cuttings that mentioned Dad.

The best bait in the most irresistible trap. Here we were again. I knew the lines to this play, and so did he.

As soon as he hung up his beige raincoat, his head was around the door. "What have you got going on, Jessika?"

There had been no direct discussion between me and my father about my treatment. None at all. That was women's business. The way he had maintained the wonderful veneer of our relationship in the face of my sickness and tears had been astonishing. Flawless.

"Oh, I'm just giving some thought to the Sonnenwendfeier," I sighed. I had the scrapbook open at the clipping from last June's summer solstice festivities—Dad on his podium, the local HJs positioned around him. One side of their faces was in shadow, the other lit by the fire. "It's only a week away, and I'm worried. Are our Kameradschaft and Mädelschaft doing things bigger and better than last year? I think we've let things slip in all the preparations for the Trafalgar Square concert."

He stepped into the room, stood at my shoulder, and watched me for a moment. I was sketching a plan for the bonfire—an ambitious basket-weave construction of logs around a belly of tinder and charcoal bricks. I like to think in that moment that I was being astonishing in return, creating a wonderful veneer of my own. I stopped shading the red centers of the flames and pushed my picture into a clear space on the table for my father's inspection. I had drawn a circle of BDM figures around the fire, their arms lifted in salute.

He picked up the sketch and . . . the doorbell rang. My heart bubbled and skipped at the perfect timing of it all. This was how it felt to conduct the orchestra, not play second flute.

"I'll get it!" I sprang to my feet and slipped out into the hall before Dad could protest.

I could see the upright, brown outline of our guest through the mottled glass of the front door, the red, white, and black on his sleeve. I took a moment to brush myself down, to remind myself that he would be far more nervous than me. After all, I knew what was going on.

I had asked him at the end of the previous evening's meeting—or rather, ignoring my mother's advice on how to speak to our HJ leader, I had told him—"We should like you to come to dinner." I made sure my announcement was not overheard by Ruby or Angelika, by Dirk or Fräulein Eberhardt, and especially not by GG, though I knew she would find out eventually.

Fisher had no choice in how to respond.

"I'd be delighted," he said, all politeness, though I could hear that he was wary. Was he accepting an invitation to meet his prospective parents-in-law or booking his ticket to a private roasting by my father for abuse of rank that evening behind the curtains?

"Felix!" I cried as I swung open the door, loud enough for Dad to hear this informal address, loud enough to bring him curiously into the hallway. Fisher had given his uniform an extra iron before walking the short distance to our home, I could tell. (Would fewer creases lessen his sentence?) I could imagine him fretting over his decision to wear trousers rather than shorts—what would look most suitable for an audience with Herr Keller: knees or no knees?

Fisher opened his mouth to say hello but, seeing my father, went straight to a salute. "Heil Dean!"

"Herr Fisher," Dad said, switching from the home voice he'd been using with me moments earlier to his official voice. "I don't believe we were expecting you."

I cut through the frost with a girlish laugh that was a little odd and surprising to us all. "I'm so sorry, Daddy." I leaned in and gave my father a short, disarming squeeze to the wrist. "This is my doing. I so wanted Felix"—I overemphasized the consonants of his name, relished them—"to help me plan the Sonnenwendfeier that in my excitement I completely forgot to ask if we could set another place at dinner. Forgive me."

I stepped forward, onto our WILLKOMMEN! doormat, and took Fisher's hand, pulling him across the threshold. What a thrill! What a strange, powerful thrill! To initiate contact, to surprise Fisher with it, the smallness of my hand around his large fingers. I felt a little breathless and silly. I kept a grip on him and turned to look at my father, to see the aftershock of this small physical action, and all its meanings, ripple across my father's face. Fisher's knuckles twitched in my grip. Dad coughed the discomfort from his throat, looked away from my fingers, his daughter's fingers, interlaced with those belonging to a younger, more virile man than he. This was what he had wanted, after all; how could he now object?

"I'm sure an extra place at dinner won't be a problem," he replied.

And we all three went into the dining room to continue our work.

On my lined reporter's notebook I had copied out some words by Friedrich Ludwig Jahn about the symbolism of the solstice flames, about how they served to fry the traitors, the troublemakers, and the liars. "I don't know if you've gotten your speech all sorted yet," I said to my father, "but I do know you are so extremely busy. I thought I would play secretary and make a start." I gave him a large, angelic grin and read aloud what I had on my page. As I did, Dad and Fisher circled one another like dogs trying to get the scent of the other's backside. Fisher refused to sit if my father, his superior, was standing. My father, in return, refused to sit until Fisher, our guest, was seated first. Fisher sweated into the collar of his well-pressed shirt.

Once they had both negotiated their way into a chair, the whole dance began again when Dad got up to pace and dictate some new words for the speech.

"Will you just sit down, boy!" my father barked—and things ran a little smoother from then on, now that restraint was gone and Dad felt able to openly, loudly, pull rank.

Moving on to the fire itself, Dad grilled Fisher on his ability to re-create the construction in my sketch, adding in his own exacting specifications for the condition of the wood and the timings of the build. *And where will you source these logs? How many boys will you send to collect them? Which boys? Why have you chosen that boy? What are his particular qualities for the task?*

Fisher stuttered his way through his answers, unprepared, understanding that though we were talking about logs, we were also not talking about logs. Sweat patches bloomed around Fisher's armpits. I'm sure he was aware of them and was willing his body not to release any more testosterone into the air, in case the alpha dog got a whiff and decided to bite.

That battle settled, I took up the issue of music and dance. "I think you should pay a visit to the Baxters' house, Felix; make sure Michael and his brothers really have made a start on their trumpet practice. Each year they say they're rehearsing into the night, but do we ever hear them, Father?"

Dad shook his head.

"Yes, Fräulein Keller," came the reply.

"And I'm thinking Ruby Heigl should work on a new arrangement of the Freedom Song," I went on. "Last year's 'Young

People Rise Up' was okay, but I think we can do something that honors the dignity of the celebration a little better. And the dance . . . Some of the moves Angelika thinks are appropriate . . . you should see them! Well, no, you shouldn't. Isn't that right, Felix?"

"Yes," he said. Then, realizing that his reply sounded all wrong: "No, no, they are not suitable in any way."

In the following silence, I looked up and met my father's gaze, awaiting his judgment on the scene I had created—his efficient, patriotic daughter and her potential suitor of rank.

"This is excellent work, Jess," he said at last. "All of it, it really is excellent."

At dinner, Lilli stared, mesmerized, at Fisher, churning her food with an open mouth. We were not used to boys in our house, especially not at such close quarters, or with Fisher's startling blue gaze and taut, imposing physique. I remembered my own fascination with the older Anderson boys next door when I was little, the swagger of them but also the awkwardness of them, being young boys trapped inside their big, masculine bodies.

My mother fussed at the stove more than usual, putting her apron on, taking it off again, apologizing over and over about how, had she known we were having a guest (an aggressive lilt to her voice, a stare in my direction), she would have prepared something rather more impressive than cottage pie. "And we don't usually eat in the kitchen when we have visitors," she emphasized for the third time, "but I would hate to disturb all those very important notes and plans you have laid out on the dining room table."

"It's quite all right, Frau Keller," said Fisher, on repeat, fielding the unnerving glare of my little sister with small, tight smiles.

Then my father tersely instructed Mum to "Just bloody sit down, Miriam, would you," chuckling in Fisher's direction afterward. *A little joke between the menfolk, there, hahaha.* And my mother did as she was told.

"Right," said Mum, eventually seated, finally picking up her knife and fork. She turned to our unexpected guest with a new vigor, perhaps realizing that in the hierarchy of the table she was still second in command. She narrowed her eyes. "So, tell me of your parents' lineage, Herr Fisher."

When the longest day finally fell dark, I was the first on our street to light a torch. Everyone left their houses—the children excited to be out after curfew with no risk of being punished—and they lit their torches from the fire of mine. Before we marched up the hill, Lilli and I did a puppet show for the littlest ones, based on the old story *Trust No Fox on the Green Heath and No Jew upon His Oath.* We'd made the puppets ourselves by stitching felt and buttons onto Dad's old socks. We handed out sweets and, once up the hill, I helped Mother serve sausages from the grill with Frau Gross. I thankfully saw little of Fisher; all his focus was on making sure that fire burned as fiercely as he'd promised.

Then it was time to join my Mädelschaft to sing the Freedom Song.

Freedom is the fire,
It is the bright vision!

I led the low harmonies that I'd insisted Ruby insert for gravitas. We danced as we sang. I was paired with Angelika, GG with Erica. We circled one another in a slow and solemn two-step, finishing in a circle as I'd drawn on my sketch, our arms aloft. That week's inspirational poster at the BDM meeting hall: TOGETHER WE ARE EVERYTHING; AS INDIVIDUALS NOTHING. As we stood around the fire, the final notes of the song vibrating through our ribs, it made sense.

It did.

I didn't want to be different. I wanted to be in the arms of the group. I wasn't fighting a battle against my mother or my father. Not really. Only myself.

We girls stayed firm, our arms lifted, as the men of the town made their somber march to the trumpet calls. Then — silence. Awed silence. My father took his place on the decorated podium. He didn't wear his black uniform often, but when he did, he looked formidable.

"Fire is a great cleanser," he told us as the heat of the Sonnen-wendfeuer beat hard against our cheeks and the underside of our lifted arms. "In its flames we see the end of treachery, the end of lies, and a death to the rebels."

Clementine and her mother were there. I'd seen them on the edges of the crowd watching our puppet show. They couldn't have not come.

"Today is the longest day, and on this day we celebrate our victory over darkness," my father proclaimed. GG was opposite me, our faces visible to one another on the edges of the flames. We held each other's gaze, our faces giving nothing.

"But today is also the day when the darkness begins again.

144

So we must work hard! We must struggle! There must be no weakness whatsoever in our hearts!" I watched the skin of GG's throat roll up and down. "Tonight we stand united as one people, regardless of our class, and on this evening we give our pledge. We put aside our own wants, we forget our own needs. We give ourselves—heart, body, and soul—to our community, this community here today and our wider community, the Greater German Reich."

When the victory cries went up from the crowd, it took my breath away. Maybe because I knew I had scored a victory of my own. I never saw Dr. Hardy again.

Perhaps this should have been a time of contemplation for me, mourning even. Though I'd clawed back my father's approval, his trust was gone. GG's friendship too. But there was no time to dwell. The concert was drawing close and things were moving fast. Maybe the tally of what I'd lost wasn't actually that high. Had my father's wholesale trust ever really belonged to me? And when it came to love and affection, my attentions were still on the house next door. On Clementine.

A few nights later, men came in the night to empty Herr Hart's garage. They lifted the door and his things tumbled onto the driveway. Heavy pots of soil smashed onto the concrete, bags of coat hangers spilled their clattering guts, boxes tipped, letting off hundreds of lightbulb bombs. It was as if Herr Hart had purposely balanced those things at the front so they would ring out like an alarm.

They woke me. That, and the screams of Frau Hart. I crept down the stairs to see my father standing, silhouetted in the frame of the open front door. He had been woken up too. Or maybe he hadn't gone to bed, because he was still fully dressed and not wearing his pajamas. At 3 a.m. Which was unusual. I worked my way down to the stair that gave the best view over his shoulder.

"You bastards!" Frau Hart was shouting. She was dressed for bed (or rather, *underdressed* for bed), chasing the men up and down the driveway in bare feet and a flapping shirt, trying to stop their progress but having little luck. Crate after crate went past, armfuls of paperwork, a typewriter (illegal), a tape player with a red-dot button (illegal), a large, clumsy piece of machinery with a handle (I wasn't sure what it was, only that it was certainly illegal). I even saw a small, flat computer like the one Dad would occasionally bring home from work. When he did, Lilli and I would pester him to press the keys and see things come up on the screen, pretending that we were controlling television. The Harts having one of those computers hidden in their garage was so beyond illegal it hurt. I couldn't understand how all those things could have been there, right next door to us, buried beneath cans of paint, piles of wood, and sacks of dried dog food for the Harts' nonexistent pet. Watching it all go past our doorway was like being a contestant on that quiz show on the People's Television where you have to remember everything on the conveyor belt—fondue set! Hunting rifle! Aaaaaannnd a bust of the Führer!

When she realized she could do nothing to stop her garage being emptied, Frau Hart turned on my father.

"You fucking bastards!" she screamed. Her voice broke

apart. Her second scream was nothing but a rasp. "You total bastards!"

Dad put his hands up, his fingers spread, in a gesture that said, very calmly, *Please quiet down, Frau Hart,* but also *Back the hell off, you crazy bitch!* I wished that I could see his face to know exactly how he felt. I'd seen Clementine's mother in this kind of state before, but seeing it again didn't make it any easier to watch. I was terrified that Frau Hart might attack my father, rip at his skin. I wanted to run downstairs, grab his arm, and drag him away from the trouble.

But also I wanted to watch.

He would send me back to bed if he knew I was there—like he had the night the Andersons and their five boys had packed up their stuff and walked in one sad line to the large, black cars. My dad had watched that procession too. I missed most of it, because I was only six and not stealthy enough to know which of the creaky stairs would give me away.

In the end, two uniformed women took an arm and shoulder each and pulled Frau Hart back onto her own driveway. As they did, Frau Hart spat in my father's face. I put a hand over my mouth to muffle the gasp, but Dad didn't recoil. It was as if he'd been expecting it, or was just so totally used to that kind of thing that Frau Hart would have to do something a whole lot more disgusting to make him flinch. It was really shocking. It was weirdly impressive.

"You'll never take our souls!" Frau Hart cried as Dad cleaned his face with a handkerchief and the blank-faced women in their sludgy uniforms yanked our hysterical neighbor toward her own front door. "NEVER!"

They took her into the house. The men continued their ant march with the boxes. I craned my neck to see if Clementine had taken up a similar position to me on her stairs. I couldn't see her. Maybe she wasn't in the house at all. Maybe she had gone. Without saying good-bye. *Oh god, oh god, oh god, oh god, oh god . . .*

"Are they leaving?" I blurted out.

My voice made both of us jump, more startling to my father than a faceful of spit.

He turned to look up at me. "Jessie?"

He was wearing his official uniform again, I realized, as he leaned toward the light of the house. Part of his uniform, at least. The shaped trousers and the brown shirt with the black tie, not the jacket. He watched me look him up and down.

"The Harts?" he asked.

I nodded.

"No," he said. "They're not going anywhere."

I let go of a huge bubble of air that I hadn't realized had been there, held down hard in my lungs. It had only just occurred to me — Clementine could go away one day. She had come from another place — one that was nowhere near as nice as here — and she could return there.

"Clementine and her mother are staying right where they are, so we can keep an eye on them," my father said. His voice was very gentle, very kind. I understood that he knew more than he was saying, but I was happy not to know. I wanted to be protected from it — the truth. I did as I was told. I went back upstairs and I went to bed.

* * *

148

The last days of June, Clementine returned to school to prepare for her exams. And I kept an eye on her, just as Dad had asked. At the front door of the Harts' house, a man in uniform kept an eye on Clementine's mother.

This was because the morning after the garage clear-out, Frau Hart had taken a chain saw to the flagpole in her front garden. And the flagpole in ours. In fact, I'm sure she would have felled every one of them on the street if Frau Gross hadn't gotten on the phone at lightning speed and sent the sirens wailing in our direction. Not that the cars could get very far. Frau Hart, dressed in Herr Hart's trousers and a pair of worker's boots, had given the poles the final kick that sent them falling across the pavement and blocking the street. You wouldn't have thought they were long enough to stretch that far, but they were. One lay with its dead-flag-head in Frau Gross's front garden; the other landed in GG's. It could have been worse, I suppose. Frau Hart could have made them topple the other way, onto our car, in through our front window, onto Lilli and me as we stood, mouths agape, in our front doorway.

Of course, it was a really terrible thing to do and it absolutely shouldn't have happened, but I wouldn't have missed it for the world. "A piece of theater," Mum had called it when Dad and the fat man grilled her for every detail in the kitchen later that evening.

None of my neighbors had intervened to stop Frau Hart's treacherous act, and I had wondered if we might all get arrested for failure to act when the Schutzpolizei eventually arrived. We had all just watched those Party flags swoop down like big red birds. But who could blame us? Who would challenge a madwoman with a chain saw? Not that Frau Hart seemed very mad that morning. She looked the happiest she had in ages.

Clementine had stood in their driveway, her arms crossed, during the whole thing. She gave a demure cheer and a clap as each pole fell. GG's youngest brother, Kurt, had tried to join in with the cheering, only because he was little and excited and didn't really understand what was going on, and GG had had to slap him across the head to make him stop. Their family got the foulest of stares from Frau Gross, as if a five-year-old's cheers were a worse crime than desecrating Party property. Frau Gross wouldn't have dared make that face at Frau Hart. Frau Gross was far too fond of having two arms, two legs, and a head.

In the end, the Schutzstaffel had turned up, as well as the Schutzpolizei. Overkill, some might say, for one skinny woman, even if she was armed with a chain saw. The men had run from their vans, leaving the doors wide open, and clambered over the hurdles in the street. Frau Hart had just finished with our flagpole and was waving her saw triumphantly in the air, but she dropped the weapon with no resistance when the men got to her. Her work was done. She let them escort her back inside the house. Clementine had tried to follow, but another man put a hand to her breastbone, keeping her in the driveway.

This sent Frau Gross scurrying across the street to our mother, who, Lilli and I hadn't realized until then, had been standing quietly behind us. Mum's face—all still and flinty—made me think of Dad when Frau Hart had spat on him. You'd have thought someone chopping down your Party flagpole at 8:30 on a Saturday morning would make you slightly hysterical. Mum was glacial — as if she too had been expecting it.

"What are they doing, Miriam?" Frau Gross was hissing, trying not to be heard by the member of the Schutzstaffel keeping watch over Clementine. "Why are they putting her back in the house? Why are they not taking her away? She's a danger! She's a danger to us all!"

My mother shrugged. "I wouldn't know, Helen." Her voice was low and flat. Her hands went up like Dad's had — *Please calm down,* the gesture said, and also *Please back off.*

"Where is Herr Keller?" Frau Gross asked, craning to look over my mother's shoulder, as if Dad might be hiding from her somewhere in the house — not so far-fetched an idea.

"Work," my mother said.

"On a Saturday?" Frau Gross exclaimed.

"Yes, Helen, it's a very busy time."

"Yes, of course." She folded her arms across the big shelf of her breasts and turned to survey the damage in the street. "I mean, where did she get a chain saw?" She tutted, raising her voice so all our neighbors would, for the record, hear her indignation. "How could she have been allowed to own a chain saw!"

All eyes drifted over to the Harts' garage, which I knew was empty. I guessed Frau Gross knew this too. As if she would have missed last night's entertainment. There were dirty patches on the ground by the garage door where the men hadn't properly swept up. Those patches of spilled soil were glinting with flakes of glass.

"My mother stole the chain saw from your garage, Helen!"
This was Clementine yelling across from her driveway.

All eyes on Frau Gross, who choked out a gasp.

"Perhaps you'd like to tell the storm trooper here if you have a license for that?" Clementine went on, sending one suspicious eyebrow skyward.

The young Schutzstaffel guy looked to my mother, as if the decision to arrest our busybody neighbor belonged with her.

Frau Gross went white. She began to gabble. "I do not . . . I have not . . . How dare you, girl!"

Clementine started chuckling. Lilli, realizing what was going on, started chuckling too. My mother jabbed her sharply in the back of the ribs.

"Ignore her, Unterscharführer," Mum said firmly, showing off that she knew a boy's rank from the design of his shoulder straps. "The chain saw is ours. Frau Hart stole it from our garage."

This, of course, made Frau Gross's jaw snap shut immediately. Lilli and I pricked up our ears. *Dad has an illegal chain saw?*

The junior squad leader nodded, as if that was all the information he needed. Case closed.

"Oh, I wasn't suggesting that—" Frau Gross returned, but my mother chopped her down.

"Get back into the house, girls!" She clapped her hands. "This isn't a sideshow."

Clementine winked at me as we went inside, and Frau Gross saw it. Of course she did.

JULY 2013

I came to this conclusion: admitting that your parents are wrong is too hard. These are the people who are programmed to love you unconditionally. Acknowledging that they haven't stepped up to the job and cared for you in the right way is close to impossible. Partly because it would mean confessing that you are as faulty as they are, because they built you, after all.

I came to this conclusion and I thought only of Clementine. Poor Clementine.

I would help her through this realization of mine.

Herr Hart had gone. Moved out. Because of his wife and her crazy behavior. This is what Dad told me.

"It's a very busy time at work right now. Herr Hart can't have that kind of distraction."

He flicked his wilting newspaper so it stood to attention. THE WORLD STAGE IS SET read the headline. There was a picture of a bronze lion wearing a jacket of red, white, and black, photographed from low down so its old, shaggy face appeared to be surveying the scene (and finding it all very tiring). Jay Acker's white-white smile glowed from an inset photo.

It was only when Dad mentioned it that I realized I hadn't seen Herr Hart for weeks. He hadn't surfaced during the flagpole incident; he wasn't at the solstice celebrations. I hadn't seen him come in from work during any of my secret visits to Clementine. He'd been gone for ages.

"Where is he?" I asked Dad.

"We've found him somewhere to stay in London, at the office," he said.

It didn't sit quite right, that Dad should help him out like that. I knew the story ran that my father had tipped off Herr Hart about the house coming up on our street, but it was clear Dad didn't care much for him now. When rumors flew around that Herr Hart had been seen doing the weekly supermarket shopping (all the women of the town sliding their carts past him, their mouths set in perfect Os), Dad was the first to mutter about how he was bringing shame on the principle of the family unit.

But Frau Hart was an unfit mother, an unfit woman, and sterilized too. So of course an intelligent man from Berlin like her husband must leave and find someone else. It was his duty.

"What, actually somewhere to stay in your office?" I asked.

Having never seen Dad's office, I imagined it like the one where Fräulein Gruber—our school secretary—worked, with a flat felt carpet and a wooden counter, two slices of reinforced glass across the front that could be slid apart when you rang the little bell. I imagined Herr Hart in a sleeping bag under Fräulein Gruber's desk.

"Yes," said Dad. "Very much nearby."

I turned the last of my alphabet cereal around in my bowl.

Sometimes a properly spelled word, something that made sense, would come together from all the swirling.

"Why are you so busy?" I asked. Emphasis on the *you*.

Mum scraped her chair back and started noisily stacking our milky bowls and crumb-covered plates.

"Jess, will you walk Lilli to school for me this morning?" she said, her voice at least two octaves higher than usual. She tried to snatch the bowl from under my chin, but I held it tight.

"I haven't finished!"

"And I don't need walking to school anymore!" Lilli harrumphed. "I'm too old. It's embarrassing!"

"Is it because of the Jay Acker concert, Dad?" I said. "Is that why you're busy?"

"Yes, Jessie," my father replied.

"Because there's lots of auditing to be done," I said. Not exactly a question. Not exactly an accusation.

Mum's thumb was over the lip of the bowl again.

"No!" I said. I wanted to have another swirl of my milk.

"Yes!" my mother barked back.

We both pulled at the bowl, my fingers turning white. I could feel Lilli and Dad watching, taking their sides. Then I let go.

Milk sprayed over my mum's hand and up her arm, making her gasp. But she didn't tell me off. She'd won after all.

"Come on, Lilli," I snapped, getting up from the table. "I don't want you making me late."

We took our last exams. IT IS ACCOMPLISHMENT ALONE THAT DISTINGUISHES ONE PERSON FROM ANOTHER was the quotation up on the wall at the BDM meeting hall. I thought it was there to

155

inspire us to study hard, but I soon realized it wasn't talking about academic accomplishment. All those years at school: I'd expected a wonderful finale. In the end, exam week was a week like any other. The exams felt like nothing, because they would change nothing. I would still go to skate camp, GG would go to the horses in Gloucestershire, Ruby would lead the local Jungmädel no matter what our results. Erica Warner might have gotten herself something a bit cushier than painting black tips on bombshells if her results had revealed her to be some kind of genius, but you didn't often see pigs flying high over Buckinghamshire.

It was a weird revelation, one that I wished I'd had months earlier so I hadn't wasted so much time trying to work out the squares on all those hypotenuses. Our lives were already sorted. The only thing that would change them was marriage. Which was both inevitable and completely not dependent on achieving an A grade in history.

I was beginning to understand the consequences of bringing Fisher into our home, though. While I was helping Mum with the washing up one evening (her turn to dry), she declared, very casually, completely out of nowhere: "Well, I suppose you'll have to decide soon whether skate camp is the right thing to do."

The heavy casserole pot slipped from my hands and plopped back into the water, slopping suds over the side of the sink and down the front of the cupboard.

"What?" I squeaked.

"Oh, Jessika! Look at this!" She went down on her knees, sacrificing one of the tea towels to mop up the spill.

"I'm g-going to skate camp," I stammered. "Of course I'm going to skate camp. Why would I not be going to skate camp?"

"Stop dancing around, Jessika," said my mother. "You're making this worse."

I lifted each of my wet-socked feet in turn to allow my mother to swab up the last of the water from the floor. I could see a line in the hair on the top of her head, gray at the roots, then suddenly brown.

"I wonder if Felix knows that's your decision," Mum said, leaning across me to wring out the cloth in the sink. She had a small smile and a coyness to her voice that made me want to shudder.

"But . . ." I didn't know what to say. I knew I would marry eventually, have kids eventually. My skating career would be short; I understood that. Once I was in my twenties and worn out, someone younger would replace me; then I'd have to find a husband, but, but . . .

"But, Rupert," I blurted. "Katrin still went."

My big sister had been seeing this lad from the boys' elite school just before she left for athletics camp. He was a soft-hearted thing who would try to hold her hand at public events while she batted him away and told him to grow a pair. Though if you ever spied them alone, they were like two little birds, heads together, pecking through the undergrowth, feeding each other scraps.

"Yes, but Rupert was . . ." Mum looked out at Lilli and Wolf in the garden, my little sister stepping a little more cautiously through the grass after that incident with Wolf's turd earlier in the year. "Rupert was different," my mother decided. "I'm really not sure that you can expect someone of Felix's lineage to wait."

Clementine, meanwhile, had no decisions to make. They were being made for her. She took her exams with a black triangle stitched onto the arm of her blouse. The only future plan she had was her date: August 13 — the day of the concert.

"All that time to have it looming over you," I said as we walked home together after the last of the racial hygiene papers.

"All that time to stage a protest," she said.

"Why?" I lowered my voice. "What are you going to do?"

"I'm going to get myself pregnant before they have a chance to whip out their knives." She made a *hi-ya!* sound and chopped her hands through the air like a ninja. "Know any big, strong boys willing to get me up the duff?" Fisher sidled into the edge of my mind and I gave him a great big shove out the other side. I shook my head. Clementine was smiling, laughing.

This was definitely not worth reporting. It was only a joke.

Because it would have been my duty to report it, if I had thought that she was serious. I was only allowed to be with my friend again because I had promised to keep an eye on her. Otherwise I would have been with the others, doing all the extra collecting and sorting and stitching and cleaning, ready for when the world's eyes were on us. If I really cared for Clementine, I must tell my parents anything she said that worried me.

"Absolutely anything," my father had said. "However small."

*   *   *

158

They knew what she was going to do.

We'd completed our uniform inspection and finished a rehearsal of the march, practicing with the new, heavier flags that had only arrived that day—huge billowing things, strung onto beautiful polished-wood poles decorated with brass Hakenkreuzen. They were totally stunning. They were pretty much impossible to lift. The boys had competed to see who could hold one up high on their shoulder for the longest time, pretending to each other that it was absolutely no effort at all. But we could see their muscles juddering. Martin Geese bent his wrist back so badly it swelled up to match the size of his head. By the third run-through of the march, the staring match between Martin and Fisher had reached maximum intensity. Fisher's hypnogaze was challenging Martin to *go on, go on, put that flag down, have a good cry, then see what happens.* Martin's manic glare, all bloodshot with pain, was silently screaming *NEVER!* I caught Fisher darting a look in my direction to see if I was impressed, and I made absolutely sure to appear as though I wasn't.

They were beautiful, though, the flags. The reds so red, the whites so bright, none of our patching-up from sewing practice over the moth holes in the black Hakenkreuzen. The way the silk fought with the breeze . . . I wished for Clementine to be there, to witness our parade, to experience that swell in the chest. Because it was truly impossible to resist. In those moments when we were all together, all singing, everything was okay. More than okay. It was how it had always been. How it always should be.

If only Clementine had heard us:

Forward! Forward!
Our flag flutters before us.
It's the flag that marks a new age,
It's the flag that leads us to eternity.
The flag that means more than death!

She would have remembered how good devotion can feel. And then maybe she wouldn't have done what she did.

After the march, we took off our drums, stored away the flags, and organized ourselves wordlessly into three neat rows of seven, which always felt like chaos because we still hadn't gotten used to the idea of mixed-sex lineups. So when Fisher asked his first question (which I absolutely knew the answer to), I was distracted. Ruby Heigl got her hand to the sky first.

"So, soldiers," he said, "who can tell me what to do if a person should catch on fire?"

He looked up from the official briefing documents. He dropped his arms so the papers covered his crotch. The positioning of the two lightning bolts was almost funny.

"Yes, Ruby?"

I let my too-slow arm slink back down by my side. I didn't care so much for Fisher's approval, but I still wanted the group to think I was better than Ruby. Also, I suspected that Ruby had gotten a whiff of what had been going on between Fisher and me. I didn't want her thinking she could elbow her way in.

"I would stop still so as not to fan the flames," Ruby began, her shoulders doing a proud little jiggle. "I wouldn't run. Then

I would cover my face, drop to the floor, and roll around until the flames went out."

A moment of quiet, which we all used to imagine Ruby rolling around on the floor, losing her clothes to the fire. Ruby quickly realized where our minds had traveled, and her neck broke out in horrible, embarrassed blotches.

"Excellent, Ruby," said Fisher.

Her shoulders stopped their wobbling. The grinning began — huge, full beam, doing awkward battle with the rash of shame that was creeping northward.

But it wasn't excellent. Ruby hadn't given the right answer. I could see Fräulein Eberhardt on Fisher's left, poking at her piled-up hair, twitching a glance down at her shoes. I could see twig-legged Dirk on Fisher's right, rocking uncomfortably up on his heels. This was no just-for-fun warm-up question. (*When hiding out in the woods, how can you best conceal yourself from approaching enemies? If you're trapped in a car that has crashed into deep water, how could you make your escape? When necessary for survival, how should you go about cutting off one of your own limbs?*) No. This question was serious.

"Excellent," said Fisher again. He coughed and took another quick look at his briefing documents. There was a clumsy silence filled with birdsong. Ruby's grin had now begun to seriously droop. She could feel it too — the wrongness. Fisher took a big breath, a different tone: "But what if it was someone else who was on fire?"

Ruby's grin went missing in action.

"Well?" He kept his blue gaze fixed on her — which was certainly an easier option than addressing the mystified stink rising off the rest of us. Our task at the concert, we had been told, was to deliver a short, rousing marching display, stand in position for the duration of Jay Acker's musical offerings, then help out with crowd management and first aid, if the Schutzpolizei and Schutzstaffel ever let us get a look in. Which they wouldn't.

Basically, we were to stand there and look pretty (the girls) or formidable (the boys). Nothing more. Yesterday's meeting had focused on the far from monumental task of how to stop a nosebleed.

Whatever Fisher was trying to do, it wasn't going well. I knew he was terrified that I would report back.

Ruby powered on through this general uneasiness, all respect to her (which it KILLS me to say). "Well, I would tell them to do exactly the same," she said, less of the shoulder action this time. "To stay still and to cover their face and to drop to the ground, then roll around."

More unconscious tics from Fräulein Eberhardt and Dirk.

The inspirational quotation poster that week: LET THAT WHICH MUST DIE SINK AND ROT. WHAT HAS STRENGTH AND LIGHT WILL RISE AND BLAZE.

Unfortunate.

Fisher still had his blue gaze on Ruby.

"And what if that person didn't want to do as you said?" he went on, which—sod it, we couldn't control ourselves now—brought about unconscious tics from all of us.

Ruby's mouth fell open. She ummed and uhhed for a moment, then decided to ask: "But why wouldn't they want to . . . ?"

She trailed off, realizing a good few seconds after everyone else that she had wandered into a Zone and should shut her trap.

After Fisher had given us a talk about the combustibility of various fabrics (*manmade fibers burn faster than natural fibers, but a combination of the two can be the greater hazard. Your uniforms, for example, are a mixture of polyester and cotton . . .*), we took turns going up to the front and pretending to be on fire. GG was my flaming person. Awkward. But also, if I'm honest, a bloody relief—to have a good reason to be close to her. She gave it her all—hysterical screaming, arms flailing, running in dizzy circles. Utterly fabulous. Fräulein Eberhardt stood there tutting. I slipped my arms into the sleeves sewn into the fireproof blanket, waited until GG was in the optimum position, and then, with a grunt of effort, I booted her so hard she fell flat onto her face in the grass. (I could still feel the concrete footprint in my own backside from where Angelika Baker had done the same maneuver on me, so I didn't feel bad.) Then I spread my arms and flung myself on top of her, like a giant fireproof bat.

"Nice work, Jessika," said Fisher with rather too much enthusiasm.

I pulled myself halfway up, GG yelping, then giggling, as my elbow dug into her kidney. Karl Pfizer in the front row was snickering. I looked up at him just as he was flicking his tongue up and down at us. I froze—a cold grip of terror. Had Fisher seen? I could report on him, yes, but couldn't he also report on me?

I looked up at our leaders. They had all seen. But it was Dirk who leaped to defend my dignity. Or possibly Fisher's, for Dirk certainly knew that he had been to dinner at our house. As if Fisher would have resisted a quiet little boast. Dirk stepped forward and struck Karl on the head several times—which was funny to everyone because Dirk is a good thirty centimeters shorter than Karl, making it quite a reach. Then Karl was immediately down on the ground doing push-ups with Dirk's muddy boot on his neck.

We were all mesmerized by the sight of it—the way Karl was sweating and letting out these small, low moans.

"Get up, Jessika," snapped Fräulein Eberhardt.

And all of a sudden I realized where I was, still on top of GG's soft outline beneath the blanket. I scrambled to standing. GG did too, dusting herself down. Her white shirt was grass stained, her navy skirt was up around her haunches.

"Look at the state of you," said Fräulein Eberhardt. The need for us girls to be both queens of combat AND pretty/presentable/alluring at the same time was taking its biggest toll on our female leader. She was growing more and more grumpy as the concert approached. Or maybe it was the further we got into the Great Integration. Because it wasn't really a Great Integration for her, but a Great Demotion. She used to be in charge, but now with Dirk and Fisher around she was only ever third in command.

"I swear you've all gone giddy," she muttered, taking the blanket off my arms and folding it for the next person.

"Yes, Fräulein Eberhardt," I said, forgetting to drop the "Fräulein," or maybe not wanting to.

*   *   *

I only left Clementine's side to go to BDM meetings.

The rest of the time, we hung out in her back garden reading magazines. When it got hot, Clementine stripped down to this tiny bikini that she said had come from Cornwall, though I'm sure Frau Hart must have run it up on her sewing machine because you couldn't get anything like that in a shop. I tried not to look too much at the lean neatness of her body, or let myself think about how she was enough. Absolutely enough.

I wore the navy one-piece Mum had bought me three years ago from Spencer's.

"Think you need a bigger size, Jess-Jess," Clementine had commented. "Got a bit of side boob going on there."

She prodded the roll of flesh escaping from the fabric underneath my armpit and said it again, delighted with this new expression of hers. "Side boob!"

I wore a light shirt over the top after that.

Clementine waited until we were outside before she took off her top and shorts, until she was standing centimeters in front of the uniformed man stationed at the Harts' back door (to match the uniformed man at the front door). This uniformed man (well, boy, really) did his best not to look or blink or react in any way, which only provoked Clementine to make a bigger deal out of taking off her clothes the next time. Arching her back. Cocking her hips.

"Maybe dieser gute deutsche Mann will get me pregnant, what do you think, Jess?" she'd say. "Was sagste, Fritz, sollen wir eins für den Führer machen?"

Whaddya say, Fritz, shall we have one for the Führer?

165

I don't know why she said it. She knew I could have—should have—reported it back to Dad. Under the circumstances, I decided to presume that the boy would say something himself if he felt it necessary. Or maybe I decided that I wasn't the right person to be telling tales on someone using a boy of rank to get what she wanted.

"She's only joking. You know that, don't you?" I told the soldier. "She's just being silly."

One afternoon I suggested we lie in the tall grass at the bottom of the Harts' messy garden. I wanted us to be out of earshot of the Fritz boy. Clementine hadn't mentioned her dad once since he'd left. I needed to talk about it, this giant elephant that lumbered across the lawn with us. I waited until she was bored of the magazines and had flipped onto her back to offer her belly to the sun.

"I'm sorry about your dad," I began. I let myself play with the dry ends of Clementine's almost-white hair.

"It's not your fault," she replied.

I let go of the tiny braid I'd been working on. "I never said that it was my fault."

"Then why are you saying sorry?"

This was classic Clementine. I would try to be kind and she would immediately chuck it back in my face.

"I'm sad for you, Clem, that's all. That he's left you. Well, your mum, I mean."

"He didn't leave us."

"He's gone, Clem."

"He didn't want to go."

Admitting that your parents are wrong is hard—that was the refrain in my head.

"Maybe," I began, very gently. "But I think you need to realize that your mum is really not well and that's why . . ."

As if on cue, Frau Hart stepped out the back door in a halter-neck dress and sunglasses, carrying a metal-framed deck chair. I watched her pry open the chair and position it on the patio so that she was facing the sun, but also so that she could read her book without the guard looking over her shoulder. The outside of the novel was covered in flowered wallpaper.

"You know he's being detained, don't you?" Clementine's voice was low and dangerous. "Against his will."

I stopped watching Frau Hart and looked back at my friend. She was still on her back, one knee bent toward the sun.

"No." I put a hand on the bare skin of her arm, feeling a buzz of strange electricity. "No one is holding him, Clem, he's . . ."

"He communicates." She pulled up her sunglasses so I could see her eyes. So I could see that she was telling the truth. "He communicates with people in America." I pulled my hand away. "With people in Canada, in Australia, all over," she went on, flicking a wrist through the air to suggest all of the many countries, all of the many people.

The blood rushed from my head toward my feet.

"What, on the telephone?"

Herr Hart is a telephone engineer in Dad's office—another well-worn refrain.

"No, Jess, online."

I edged back from her and dragged the rug taut beneath us. "What line?"

She stared at me. She narrowed her eyes. "Is that a real question, Jess? An honest one?"

"Yes . . . Well . . ." I understood what online meant, that there was this technology. I'd seen it on the People's Television. But it was only for our top people. Certainly not some lowly telephone engineer, or some girl . . .

"Because I really need to know," Clementine said sharply.

"Well, y-yes, then," I stammered. "I guess it is a real question, because I don't know how . . ."

"Has he got you locked up too?"

I shook my head. I didn't understand.

"I mean . . . metaphorically." She flipped onto her side and propped herself onto one elbow.

My mouth dangled open. The words . . . None came.

"Let's stop this," she went on, "because the damage is already done. Me, my mum and dad, we're near the end now. Let's just come out and say it."

"I don't know what you mean." A horrible panic was tightening my throat. This was too much. I wanted to pull her close to me, never let her go. But instead I was edging away. She was holding my head over a box full of snakes and she was about to open it and push my nose inside. She closed the gap between us. She cast her eyes quickly to where the guard was sweating in his jacket, to where her mother had hitched up her skirt to show her thighs to the sun. Clementine's breath was against my neck. "I know why you're here and not off polishing up all those portraits of the Führer. I know that you report back. I know that you always have, right from the start."

168

This was awful.

"It's not like that, Clementine! I look out for you!" I think I really did believe that.

I went to sit up, but she pushed me back.

"Okay, however he sells it. Whatever he calls it. I get it. I'm not cross with you. We all do what we can to survive. You do it with a good heart, I think."

"I'm innocent, Clementine," I said.

Painful tears were pricking at my eyes. My breath was short.

"Maybe . . ." she said.

"I am, Clem! I am! I love you. I really love you."

"Shhhh." She slipped her whole arm around my shoulders to stop me from leaping up. We both darted our eyes across to the guard this time. He wasn't paying us any attention. He was watching passenger jets cross in the very blue sky. From where Frau Hart was sitting, it would have looked like we were hugging, or wrestling. Just being playful.

"It's fine, Jess, it's fine," Clementine whispered. "I love you too."

But not enough. I knew that I wasn't enough.

"We only let you see and hear what we want you to," she said. "I don't think we would still be here if it wasn't for you. If we weren't friends. We learn things from you too, you know."

I couldn't bear this, the truth of it. I tried to shake off her grip, but she clamped it tighter.

"But I need to understand," she went on. "For myself, I guess. I need you to be honest with me. We can't be friends anymore if you refuse. You know where your information goes, don't you? You know what happens when it gets there?"

"I don't know anything!" I gasped. I sounded hysterical. I felt hysterical. I couldn't let myself know it.

"It's okay," she soothed. "It's okay. It's okay to admit it."

"I don't know anything!" I said, quieter this time.

"So you don't know where my dad is?"

I stared into her green eyes, her pupils jerking from left to right as she held my gaze. I nodded.

"Where is he?"

"He's staying at the office," I whispered.

I hadn't told her anything she didn't already know.

"And what office is that?" she pressed.

"My dad's office, your dad's office."

"And what office is that?"

There was just the sound of our breathing for a moment, hard and faltering. Sweat was building between the bare skin of her arm and my shoulders.

"What office is that, Jess?" She drilled the question down into my cheek. "What office is that?"

"Erzähl mir, wo du vorher gewohnt hast," I gasped.

Tell me about the place where you used to live, before.

"Nein." She shook her head. "Ask me about the place I'm going to instead."

"No."

"Ask me!"

"If there is something wrong, Clem, our parents will sort it out. It's not up to us; we're children, we don't need to—"

"We can't wait for them, Jess. When you get old, you get scared. I'm not scared. Ask me!"

"No!"

"Ask me!"

"Wohin gehst du?" *Where are you going?*

"An einen Ort, von dem ich nicht zurück kommen kann," she replied.

Somewhere I can't come back from.

"No, you're not! Stop it!" It was a last desperate order. I wrestled free of her grip. She let me sit up. I straightened the straps of my swimsuit. I was properly crying now.

She gathered her legs into her chest, folded her arms across them, and pushed her face down into her knees. I took a tissue from my bag and blew my nose. The guard looked our way briefly at the sound of it. I smiled. He looked away. Clementine's mother, though, couldn't be torn from the pages of her book.

Clementine lifted her head. "All I'm saying is, I know my cause, Jess. I know who I stand for."

The sun was sparking through the leaves of the willow trees behind her head, creating starbursts, making her seem like a goddess, making her seem immortal. I looked at the smudged red triangle that she had drawn on her upper arm in felt-tip pen.

"But it's going to get you killed, Clem." My voice was just a husk. I couldn't look at her anymore. "I don't want you to get killed."

She crawled over to me and wrapped her arms around me. She squeezed me very tight.

"It's better to live a short honest life," she said into my ear, quietly but very definitely, "than a long, long, long one in the dark."

Her mum was looking over at us now, her gaze level, sure and unblinking.

"Help me," Clementine whispered. "Don't be scared."

I squeezed her back as tightly as I could.

"*The time is out of joint,*" Clementine went on. "*O cursèd spite, that ever I was born to set it right . . .*"

"*Hamlet,*" I croaked.

"Me," she replied. "Us. We don't have to tell them everything."

AUGUST 2013

The night before Dad went away, we all sat together watching a program about the Reich's supercomputers. Mum and Dad were sitting on the sofa; Lilli and I were on the rug. A camera panned along banks of black towers humming quietly to one another. Then it went in close on a sleek, flat touch-screen. A man in a white coat was being interviewed about what we were seeing. The men always wore white coats on those programs, whether they were experts on the space program or an authority on how women could make their houses cleaner.

Trust me, said the coat. *I'm a scientist.*

"Our great nation has the fastest computers in the known world," said the man. (Clementine's voice: "But they might have MUCH faster computers in Russia, or Japan, or America.") "They enable us to do almost everything, from predicting the weather accurately"—he gave a little grin at this, as if a bit of rain was the most ridiculously trivial thing for a supercomputer to be worrying about—"to creating weapon simulations that ensure Germany is the safest and most formidable country on Earth."

The camera moved across a panel of men from the security services. Each one was sitting, focused, hypnotized, by the flickering monitor of a small, flat computer that opened like a book. They were wearing headphones and listening in on "dangerous conversations," though the white-coat man didn't explain who these "dangerous conversations" actually involved.

He didn't need to, I suppose. Everyone knew that "dangerous conversations" went on between evil terrorists with bombs in their briefcases. The camera went in close on one of the men's screens to show a moving, jagged bar code — a sound wave. This was a bad person's voice in all of its terrifying detail.

Lilli was suddenly up on her knees. "Look, Papi!" she squealed. "You've got a computer like that one!"

"No, I haven't," said Dad. *Slam*. Like a door being shut in her face.

"Oh," said Lilli.

I let my eyes slide from the screen to my sister. I watched her smile fade, her brow crease. She sat back on her heels.

The man in the white coat was saying how he was going to take the back off one of the computers now and show us its brain. I kept watching Lilli, though. I wanted to see what was going on in *her* brain. Which of her memories was winning the fight? Was it Dad all of those evenings, sitting in the dark of the dining room, focused intently, hypnotized by the flickering monitor of a small, flat computer that opened like a book? Was it the sensation of her little nail-bitten fingers once or twice being allowed to touch its delicious keys? Or was it that moment — the one where Dad shot her down and told her she was wrong?

I guessed the last one. It packed quite a punch.

I looked back at the white-coat man. He'd pulled out the

processor — a thing no bigger than a Curfew Mint — and then from inside it he extracted something so tiny he had to hold it up to a microscope with a pair of tweezers. It looked like a robot spider.

"This," said the man in the white coat, "is what's doing all the work."

He seemed terribly pleased with himself, and I think we were supposed to feel the same.

That day in the sun, Clementine had made me take home a stack of magazines.

"I already have this one," I said, handing back the issue of *Das Deutsche Mädel* with the April 20 celebrations pictured on the front.

"No, you don't." She pushed it back toward my chest.

"Yes, I do," I said.

"No, you don't."

I opened my mouth to argue but, after our earlier admissions, I didn't have the strength, or the authority. I took it.

When I got home, I left the stack of magazines on the chair in the hall while we ate dinner. Dad ran through his list of questions for me, ticking boxes and making notes.

"Is that all?" he kept prodding. "You're sure? Nothing else?"

Mum watched, slowly coming to the boil because Dad had brought paperwork to the meal table AGAIN. I was the one who felt the full steam of her annoyance, though, once we'd finished eating. It had to come out somehow.

"Er, excuse me, young lady, do these magazines live in the hall?"

Off we went.

"Do you think I was put on this earth to trail around after you, putting away your things? Do you think I enjoy it?"

It was best never to answer these questions, even with a shake of the head.

"I suppose you think that I have nothing better to do than tidy up!"

The vein at her right temple began to swell. I thought she might have a nosebleed.

"Get these to your room. NOW."

I grabbed the magazines. It took all of my restraint to go up the stairs without stomping.

Do you think I was put on this earth to trail around after you, putting away your things? YES, I wanted to scream in her face. *ACTUALLY! That's all you do. Tidy away! Tidy away Dad's things! Tidy away me!*

I tossed the magazines onto my bed and, with my restraint all used up, slammed the door behind me. I flopped onto the floor and tipped my head back against the bed, smacking it against the duvet a few times until my neck hurt. That was what made the Hitler's birthday edition of *Das Deutsche Mädel* slip from the top of the pile, slide over my shoulder, and spill onto the carpet. It fell open on a large picture of a girl. A terrifying girl. I jumped to my feet. I had read this magazine — at home and in the doctor's waiting room. I knew it front to back. There was definitely no picture of any terrifying girl.

I crept forward, crouched over the magazine, and flipped it back to its cover. Yes, this was *Das Deutsche Mädel*. Yes, this was the Hitler's birthday edition. I turned back to the page with the girl. She was one of the most in-demand celebrities of our time, the piece said. She was a singer, though the interviewer didn't ask her very much at all about music or songs. They wanted to know what she thought about money and what kind of boy she "fancied" and which part of her body she liked best. I couldn't imagine she liked anything about her disgusting self. She had nails like claws and metal through the tops of her ears. There were things drawn on her arms, and her lips were as red as blood. Her short hair was two different colors. Black underneath, blond on top.

I turned the page, to a cluster of smaller pictures of the girl. In one she was wearing a bikini like Clementine's. In another picture she was basically naked, covered only in a lace curtain dress that didn't conceal the sides of her breasts. She was offensively thin.

I threw the magazine across the room—because it was dirty, because I could almost feel the cancer crawling across my hands. I sat staring at the thing. It was a dead rat, one of Wolf's turds—something I didn't want to have to deal with. On the cover, the Faith and Beauty girls were still there spelling out WIR GEHÖREN DIR, completely unaware that there was a grotesque, alien girl inside their pages telling me I should just *"Get out there, live without regret, do it!"*

Whatever "it" was.

I crawled on my hands and knees back to the magazine. Using the very tips of my fingers, I opened it up again. There was a page of letters from readers, decorated with images of two different starving women. Neither of them had many clothes on. One was pulling down the waistband of a pair of too-tight trousers, as if to show us how painful they were, though there were no marks on her skin to back her up — her belly was weirdly smooth. The other shocking woman had a garland of flowers in her hair and no top. The words I AM FREE were painted across her naked breasts.

I carried on reading, though I knew I shouldn't. I had to figure it out. Clementine wanted me to have this. There must be something I was supposed to understand. I went through the readers' letters on the page. What were "sex tapes"? What were "plus sizes"? What did Clementine want me to grasp from all this?

I tried the next page — a man wearing just a pair of boxers was kissing the shoulder of an arrogant girl in a fluffy black dress. Further on, another man in just his boxers, this time for a medical article. Arrows pointed to the parts of his body that scientists say should be touched to increase blood flow to the penis. I thought of Fisher, that he seemed to know where to put his hands on me without the help of any magazine. Or maybe there was a corresponding edition with instructions for men? A gentle throb started up between my legs at the thought of it. I quickly turned the page. Here was an article about a terrible "crime" illustrated with pictures of Untermenschen with brown skin and fat noses shouting and holding up signs. I AM A GIRL NOT A BODY TO BE USED said one banner. Yet the terrible "crime" had not been committed by these awful people, the crime had been done AGAINST one of them. A rape. What Commie bastards do to nice German girls.

I went over to the baseboard and pulled out Clementine's notes. There was the word again.

178

Nine countries ~~taken~~ raped!

It was the first time I had ever really thought about what the word actually meant. Before, it had just been a word. A vague idea.

We traveled into London for rehearsals every day during that final week. I was instructed to shift my skating practice forward to 4 a.m. so I could be at the station with the others to catch a train at 6:30 a.m. Ingrid was furious.

"If I'm to teach all the little ones right up until midnight, then when do I actually sleep?"

Just like when Mum was fuming about something, I knew that it was best to keep quiet, be the punching bag.

"All for a stupid boy," Ingrid muttered as she laced her skates, "who can't even find a pair of trousers to fit."

"Is it, though?" I asked her. There was something fake about her fury, like when a skater cheats by starting the rotation of a jump on the ice. That's much easier than doing it for real in the air.

"Is it what?" Ingrid arranged her knitted warmers over the top of her laces and hooked them under the heel.

"Is it just a boy, though? Is it just a concert?" I looked over Ingrid's shoulder to make sure we were alone, that the man who drives the ice resurfacer had left to take his morning tea. Ingrid followed my gaze and did the same check. I lowered my voice. "Or is this them doing their hardest to control something they just can't control?"

Ingrid gave a painful sigh, closed her eyes. "Probably," she whispered. "But let me tell you . . ." She was up then and stepping past me. "I am far too old to be getting my hopes up."

I watched her take to the ice, launch into great swirls of backward crossovers that I could see were cooling her down just as much as they were warming her up.

While Ingrid wanted to know when she might sleep, I wanted to know when I was supposed to eat. For my breakfast, I was forced to stuff some of Mum's Zimtschnecken rolls into the pockets of my BDM jacket and eat them on the train.

I had thought that these trips might be an opportunity to travel into London with Dad. I wanted to get a glimpse of his morning routine, of another version of him. Not the man we got at home. The other man. Perhaps the real one. But Dad was drafted to work from London 24/7 that final week. He packed a suitcase on the Friday, the morning after we sat together watching the television program about the supercomputers, kissed us all good-bye, and said he'd be back after the concert.

"Where will you be staying?" I asked.

"At the office."

"With Herr Hart?"

"Yes," said Dad. An uncomfortable yes.

I pictured my father rolling out his sleeping bag next to Clementine's dad, on the floor of Fräulein Gruber's office, wishing each other night-night before turning out the lights. In the battle inside your brain, often the made-up image is more powerful than anything else.

*   *   *

We didn't sing.

There was excitement in the train car, but it was regimented, scary. We'd been told too many times that all the world's eyes were on us, that the images from the concert were being broadcast across the globe, that this was the first time we were letting those other, lesser nations get a glimpse of our beautiful Reich. Telling us this was meant to be motivating, to fill us with even more passion, but it only left us frozen.

At our last meeting, Fisher had opened up the knowledge section by asking: "Soldiers, what should you say if an American journalist asks you about living in the German Reich?"

Ruby Heigl's hand flew up in the air. Of course it did. I think her question-answering reflex had developed in the womb, way ahead of any reflex to suck, cough, or gag. But of course the question was entirely rhetorical. Fisher had the EXACT things that we should say to an American journalist if we got asked about living in the German Reich. They were written on the sheet of paper in front of him.

"Let's practice, shall we, battalion?"

We recited back what Fisher read out to us. *"As youngsters we have been taught the value of camaraderie—and not just textbook theories, but in the thousandfold experiences of our everyday lives."*

The words felt weirdly familiar, lines from a school play that you'd been in ages ago and thought you must have forgotten.

That finished, we were informed that if we did come across someone claiming to be an American journalist, then they were on our soil illegally, because American journalists couldn't be trusted to have access to our great nation and not abuse it by planting a bomb or something. Either that or they were lying about being an American journalist, so they were probably a spy.

So, then (asked nobody), when would we ever get to say our lines?

Fisher attempted to lift the fog of confusion by making us practice our restrain and detain techniques. We each took our turn in the middle of the circle, pretending to be an illegal/fake American journalist. I was chosen to go first — and I was lost. What did an illegal/fake American journalist in need of restraining actually look like? I decided to stand in the middle of the circle, tip my head back, and scream. It may have been wrong, but just like Ingrid's series of workmanlike backward crossovers, it made me feel better.

"Interesting interpretation," I heard Fräulein Eberhardt snicker to Dirk as I took a breath.

"In you go, Fräulein Baker!" yelled Fisher. "Go! Go! Go!"

Angelika leaped forward, put her head to my chest, and clamped a hold around my neck. She yanked me backward. The hand that she smacked across my mouth smelled of grass and mud from the squat thrusts and push-ups we'd done earlier in the meeting.

"And release!" instructed Fisher. Angelika let go. I shook my head to get rid of the little white dots dancing in my vision. My glance landed, quite by accident, on GG. I thought of the smell of her that day on the cross-country run when she'd grabbed me. From the less-than-a-second that our eyes met before flickering apart, I would have bet everything that she was thinking of it too.

*   *   *

No one on the train made eye contact with anyone they did not know. All the world's eyes were on us and they belonged to fake American journalists. And spies! And TERRORISTS!

Even Ruby Heigl understood that this wasn't the time for a singsong, and she'd been known to strike up a verse of "Eine Flamme Ward Gegeben" at a public hanging just so she could make it all about her. Instead we stared out of the windows. And at each other — safe faces.

"How can you possibly eat at a time like this?" Angelika Baker muttered as I stuffed the Zimtschnecken into my mouth. "Just watching you is making me want to puke."

Angelika had woven little red, black, and white ribbons through the French braids that started at the front of her head and worked their way around her scalp like a mountain road. Or rather, Frau Baker had. No one had enough hands or mirrors to have attempted that construction by themselves.

My hair had been rushed and would probably work loose the second we started marching. I could feel the pastry grease smeared on my chin. But I had to eat, even if it made me feel queasy, or I would collapse later from jelly legs after all that skating practice. I didn't want Fräulein Eberhardt seeing me swoon and thinking it was because I was too excited about a stupid boy who couldn't even find a pair of trousers that fit.

Because, actually, we'd all forgotten about him. When Ingrid had mentioned him that morning, there had been a brief moment when I'd honestly caught myself thinking, *What boy?* Even the girls who had gotten a thrill from Jay Acker at the start had lost interest. In the beginning his song was weird and exciting and new, but after hearing it day in and day out on the People's Radio, it felt normal and tired and obvious. Maybe if they had given us something new, we would have stayed enthralled. Instead those repeated words got stuck in our heads.

You have me in your arms
In your prison
Yet I'm feeling free
How can it be?

It had become something of an earworm. The song went around and around and around and around until you were forced to sing it out loud, just to set the pest free. The opening piano notes were enough to make you reach for the radio's off switch. Is that what it would be like when he finally stepped out onstage to sing? Thousands of German kids groaning out a sigh and ramming their fingers in their ears?

All this, for that.

When we got to Trafalgar Square, we were escorted straight to the grand hotel that we would be using as our base. We stashed our flags and supplies in one of the larger meeting rooms and were given a tour of the public areas by a pretty, bossy girl with looping braids. It was the most stunning place — beautiful, so stylish — yet the bossy girl acted as if it was all nothing — irritating, even. The lighted pillars, the screens made from suspended cord that shimmered as someone passed, all of those high-powered men and women in pristine uniform, sitting around the lobby in little leather seats with molded feet having Kaffee und Kuchen—oh, it was all so TIRESOME to her.

We were taken down the glass-paneled stairs to a moody lower-ground floor where the walls were coated in a textured navy blue, and directed toward the bathroom to freshen up. The bossy girl didn't come in with us, so that meant we were free to strike poses in front of the two-meter-high gilded mirror and squeal with delight at the sensor taps. We used two cloth hand towels each, just because we could, and rubbed the lovely hand cream into our skin, right up to our elbows. Fräulein Eberhardt hissed out a few "Calm down, girls," but I'd seen her pout her lips as she looked at her reflection in the mirror. She was as swept away by it all as we were. In a tense day, it was a longed-for moment of release.

Back upstairs and back on our best behavior, a high-ranking man from the Schutzstaffel led Fisher, Dirk, and Fräulein Eberhardt up to the top floor of the building. We went too, following behind in a neat line, our hands behind our backs, but all of the Sturmbannführer's words were directed at the older three, as if he didn't quite know how to speak to young people, especially not girls. I got a nod, of course. He had to acknowledge me.

He led us through a gorgeous suite with a vast landscape of thick-pile carpet that made you worry about the fact we were all wearing shoes, past a purple-quilted bed and a door giving us a peek into a marble-sinked bathroom, then out onto a balcony that ran along three sides of the building. It had the most amazing view of the square and the city. The streets were dressed in red, white, and black as far as the eye could see. It was one of those moments, staring down on the domed rooftops of our elegant capital, where an intense rush of love for the Fatherland was unavoidable.

But we hadn't been taken up there for the view. We were there to see the rope ladders that were stored by the railings of the balcony.

"Another potential escape route," said the Sturmbannführer.

I wanted to ask if we were the ones who would need the escape route, or if we were to stop others (Journalists! Spies! Terrorists!) from using the escape routes. Then I realized the clue was in the ladders. As if we would be providing means for the enemy to make their run for it. But then another question—if it was us making the escape, what exactly would we be escaping from? (Journalists? Spies? Terrorists?) No one asked. Not Fräulein Eberhardt, not Dirk, not Fisher. I assumed it would all become crystal clear when the general escaping started to happen.

The Sturmbannführer turned and walked back through the glass sliding doors of the hotel suite, and like the tail of a snake, we followed. It was a moment's job, I thought, to flip one of those ladders over the side of the balcony, to make it an entrance route as well as an exit. It seemed to me that this was something the Sturmbannführer hadn't considered—that people might want to get in as well as escape. I quickly pushed the thought from my mind before I felt compelled to say something out loud. All I had to do was stay quiet, but that felt like an impossible task, treacherous. Even though I had nothing to tell, not really. No details. But I had a feeling, an understanding that couldn't be shaped into words . . . I had that.

As we passed the bed, I let my hand fall away from behind my back to stroke the silkiness of the bed linen, just to distract me, just to see if I dared. The excess and the decadence of this room — it was all wrong. But it existed, for someone. I wanted to touch it. I saw that GG, immediately behind me, had let her hand drop to casually do the same. Our hands traced the same line along the neat stitching. I didn't risk turning around to see her smile. But I knew it would be there.

The Sturmbannführer escorted us outside next, through the square, past the statue of Himmler, past the lions in their flag jackets, and around the fountains where mermaids and dolphins and tritons flipped around in nothing because the water had been drained away. This would be our route to the vast stage beneath the pillars of the National Gallery. This monster stage had huge red, black, and white wings. Television screens were suspended where the monster's horns might be. None of us had ever seen anything like it. Not even at the birthday celebrations on April 20. Fisher hollered back to us the instructions he was receiving from the Sturmbannführer. We couldn't hear him ourselves, now that we were out in the open. Helicopters were circling and light aircraft were crossing overhead, leaving strange trails.

We passed other groups of HJs and BDMs, picking up snatches of their instructions from their SS escort. We straightened our backs and eyed them suspiciously. They eyed us back. Usually in situations where we met other troops, the girls would be giggly, checking out the new crop of boys. The boys would be swaggering, trying to impress. Not that day. This was the enemy. What songs and marches did they have up their sleeves? Would they be putting on a better show than us? Could we honestly say that our troop had done all we could to prepare?

Once our instruction was over, the order for the shooting came. Wehrmacht boys started working their way through the square, picking off the gulls and pigeons. Each soldier had a dog at his heel to retrieve the bird corpses to put into their sack. A man in a bright-yellow jacket followed, hosing away the blood.

The gunshot continued all week, every day. The pigeons didn't seem to get the message that this wasn't a safe place to be. Or maybe they were up for the fight. They kept on returning, in their battalions.

AUGUST 13, 2013

Our moment arrived.

The square was an unending mass of upturned faces, bobbing on a sea of white and brown shirts. Special instruction had been given that we should remove our jackets because of the heat.

The crowd joined in with us as we sang—one voice—so that it was never very clear if we were performing or them. I don't remember if we made any mistakes. I'm sure we were perfect. The routine was etched so deep into our muscle memory that none of us was conscious of it anymore. We just did it. Like when you properly nail an ice routine, you don't worry about which foot, which edge, which way to turn, what speed to reach—you just go. And that frees you up to concentrate on the emotion.

So what was my emotion on that stage as we marched and sang and banged our drums and waved our flags? A sort of terror, I think. An anticipation of something beyond this, bigger than this. I thought about Clementine—could she see me? Because she said she would find a way to be there, somehow, to see history happening right now. And also to say good-bye. She promised me she would say good-bye. I thought about my father, who could certainly see me, supposedly making him proud. But mostly I thought about myself—which version of me was on display that day? Good Jess? Bad Jess? Moments earlier I had saluted and curtsied to a lineup of dignitaries in the hotel lobby, a lineup that included my father. I was but a few meters away from our dear, great Führer. Did I tremble? Yes. But I'm ashamed to say my overriding emotion was one of regret—the regret that I could not enjoy it more.

When we finished our march, we stayed on the stage, just as we had rehearsed over and over. Each of us had our own small X taped onto the floor. Miss it at your peril. On the day of the actual concert, there were Wehrmacht boys just beyond the footlights, on the stone stairs, holding their rifles, and I had to wonder if they'd been put there to pick us off like unwanted pigeons should we stand out of line. We eyed them when we could—and the small monitor screens next to them showing what images were being relayed to the people at home and the people around the world. It was confusing, because there we were standing upright on the stage, looking pretty/formidable, ready to be the human scenery to Jay Acker's performance, but there on the screens was footage of us marching ten minutes ago. The day's so-called "live" events were going out with a time delay. If we had messed up our march, would they have cut it? Were they going to edit out parts of Jay Acker's performance?

He had arrived that morning.

No one could hand-on-heart claim to have actually seen him, but we knew he was in our midst because this weird, electric ripple had gone through all the HJ and BDM troops waiting in the hotel for the show to start. We squinted through the quivering cord screens and craned our necks around doorways, eager to be the first to see a real-life American, but we only caught glimpses of his entourage — fat men dressed strangely, in pajamas and farmer's trousers, with hooded jackets, as if this trip to our great nation was an everyday event and really not worth dressing up for. It didn't quite occur to us that these fat men counted as a sighting of a real-life American too.

There were also women in the entourage, dressed a little like the women who had clambered over Frau Hart's fence, and very much like the women in Clementine's camouflaged magazine — tight, painful trousers, snug little sweaters that left a strip of belly skin exposed. These were the wives, we guessed, or secretaries. They bustled around, carrying flat touch-screen computers — computers that were nowhere near as fast or as super as ours, especially not in the hands of these women who chewed gum like idiots and jabbed at the screens, sighing and squawking out their every thought.

"How are we supposed to make this work if we haven't got the fucking VPN we were promised?"

It didn't seem to occur to them to ask the pretty, bossy girl with the looping braids for what they needed. It would have been brought to them straightaway. I think they utterly underestimated our efficiency.

Once positioned on our Xs on the stage, we stood with our backs to these American people as they waited, chatting in the wings. I did wonder if the gunfire might come from behind us, not from the Wehrmacht boys out front. We could be shot right in the exposed parts of our necks and fall neatly in our rows, on top of one another, like dominoes.

After our songs and marches (were we the best? In the end it didn't really seem to matter) Herr Dean gave his speech. Onstage, we weren't allowed to move or react, but the girls in the front of the crowd, the girls specially selected to stand on the raised stone sections to our left and right, did enough of that for all of us. They clutched one another and jumped up and down, squealing and gasping. We saluted and gave our victory cries in unison, our fingers quivering, while behind us came unmistakable whispers of "Jesus Christ" and "fucking hell," in weird elastic accents. When one American voice raised itself to something closer to a mutter, we heard a scuffle break out. Then quiet. But we were good. We stayed still, we faced forward and listened to our Führer's wonderful words about music and art and youth and the German spirit.

Then all of a sudden, it was happening. HE was being introduced, being called out onto the stage by our dear, great Führer. I thought the whole square might implode from the incomprehensible excitement of it all. Here was one god introducing another! Well, in a way. And then THERE HE WAS—this pure-blood boy, this first American on British soil, on any German soil, in over sixty years, one of the most in-demand celebrities of our time and . . .

He was very small. Like a squirrel.

And in the same way his entourage hadn't bothered to dress up for this momentous occasion, he hadn't either. Here we were bestowing a great honor upon him and he had chosen to wear too-big shorts in the colors of a tiger. They were slipping down low over his tight black underpants. He walked from the side of the stage in a stuttery, lopsided way, which made me think for a moment that he must be damaged (. . . *the diseased, the damaged, the dissolute* . . .) before I realized it had something to do with his huge, clumpy running shoes that were clearly the wrong size, these things not being so readily available in his country.

No one in the crowd quite knew what to do. There had been this buildup of pressure, this massive intake of breath, but no one dared let it out. There was an awkward smattering of applause, which stopped as soon as it had started when the few realized the many weren't really going for it. How were we supposed to worship this boy when our true hero, our Führer, was already before us? And actually, were we supposed to worship him? The inspirational poster on the wall of the hotel reception that day read: WE JOIN IN THE PRAYER OF A GREAT GERMAN: "AND THOUGH THE WORLD WERE FILLED WITH DEVILS, WE MUST STILL SUCCEED."

Was this the devil the poster was talking about? Someone to succeed despite of? Was this a Trojan horse? Nothing but a great big challenge? Because we German people like a challenge—it's a chance to show our mettle.

Some odd little squeaks and gasps came from across the square.

Jay Acker seemed unfazed by this almost silent reception. He unzipped his hooded pajama jacket as he made his way to Herr Dean's podium. Without missing a step, he took the jacket off, bunched it up, and tossed it at one of the HJ boys standing in the front line of the formation up onstage. It hit his uniformed chest and flumped onto the floor. The HJ boy did not react at all, not for a second—which we were all thinking was pretty impressive, until there was a cross little bark from below the front of the stage that made the boy quickly drop to his knees and retrieve the discarded item of clothing.

Underneath the pajama top, Jay Acker was wearing a white vest. Underwear, basically. There was writing and drawings all over his arms—foreign letters, flowers, the face of a dog, and . . . a big, red triangle on his deltoid muscle. We saw it. Herr Dean saw it. We saw Herr Dean see it. We saw him hesitate to offer a handshake, especially as the boy hadn't saluted. But we also saw Herr Dean glance down at the photographers poised at the front of the stage, ready to catch this momentous image. Our Führer took the boy's hand, maneuvered him so the shoulder with the triangle was away from the cameras, and clamped an arm across his back to freeze the pose. The cameras flashed, blinding all of us who were standing behind.

Before our eyesight had a chance to return, the orchestra struck up its chord to play our Führer off the stage. It was time. IT WAS TIME! We blinked away the comets dancing across our vision and . . . the boy ran away. Offstage. Gone. Where to? Wohin? The desire to turn our necks was just too too much.

But there was no chance to ask ourselves any more questions. There was an almighty sound. ALMIGHTY. The loudest gasp you have ever heard, and it burst free of the speakers. "AAAHHH!" Like a pressure cooker firing off its lid. It made all of us onstage leap thirty centimeters in the air. Up started the solid beat, the *ting-ting-ting* of a cowbell over the top. Then an echoey, disembodied voice was telling us to dance. But to what? Because this wasn't music. This was the sound of sandpaper going back and forth. This was a woman yelling like

194

she was a kid in a playground, calling someone else her "baby." A synthesizer kept starting a tune but never really finished it. It was the weirdest, weirdest thing. "Owwww!" cried the woman on the music, like she'd trapped her finger in a door. And all the time we had to keep our faces forward, looking pretty and formidable.

"Come on, Great Britain!" said a man with a microphone who hadn't bothered to learn the correct name of our country. He bounded onstage. He stuck out his lips like a monkey, jerked his chin to the beat, clapped his hands above his head, making the microphone *thud-thud-thud.* The suggestion was we should do the same as him. But no one did. Because who was he? This wasn't Jay Acker. Why should this stranger be telling us what to do? All the kids in the square were staring up, white faced, at the television screens above the stage, screens that, being onstage, we couldn't see. Or else they were searching for the faces of their troop leaders in the crowd, or Herr Dean himself, looking for clues as to how to behave. But our leaders were only doing what we were doing—staring forward, enduring it. This was awful.

Then the "music" changed. THANK GOD. But— DISASTER—it had been put on at the wrong speed. Either that or the tape player was chewing up their cassette. Yet they let it run for the longest time without sorting it out—this weird monster voice saying something that we couldn't understand about parties. The voice of a girl wobbled over the top—worse than Angelika Baker milking a solo.

"Yeah! Yeah!" bellowed the microphone man at the end of every line. Again, I think we were supposed to join in. We didn't.

"Who *is* he?" mouthed the lips of just about everyone in the crowd.

They were all getting itchy. This wasn't what we wanted, what we expected.

But that's when the song came on.

A single quivering violin snapping everyone's jaws shut — just like that.

Jay Acker's voice — strange but clear and delicious, singing low, full of something, luring us in, talking about how in the very beginning there was no light, no color, and how he sometimes felt like he couldn't go on, but then, but then . . . Oh goodness! There came a piano, a cry, a WONDERFUL EXPLOSION.

OH!

I had never felt anything like this before. Never. No, that's not true. It felt like being kissed, like being touched, like watching the person you love swing through a shaft of the last summer sun. The stage spots danced to the same frantic beat as the song. Jay Acker leaped across the stage, telling us we were LUMINOUS, we were LOVED, we were BLESSED, we were TOGETHER. WE WERE ONE! And you almost couldn't notice it to begin with, because it grew so gradually. But we were moving. It was impossible to stay still. We tried, because we were terrified of being punished, but somehow this was stronger. The audience was rolling in waves, like a beautiful sea, the lights painting them pink, then blue, then yellow, then pink again. GG grabbed my hand in the excitement, because no one would notice, because everyone in that square was doing something they shouldn't. I squeezed it back. In front of us the kids had their hands in the air. They clapped, they bounced, they sang. They worshipped this devil, this truth, this light.

It was awful. So BRILLIANTLY awful that I entirely forgot, about the something beyond this, the something bigger than this.

And then she burst onto the stage.

I didn't know that it would be this. She'd told me her family was going to escape. That the concert would be their "final day." Their summer holidays in Cornwall were all about meeting their connections and planning their route out. People had done it before, she said.

"But you don't know anyone in America," I said, scared for her.

"Oh, I know plenty," she replied. "I speak to them all the time."

She communicated via short little messages on a program on the Harts' illegal computer. Her dad knew how to stop everyone else in the Reich using the networks, so of course he knew how to do it himself and go undetected. She spouted a bunch of initials at me, systems, communication routes, ways to distribute information—her father's value.

"But have you ever actually met these people you're talking to?" I asked her.

"No."

"Then how can you say you really know them?"

I didn't tell my father; I did as she asked. I thought I was helping her to escape. But it was a fantasy. Why didn't I see that? There was no longer any chance that that could happen.

197

My hope had made it real, because I was willing to let her go. That was how much I loved her. I knew she would be happier somewhere else. Somewhere nicer than here. But nothing nice could come of this. It was just like she'd said. She hadn't been taunting me—Clementine was going somewhere she couldn't come back from.

She was wearing her BDM skirt and necktie, but she had removed her blouse. The title of Jay Acker's song, FEELING FREE, was scrawled across her small, bare breasts; red triangles were drawn on her arms. She had a Party flag around her neck like a cloak, which is what I think fooled everyone, stopped anyone from reacting straightaway. The Americans thought this was something to do with us. The Germans thought, obscene as it was, it was something to do with the boy's song. She was a devil that we all had to endure for the greater good. She had found her own microphone. It seemed rehearsed. And I suppose it probably was. As much as it could have been.

"I WANT TO BE FREE!" she screamed over the song. "BUT WE ARE NOT FREE!"

Jay Acker turned to look at her across the stage. He seemed puzzled for a moment, then beamed. He was pleased at the intrusion, and because he was pleased, the crowd, lost in themselves, was pleased too. They cheered her on. But I couldn't. Because now I understood what she was going to do. Had I always known, on some subconscious level? I could smell her—the stench of gasoline.

We stayed on our Xs. We did as we were told. I alone was pinned there by the awful realization of what I had done by keeping quiet, by the awful realization that no matter what I did, I couldn't truly save her.

"WE ARE THE DEVIL! WE ARE THE CHILDREN OF DEVILS!" she screamed.

"Yes!" the crowd screamed back, not really understanding.

"GERMANY AWAKE! DEUTSCHLAND ERWACHE!" she cried to the heavens, a fist to the sky. The lights danced around her like colorful moths. She was irresistible.

"DEUTSCHLAND ERWACHE!" the crowd echoed. It was a phrase we knew and understood from one of our own songs. Historic. And here she was, changing that history.

She hollered her last words, borrowing them from Jay Acker's song. "I AM LUMINOUS!" she cried. "I WILL SHINE ON!" And then she flicked the wheel on the lighter in her hand. "Good-bye," she gasped. To me, for me. She did just as she promised. She said good-bye. Then the microphone dropped to the ground with a horrible clunk.

The fire ate her up. The flag, her skirt, her hair. The ticker tape dancing in the air became a swarm of fiery butterflies.

Clementine curled into the flames, but she refused to fall.

Everyone just watched.

Like this wasn't a person at all.

Like she was just the burning logs of a Sonnenwendfeuer on summer solstice eve.

Do you ever feel like you are not your body? That you are trapped inside of it? A soul, if you like. Though I'm not sure I believe in magic like that. You want to climb out of your skin, get a proper view of yourself. A proper view of reality. Or unreality. Because in that moment you can see that everything is just a construction. It's all fake. But even though you want to leave your body behind, your greatest wish is to be reconnected with it. You want to be part of the world again. But you can't do either of those things — leave or go back — because either way you're trapped. Do you ever feel like that?

I left my X.

I didn't make the decision to do it. I didn't break the rule on purpose. My body moved without any conscious thought. A well-trained reflex.

I ran to the HJ boy holding Jay Acker's jacket, snatched it from him, slid my arms inside, back to front, the hood over my face. All this happened in slow motion, though it could only have been seconds. *Manmade fibers burn faster than natural fibers, but a combination of the two can be the greater hazard.* I ran toward the person on fire, kicked them hard on the backside, made the hungry fire spill onto the stage, then I threw myself on top.

LET THAT WHICH MUST DIE SINK AND ROT. WHAT HAS STRENGTH AND LIGHT WILL RISE AND BLAZE.

I lay there with the taste of gasoline in my mouth, the fog of smoke in my lungs, triumph in my heart, until the fire went out.

I left my X.

I didn't make the decision to do it. I didn't break any rule on purpose. My body moved without any conscious thought. An instinct that can't be taught. Love.

I ran to the HJ boy holding Jay Acker's jacket, snatched it from him, slid my arms inside, back to front, the hood over my face. All this happened in slow motion, though it could only have been seconds. *Manmade fibers burn faster than natural fibers, but a combination of the two can be the greater hazard.* I ran to my friend on fire, my best friend, the only person I have every truly loved, and kicked her hard on the backside, made her and the hungry fire spill onto the stage, then I threw myself on top.

THE TIME IS OUT OF JOINT

O CURSÈD SPITE, THAT EVER I WAS BORN TO SET IT RIGHT.

I lay there. We were one, the taste of gasoline in our mouths, the fog of smoke choking our lungs, something unquenchable in our hearts, until the fire went out.

I left my X.

zwei

They pulled me off her.

I don't know who they were, I only felt them. I was blind. Someone slung me over their shoulder — a man definitely, a soldier maybe. I was carried at some speed back to the hotel, my body bouncing with each step.

"Out of the way! Out of the fucking way!"

Once in the lobby, they pried open my eyelids and poured in drops that stung like hell.

"It's just the blast of the heat," said a voice. "Just the effects of the smoke."

The world came back, smeary and unreal. Fuzzy green explosions in the blackness first, which turned out to be the small, circular spotlights set into the lobby floor. Then I could make out pillars, chairs, feet, people, my Mädelschaft, our Kameradschaft. They had all retreated from the square to regroup.

"Ugh!" Ruby Heigl was all of a sudden in my face. "You know you have absolutely no eyelashes left." She spoke as if my swollen eyes were the worst thing she'd seen that day.

"Do they hurt?" she asked, a little quieter now, almost kindly, I thought.

I couldn't speak. I knew I would cry. I looked down at the dark, putrid stains on my skirt and socks. I stank like burnt bacon. I nodded.

"Well, you're all right, then," she snapped. "Because if it was a third-degree burn, you wouldn't feel a thing."

The Wehrmacht boys drew down the roller blinds in the reception lobby. Walls of glass became walls of fabric. This muffled the chaos outside but also made it louder somehow, because now our minds put images to the sounds instead. The blinds had been rushed — they hung at different lengths, just a centimeter here or there — so the pretty, bossy girl with the looping braids came out from behind that huge sweep of a reception desk and made it her job to correct them. The day had been mangled beneath the wheels of a steamroller and there she was tying a ribbon around it all, thinking that would make everything fine.

Clementine's voice was in my head: "It's all window dressing, Jess, nothing but window dressing."

My sight had returned too late.

I didn't see what they did with her. And I'm not talking about her body, an empty shell without a soul, but all of her. Because she was still alive. I heard her screaming — I'm sure I did — as I was carried away.

I was frantic to ask. Someone would know. GG would have seen. She was right next to me on the stage. But when she came over to my corner of the lobby, her face white with shock, I pushed her offered hand away. *Did you know?* Her eyes were asking. *Did you know this was going to happen?*

I shook my head.

Then I was told to stand.

This would be my good-bye, I had started to believe.

I was taken away. To that small meeting room along the marble-floored corridor. With Fisher. With the fat man — the man I knew, yet didn't.

I thought about asking them, before Fisher started his cross-examination. *Is Clementine going to be okay?* Because if my fate was already sealed, asking this could bring me no more harm. But I didn't ask. Mainly because it was a really stupid question. Alive or dead, Clementine Hart was never going to be okay again.

The fat man quickly got impatient with Fisher's questioning. His grilling of me had started well — persuasive, authoritative, no hint of any particular softness — but it went nowhere fast. The fat man huffed and puffed and readjusted his position against the wall. He must have known what Fisher was to me, to the Kellers. It was as if he expected him to fail, *wanted* him to, even. The fat man made the portrait of Herr Dean behind him scrape against the plasterboard. Fisher began to repeat himself and fumble. This was his chance to impress. This was the moment he'd been waiting for all his life — a great big crisis he could stand on top of, hands on hips, and demonstrate his brilliance. He was sliding down the side of it.

I tried to help him. And myself. "Shall I run through things exactly as they happened, Fisher, or . . . ?"

The fat man planted his grip on Fisher's shoulders. No words were needed. Fisher got up and the fat man dumped himself down opposite me in his place, the leather of the seat doing a fart as he did so. It made me want to laugh — even after everything — because what a relief it would have been to let go with a fit of hysterics. I wanted to gather together the Mädelschaft and take them down to the basement bathroom again and make faces in the huge gilt mirror, wearing silly hats made from the cloth towels. As if nothing had happened.

The fat man coughed phlegm from his big, barreled lungs. Fisher took up a position by the door, his head hanging, like a puppy that had messed on the carpet.

"Do you know who I am, Fräulein Keller?" The fat man leaned forward on his elbows, so far forward that the heat of his breath was burning my sore eyelids.

Yes, I wanted to say, *you are Frau Hart's very best customer,* because GG's story was much preferable to facing up to the real reason the fat man kept visiting Frau Hart and Clementine, why he was in our kitchen the evening after Frau Hart chopped down the flagpoles, why the Harts had been moved into the house next to ours in the first place. Believing that he was a sweaty, sex-hungry brothel-goer, that Frau Hart was an asocial prostitute, was so much nicer than reality.

"Yes," I said to the fat man. "You are Herr Hoffman. You work for my father."

"So let's get everything straight before he gets here, shall we?" He opened his eyes wide. *Okay, little girl?* I was beginning to understand what this was. I nodded slowly. Just outside the door a man started shouting — no, shrieking — in German.

"Alle in die zugeteilten Räume! Sofort!"

Go to your designated room! Now!

There was the satisfying *ch-chunk* of a gun being readied.

"Whoa, man, cool it, cool it," came a high-pitched American voice—a man's voice. I don't think he'd understood. *The Americans are lazy people,* I had been told at school. *They are falsely convinced of their own superiority so they do not attempt to learn the languages of other, greater nations.* But this man understood the gun. There were boots in the hall, then quiet. Herr Hoffman waited for this short audio play to be over before he began again. I wondered if he needed to hear it, to know what was going on, or if he needed me to hear it so I knew what was going on.

"Fräulein Keller, were you complicit in Clementine Hart's act of terrorism this afternoon?"

"Sorry?" My head was still outside the door, still staring down a rifle.

"Sorry for what?" Herr Hoffman snapped back. "Sorry that you don't understand? Sorry that you were complicit . . . ?"

I was back in the room.

"I'm very sorry that I didn't hear you, Herr Hoffman." I used my BDM-lineup voice, my soldier voice.

Fisher lifted his head. He was no longer the lowest person in the room.

"We'll try that again, shall we, Fräulein Keller? Are you ready?"

I swallowed, nodded.

"Were you complicit in Clementine Hart's act of terrorism this afternoon?"

What a word. Why that word? Because with a word he'd changed it. It wasn't terrorism, I was sure of it. That was done by men with bombs in their briefcases who made friends with wily American journalists. Clementine was a girl (*is* a girl) who was desperate (*is* desperate). Herr Hoffman didn't know what he was talking about. They had driven her to it. They had made her. Left her with absolutely no choice whatsoever. What did they expect? If anyone in this room was complicit in any act of terrorism, it was him.

I shook my head.

"Aloud, please, Fräulein. Were you, Jessika Davina Keller, complicit in Clementine Hart's act of terrorism this afternoon?"

"No." It wasn't a lie. I had only wanted her to escape.

"Say it."

I had only wanted her there, selfishly, to say good-bye.

"I was not . . ."

"No!" He slammed a hand on the table. I flinched. Fisher flinched. This was how it was done. Fisher had much to learn.

"I, Jessika Davina Keller . . ." said Herr Hoffman, feeding me my line.

"I, Jessika Davina Keller . . ." I parroted.

"Was not complicit in Clementine Hart's act of terrorism this afternoon."

"Was not complicit in Clementine Hart's act of terrorism this afternoon."

"Again!"

"I, Jessika Davina Keller, was not complicit in Clementine Hart's act of terrorism this afternoon."

"Again!"

"I, Jessika Davina Keller, was not complicit in Clementine Hart's act of terrorism this afternoon."

212

"And do you condone acts of terrorism against the Greater German Reich, Fräulein Keller?"

"No."

"Sag es!"

"Ich, Jessika Davina Keller, dulde keine Terrorakte gegen das Großdeutsche Reich!"

"And is she your friend?"

He was switching languages quickly, on purpose, to make me lose the thread. "Am I friends with . . . ?"

"WITH CLEMENTINE AMELIA HART!" he shouted—shrieked—using the same voice as the man with the gun outside the door. "WITH THE TERRORIST CLEMENTINE AMELIA HART! IS SHE A FRIEND OF YOURS, JESSIKA DAVINA KELLER?" His spit landed on the surface of the lovely, glossy table. My ears rang. My body began to shake again, my teeth began to chatter. Fisher and Herr Hoffman were sweating.

"Was she a friend of yours?" he said quietly now, remembering all of a sudden who I was. He didn't really want to make me cry.

I had no choice. I shook my head.

He was almost whispering now. "Was Clementine Hart a friend of yours?"

"No," I whispered back.

"Was she ever a friend of yours?"

"No."

"What was she?"

What IS she? What IS she? What IS she? I desperately corrected him in my head to keep her alive.

"Ein Staatsfeind," I said. *An enemy of the state.*

213

Maybe I was outside of my body then, looking back at myself, when those words came out. Maybe my body was speaking, not my soul.

"And what happens to enemies of the state, Fräulein Keller?"

His eyes were unblinking. The whites had edges of yellow.

"Death," I said, my stomach clenching at the word. I would not let myself cry. I pitched my gaze upward, my chin too. The profile of a perfect deutschen Mädel.

Silence.

Then: "Ja, gut," said Herr Hoffman, chirpy almost. Job done. Fisher's head bobbed into a fully upright position. Herr Hoffman pushed himself to standing with a grunt. "Well, I'm glad we have agreement on this, Fräulein Keller. You are free to go."

Fisher saluted. For a moment I thought Herr Hoffman would shake his hand. But no. He reached past him and straightened the portrait of Herr Dean on the wall. He tutted at Fisher as he did this, as if he held him responsible for its wonky angle, as if he held him responsible for everything unsatisfactory in the room.

"Watch her until Herr Keller gets here, will you?" said Herr Hoffman, and he slipped out the door with a wink.

Silence.

No, not silence.

Zwischenraum. The space between.

"Jessika . . ." Fisher said.

I didn't reply. There was nothing I could say.

"Jessika . . ."

"What?" The word came out like a dart.

"Are you okay?" he asked gently.

"Yes," I said. "I'm fine."

He started to move away from the wall.

"I'm fine," I repeated a little louder, keeping him where he was. "My father will be here any minute."

I was alone for a long time, in a room with a short metal bed. I had a rough blanket, a sink with only the cold tap working, a bucket (for the obvious), no radiator. I'd realized what was going on before they took me by the arm and steered me in, locking the door behind me. But maybe not on the journey over. I let go of the lie when I saw the gate.

I was here to work, and that work would set me free.

In the first room, a sign was hung around my neck with the name of the place and a number.

23674.

"Look left," said the woman in the gray smock, blinding me with the flash. "Look right," she said, blinding me again.

In the second room, she took away my watch, my necklace and Party pin. I handed over the small purse of money Mum had strung around my neck before I left. If she had known, I told myself, she would never have given me this. Next I removed my clothes—my BDM jacket, my tieslide, my necktie, my shirt, my skirt, my shoes and socks. My bra next, then my underpants. I signed them away, along with my trunk.

"When will I get them back?" I asked, feeling silly to be speaking while completely naked.

The woman shrank down further into the collar of her gray smock, adding more chins to the two she'd had from the start. "When you are good" was the reply.

My dressing down from Herr Hoffman was not the end of it. I was punished, and in the most ingenious way. They gave me what I had always wanted. They made me their hero.

My picture was in the newspaper — the national one, not just the local — and I was interviewed for the radio. Then — the pinnacle — a crew from the People's Television came to our house. They filmed me in our living room, sitting next to my mother, who was told to beam with pride, while Lilli sat at my feet, as if I were a god, or she my dog. (They tried to get Wolf to sit in too for what they called the "ahh factor," but he would only keep still if provided with something to chew. The sound of him cracking bone with his back teeth was too loud to accommodate, so he was shut outside in the garden and the microphone hardly picked up his whimpering at all.)

What choice did I have but to go along with it? And anyway, hadn't I always wanted to be loved like this? As long as I didn't think too much about why I was there, I thought I might come to enjoy it.

Before we recorded the piece for television, I sat down with the interviewer to work out exactly what I would say.

"So you actually went blind for a few moments," gasped the woman in the neat peppermint-colored suit. "What did you expect to see when you could open your eyes again?"

She was one of the People's Television's main hosts—but only for the interviews with wives and daughters. And animals. They got a man to do the stories about money and war and industry. She was incredibly pretty, with large, impossible eyes, which meant the old-fashioned suit she was wearing didn't exactly look awful. Her hair was styled all high, sharp, and rigid. Her lips were painted a very vivid red. "To show up on the camera," she explained, as if it were a terrible chore to be allowed to wear lipstick.

"Well, I could hear screaming and some fighting," I answered, "and when we got back to the hotel there was the sound of glass breaking outside, bottles and things like that, so I thought, oh god, this is bad, this is . . ."

"Oh, HAHAHAHA." The woman cut me off with the loudest, strangest laugh. She seemed to think I was telling a joke.

She grinned at my father. *What an adorable daughter you have, Herr Keller!* the grin said. But it was also a little flirty. I glanced at Mum to see what she was making of it all, but she had her eyes tightly shut while a girl in a checked skirt and black blouse was poofing powder onto her face. Our living room was all activity—men setting lights, mounting cameras on tripods, Lilli bothering each one of them in turn with her questions. Through the window, I could see Frau Gross standing across the street, craning her head around the television crew's van, trying to see what was going on.

"No, we won't say that," the woman in the peppermint suit told me sweetly. She clutched my knee to stop me skipping off in any more giddy directions. The newspaper and radio people hadn't wanted my real answer to that question either. I thought the television people, in the whole hierarchy of things, would be more discerning. They would like this injection of excitement. But in the end, they flattened out the story like everyone else. I just couldn't see how I could be a hero if we hadn't been in any danger in the first place. I was only trying to help them. Or maybe my ego had let me get swept away with it a little. The live broadcast of the concert had been stopped before the fire, thanks to that time delay. No one had seen this part, when she had . . .

I wouldn't let my mind go back to it, not properly. I just couldn't. It was too much to bear. The sight of my friend, like that . . . So really I was only making up my own safe story, just like they were making up theirs.

"You must have heard the crowds cheering your quick actions," the peppermint lady said. "You must have expected to open your eyes to the hugs and kisses of your comrades?"

She positioned the question so that saying anything other than yes would have sounded completely idiotic.

"Oh, um, yes."

"So shall we say you were carried back to the hotel by the crowd, passed across that joyous sea of arms?" She was a little bit in love with this image.

"Okay," I said, because I didn't want to disappoint her, or my father, who was watching carefully from the sidelines. She beamed a big-teeth smile. "And, gosh, how did that feel? Being carried like that?" Her eyes were shining, making it all instantly true—that joyous sea of arms.

"Um, wonderful?" I suggested.

I saw that Dad was nodding encouragingly, so I came up with more words.

"Thrilling, unexpected, totally overwhelming . . ."

They needed some pictures to "cut away to" during my interview, so they came and filmed me skating.

Ingrid had hugged me so tight that first time I'd returned to the rink.

"Is everything all right?" she'd said into my hair.

"Yes," I said. "I think so."

She continued to hold me close so she could speak quietly.

"Is everything to go on as always?" And I realized she wasn't really worried about me. No, that is unfair—she wasn't *only* worried about me. Her life, I saw, was inescapably associated with mine.

"Yes," I said. "You're fine."

"I'm so pleased," she said, louder now, patting my back and moving away. Then she set about getting me into the pole harness so I could work on my triple axel.

When the peppermint lady and the People's Television crew invaded the rink, disturbing the hushed focus of our practice, Ingrid had to work hard to hide her irritation. She stamped her blades impatiently against the rubber flooring as the makeup girl straightened her hair and powdered her nose.

"It's so cold in here, isn't it?" the girl kept saying as she teased the strands of Ingrid's bangs. With each repetition of this stupid rhetorical question, I expected Ingrid to swipe a paw at the girl's unsuspecting face.

The crew played around endlessly with the lighting available until it fit the mood they were trying to create, until we were all frozen to the bone waiting. At last I did my routine to Bruckner's *Fantasie*, but I was so cold and nervous that I went wrong in a number of places. I knew I was letting Ingrid down, denting her pride, in front of all these people.

"Don't worry," said the peppermint lady. "We'll edit it to make you look fantastic."

"She is fantastic," Ingrid hissed.

"Oh yes, yes, she is! Absolutely!"

The peppermint lady may have been tall and blond and magnificent, but no one would have fancied her chances in a fight against small, dark, catlike Ingrid.

They also filmed me giving a talk to the Jungmädel.

Ruby Heigl, their new troop leader, was made to stand aside, her face like a puckered balloon as she led the cheers and rounds of applause for me. The television crew filmed her doing an introduction, which she was asked to redo over and over again.

"With a little more passion, Fräulein," said the director, a slim, good-looking man with a wave of blond floppy hair and a lovely patterned tank top. "This is our national hero we have here!"

The girls stared up at me, openmouthed, when I began to talk, describing how I had run from my position on the stage, grabbed the jacket, and plunged into the flames. Then, without any prompting at all, I found myself telling them that I had been carried back to the hotel by the crowd, passed across a joyous sea of arms.

No one came back for hours. I was shivering. I wanted to curl up in the chair behind the desk, but guessed that would be against the rules. Would a good girl put her naked self on a wooden seat that would later be used by her superiors?

I had to get my stuff back. It wasn't about the things. It was about proving that I was good and I deserved them.

I shifted my attention away from the chair to the slatted blinds. But, oh god, even in a half-empty room I couldn't help but find temptation. Now all I wanted to do was open the blinds and see daylight. I wanted to look around and try to place where I was. (Of course, I did know where I was; I wasn't stupid. But I only knew it by name. Just as a concept or an idle threat. Not as a real place, positioned on a real piece of landscape, reachable by real people, like me.) But I didn't look. Because there was a camera mounted on the ceiling in the corner watching my every move.

When the man in the white coat walked in, I was lying on my side on the floor, hugging my knees, almost asleep.

"Aufstehen!"

I stood, trying to keep myself covered with my arms. He

pulled a flashlight from his top pocket and shone it into my eyes. Another blinding.

"Look up . . ." he said. "Look down . . . Look left . . . Look right." I did as I was told.

"Now open your mouth. Say ah." He counted my teeth.

The light went off. He ticked and scribbled into his folder of paperwork, gave me occasional disappointed glances as he wrote. I wondered if I would feel any less humiliated if I just let my arms drop. Standing there with one hand clutching a breast and the other between my legs wasn't feeling anywhere close to respectable. But I didn't have the nerve to let go. I thought about what his notes might say. *Good height, sturdy build, features well within acceptable limits, no clear outward signs . . .*

He didn't have a stethoscope or a pump to measure my blood pressure. I was only going to be checked like a dog or a horse, for my shiny eyes and solid teeth.

Then he said, "Are you hiding anything on your person?"

This made me choke, almost laugh. It also made me drop my arms. I wanted to show him that, despite his expert's white coat, he was clearly being an imbecile. How could I be hiding anything on my person when I wasn't wearing any clothes?

The doctor's face stayed steady and serious. He looked me up and down. But mostly down.

And I really had done so well up to that point, managing not to cry, but my voice cracked when I said, "Please don't."

Wait until my father hears about this! is what I should have said. *Wait until he hears of this insult to his rank and family!* But I was too shocked.

A nurse came in.

"Shall I cut off her hair, Herr Doktor?" she asked as she passed him in the doorway.

My hands went instinctively to my head. I didn't care about covering myself up anymore. I'd thrown away my dignity.

"No," muttered the doctor. "Just make the usual checks for contraband."

And the nurse did exactly as she was told.

We sat down as a family. And I confess, I was excited. It was the night we would watch my interview on the *Evening Show* on the People's Television. Mum had prepared us drinks and snacks. (Drinks and snacks, in the living room! A total infringement of the ban on anything that could potentially stain the best furniture.) This was a very special occasion.

We sat through the previews for the week's dramas, the weather report predicting a drop in temperature, the tension building all the while. This is what it must feel like, I thought, to be a famous actress arriving at the Kino Babylon in a silk dress, ready to see your face on the big screen. I had been seduced by it all, this hero worship. I had swallowed the wonderful pill. And then there it was, straight off the back of the *hello*s and *welcome*s, while my head was still in Horst-Wessel-Platz signing autographs — my face!

"Look, look, look," gasped Lilli. "Our living room!"

In which we were currently sitting! Having drinks and snacks!

Mum let out a delighted squeal. Lilli grabbed hold of my arm, digging her nails into my skin with her excitement. I felt so sick I thought I might actually be sick.

But it was the oddest thing. The peppermint lady's hair didn't look nearly as tall and sculptural as it had in real life. The screen reduced it somehow. For me, the camera lens had the opposite effect. I was bigger. Sort of grotesque. It didn't feel like watching myself at all. The girl traveling across the rink in a wash of pink light, all snappy and breezy, her upright spins as neat and tight as any Dani Hannah could manage . . . that wasn't me. The girl looking so cocky and sure as she stood in front of the Jungmädel telling them they must always be ready, always be prepared, because evil lurks behind every corner . . . that wasn't me either. The girl sitting on a sofa with such an admiring mother and sister, telling a lady in a peppermint suit about "a sea of joyous arms" . . . that certainly wasn't me.

Yet it was. It was my shape and outline.

But my soul?

That wonderful pill was stuck hard in my throat.

When our moment on-screen ended, Mum, Dad, and Lilli began applauding, babbling and cooing about what they'd just seen. I didn't join in. The program returned to the male host behind a desk. Time to discuss the serious stuff surrounding the Jay Acker concert. The host didn't call it that, though. The name Jay Acker had been crossed out. The day was now known as the Concert or sometimes the Incident. Did the boy go straight back to America? In the buildup, there had been talk of him seeking asylum in the Reich. Since the Incident, no word.

For days they'd been promising to reveal the identity of the "terrorist." I somehow knew that tonight would be the night, because Dad was carrying himself looser, a button undone at the top of his shirt, his cuffs rolled up. He had stayed over in London, at the office, the night before my first interview, and when he came back he was fired up again, not brooding. He'd seemed ready to throw his energies into home. Into me. There was a momentum, and I felt part of it. The television interview had been the culmination of something.

In contrast to Dad, I was coiling tighter and tighter. They hadn't asked any direct questions about her in my interviews—not her as an individual, only her as an abstract concept, her as a fire to be put out. I was grateful for this, of course. How would I have even said her name without collapsing into despair? But the silence, it was ominous. I couldn't figure it out, how they were going to do it. How would they tell the nation that this "terrorist" was our neighbor, my friend? Someone right under our noses, someone on our watch, someone whose father worked with my father? Someone who was one of us.

"Authorities have today revealed the identity of the terrorist who made an attempt on the lives of our young people . . ." said the host. I was breathing so fast I felt dizzy.

Her picture filled the screen.

She was an American, they said.

She's called Amanda Levy.

She's a Jew and a Bolshevik sympathizer, they told us. The girl in the picture had a cross and messy little face just like Clementine. She was wiry and white-blond, the same as my friend. But it wasn't her. It was a picture of someone else.

My mouth opened, ready to argue, but what could I say? Who would I say it to? Mum and Lilli were still squealing about their television appearance. And my father . . . I didn't dare look at him. But I could feel him looking at me.

Next on-screen was a series of images of men with dark skin and misshapen features. These were also Americans, they said. These were the men who had instigated the plot. They had taken this Amanda Levy girl under their wing. She was an "asocial" and an "idiot," they told us (so not a calculating political sympathizer after all). She had been their puppet.

It made no sense.

That's what I would have said, had I had the courage to speak. *No one is going to buy this, because it doesn't make any sense!* All those people at home may not have seen her face, her real face, but they would have heard me in my interview—only moments ago on that very program!—clearly saying how I wanted to save my friend. Yes, I had said that. I had managed that much. I had leaped onto the flames, I told the peppermint lady, because I wanted to save "my friend." And now they wanted everyone to believe that I was friends with an American! With a Bolshevik sympathizer! With a Jew! How could I be a hero to them if I was friends with an American Bolshevik-sympathizing Jew? How could my father let anyone believe that his daughter was friends with . . .

No, that's not what I had said.

I hadn't said "my friend" at all.

Of course I didn't. They wouldn't have allowed that.

I'd been asked to say something ever so slightly different, the distinction barely registering at the time. I'd said yes to everything just to save my own skin.

They'd asked me to say "my friends."

I leaped onto the flames, I told the peppermint lady, because I wanted to save "my friends."

Just one letter—and I had crossed out her name, erased her message.

All that she'd done had been for nothing.

Even the people who were actually there, seeing it with their own eyes, hearing it with their own ears, they were too drunk on the music. And suppose just for a moment they weren't— would any of their memories have survived the debriefings we were given to help us "understand" what had happened that day? Even within our own Mädelschaft and Kameradschaft, the people who knew and recognized her, would any of them have managed to hang on to their belief that they had seen her—Clementine Amelia Hart—so desperate to be noticed, so desperate to be heard, that she had set herself on fire?

That's not what you saw, the visiting Schutzstaffel officer had said in our debriefing in the meeting hall. He'd said that without having to say it at all.

"This was the act of a terrorist," he told us, slowly, methodically replacing her face, her very existence with a word— *terrorist.* I could see it now—the process of it, the system.

"And we do not engage in discussions about the motivations of terrorists," he went on, "for there is no justification for acts of violence against the Greater German Reich. We simply condemn their acts," he said, "and then we seek revenge."

It was only me. Her message had reached only me.

Sitting in the living room that evening with my family, I spat out that wonderful pill. It tasted bad. Very, very bad.

On the television, the man behind the desk was summing up, declaring this tragedy "a victory." Enemies of the state had been captured before they could do any damage because we had infiltrated and dismantled their intricate but naive little plot.

"And all this has been achieved," the man said, switching from a straight face to this strange little grin, "with the help of the Reich's favorite daughter."

A smiling picture of me in my BDM uniform came onto the screen, the wind whipping up the loose strands of my hair, my eyes on something pleasing in the distance.

I had killed my friend. Me.

In came a female warden, all jaded around the eyes and gnarly at the edges. Rough, basically, despite her starched collar and scraped-back hair. I was given a pile of gray things — a smock, a large pair of underpants, some rubber clogs — and told to dress. The warden stood and watched, her head tipped to one side as if calculating the marks she might give me for technical merit and presentation.

"If you are good," she said while I buttoned up the front of the smock, "you will earn yourself a bra."

She handcuffed her wrist to mine and we left the room. We walked along a white hospital corridor and through a series of locked gates, stopping outside a flat steel door with a sliding shutter.

I was expecting the worst, so it came as no surprise — the metal bed, the bucket toilet, the cold. The window had bars and frosted glass that let in milky light but offered no view.

But I didn't care about that now. I didn't need to work out where I was. I had decided to absolutely refuse to believe that this place existed. This place was nothing but a concept and an idle threat. I wasn't here. Soon they would see that I was good—and then I'd be set free. I'd go back to my family. We would forget that all of this had ever happened.

I was left with a white cloth rectangle printed with the same number from the sign they had hung around my neck. 23674. I'd been instructed to sew it onto the front of my smock. Along with a black cloth triangle. *Vagrants, beggars, idiots, workshys, the diseased, the damaged, the dissolute, alcoholics, prostitutes, pacifists* . . . I pulled my smock up and over my head, baring my chest to the cold, ready for the sewing. I would show them exactly who they were dealing with via the beauty of my invisible stitching. But I didn't get the chance. The gnarly warden returned after just five minutes, demanding I hand back the needle and thread.

"Come on! Come on!" she barked, forcing me to switch to big, lazy loops to get the work done fast. The untidiness of it made me want to cry.

After that, with nothing to do, I spent my time on my back, on the lumpy straw mattress. I picked at the edges of the white rectangle and the black triangle on my chest, making the stitching even worse. I listened to the distant hum of the motorway, to the birds, to the wind in the trees and the sirens that went off at all hours of the day but didn't seem to have any relevance to me. I heard orders carried across the breeze, the trudge of feet, sometimes metal against stone, the squeak of a wheelbarrow. At night, I heard the conversations of owls, the whistling of bats, the screams of foxes—nature doing what it had always done for years and years and years.

I would wait this moment out. I took my inspiration from Ingrid. Wasn't that how she was treating her whole life—as

233

one long wait? Keep your head down, keep safe, allow time to move on. I just needed to remain still until things changed around me. This went entirely against everything I had ever been taught, though. You must do! You must work! You are nothing but your actions! I had never been still. Never been allowed to. Even when I was sick.

But this stillness became strangely, weirdly, sort of . . . nice.

Every so often I had to move, of course, or I would be overwhelmed by the cold. I did bursts of jumping jacks and squat thrusts to help keep the blood flowing. When I did this, I pretended I could hear Fisher's voice shouting out the order. I imagined Fräulein Eberhardt crouching beside me, hissing insults into my ear because I wasn't doing the leg thrusts right. I made myself feel Dirk's boot on my neck, the smell of grass and mud up my nose. This was also strangely, weirdly, sort of nice. I was wishing for normal, I suppose. Because I knew what to do with that.

The day after the screening of the television interview, the men came with their flatbed truck. A team of efficient-looking women in housekeeping smocks pulled up in a small red car.

Up until then, the Harts' house next door had been a dark, looming question waiting for an answer. Or rather, a question waiting to be asked—a question even Frau Gross wouldn't have dared put to my mother. When the truck and the red car turned up, Frau Gross was straightaway in her front garden, gloves on, trowel in hand, pulling up nonexistent weeds.

The men did the heavy lifting and packing, while the women sorted and cleaned. I watched what I could from my bedroom window, my arms resting on the flat top of the trophy I had won at the Reich's sports day for the BDM the year before. Later I watched from a deck chair in our back garden while I pretended to read a magazine, enjoying the benefit of Dad's shorter fences. An image came to me as I sat there: me, looking down on Dad through the gap in my bedroom curtains, his sleeves rolled up, his brow all sweaty in the moonlight, as he took a chain saw to the heads of the Harts' new leylandii. I couldn't understand where it had been hiding, this memory. What door had I opened to let it out?

Frau Gross would have given anything to have this front-row seat on proceedings at the Hart residence. I would have given anything for it not to have been happening at all. I should have been down at the tree swing by the river, watching my friend glide through sunlight, collecting leaves in her hair and dirt on her heels, as she talked me through the seduction of a grilled banana.

The clearance team didn't build a bonfire in the garden or throw everything on the back of their truck for landfill as I expected. Each item was handled very carefully and methodically. Two women went into the back garden to make the most of the last September sun and laid out the Harts' clothing on the picnic table, holding up each piece for inspection — Herr Hart's black V-neck sweaters and gray trousers, Frau Hart's billowing shirts and skirts, Clementine's uniform and that striking bikini — folding the ones that passed their test, placing them in sacks like the ones we used when distributing clothes during the Winterhilfswerk. As they worked, they chatted about their families and people they'd seen on the main street the day before. Snatches of their conversation cut through the birdsong.

She's looking tired, don't you think?

But their son has always been good like that.

If you just add a bit of warm water to the mixture it turns out fine.

It was all so horribly ordinary. Did they not have any idea whose things they were touching?

I saw them box up dishes and bed linen, watched them throw the living room rug over the washing line for a beating before rolling it up and taking it back inside. Frau Hart had some nice pieces of silver jewelry. The sight of them suddenly came to me, sharp and clear in my head—lovely delicate stud earrings with falling flowers rocking on a chain link as she moved. I wondered who would be getting those.

The following day, the Sunday, I overheard Dad talking to Lilli in the garage as he fixed her bike. The chain kept slipping, making her heels strike off the pedals. She had red scrapes up the insides of both legs. Mum had sent me from the kitchen with glasses of orange juice—"for the workers!"—and I was carrying a bag of cookies in my teeth.

I was just about to turn the corner around the wall from the side passage to the front driveway when I heard him.

"Good news, Lilli; we have new neighbors moving in soon."

I stopped dead, hidden by the wall.

"Oh?" I heard Lilli say. She sounded bored. She wasn't interested in helping; she just wanted the bike fixed. I listened. There was the *ting* of something metal hitting the concrete floor of the garage, then the *tick-tick-tick-tick* of the bike wheel being spun. *Ask him*, I thought, my teeth gritted tightly against the paper bag of cookies. *Ask him*. She did.

"Where's Clementine gone, then?" Her voice was all high and innocent. Casual, because she didn't realize she needed to act it. I held my breath.

A pause, then . . .

"To music college," Dad said.

All the air went from me, all the blood, all the bone.

For a moment, I became my little sister; I let myself believe him. Because I wanted to. I wanted Clementine to be there, in a light and dusty classroom, banging out something passionate on a beautiful grand piano, her hair falling with the movement, learning to love a bit of Wagner after all. Because if it was true, I could write her a letter, exchange news—my preparations for skate camp, her new life at college, who I'd seen on the main street, who was looking tired, whose son was being good, the everyday and the ordinary. But I knew I mustn't trick myself. It was so easy, so comforting, but I mustn't.

I returned to my own body, my own mind.

I willed another thought out to my sister on the other side of that wall. To ask about Clementine's parents. My tears dripped onto the bag of cookies, soaking into the paper.

Lilli didn't say it, though. I doubt if Herr und Frau Hart, being grown-ups just like any others, had ever registered as real people to my little sister. Dad carried on.

"This new family," he said, "they have a little girl exactly the same age as you."

And, oh, the whole world joined up in a perfect circle.

"Yeah?" said Lilli, sounding interested now.

I tipped sideways. I slid down the brick, sandpapering my arm. I set the orange juice on the floor very carefully, the cookies too. I crouched there, crying as quietly as I could, fat, hot tears rolling down my chin and arms. Someone had lifted the corner of the grass, like it was only a carpet, and revealed beneath the clockwork mechanics. I was much happier when I believed it all to be natural, magic even.

I stayed on the ground until the tears stopped and my breath was my own again. I wiped my face and the wet streaks from the paper bag of cookies. Then I lifted my father's glass of juice close to my mouth, hawked up a mouthful of phlegm, and I spat.

The sessions began. Three of them each day. They would happen at any point, even during the night. I think they were trying to surprise me by switching the times around, but the sessions were the only thing I was ever expecting, so as surprises went, it was pretty useless. I felt sorry for them, if that was the best they could manage.

A female warden would collect me and walk me down a series of windowless corridors to the chosen room. Every movement around the building was done with handcuffs, which only ended up making me believe I was terribly important or terribly dangerous, or possibly both. The opposite of what they wanted to achieve, I'm sure. I began to feel really exceptionally sorry for them.

Once inside, the warden would instruct me to sit on the hard chair, opposite a man in uniform at a desk. She'd free herself of me, then turn on her black, ugly heels and leave the room.

"So, Fräulein Keller," the man would say—big, patronizing smile, a pair of fat fingers pushing down the red dot and the arrow on the tape player at the same time. "Let's start at the beginning, shall we?"

The first time, I cried and told my interrogator that I had already done this with the fat man, Herr Hoffman, and with Fisher (I was told off for not calling him *Herr* Fisher — you can't win). "And do you *know* who my father is?" I wailed.

"Yes," said the uniformed man. He slid a sheet of official paper across his desk so I could see the ink. "This is his signature on the order that brought you here."

I think it was then that I stopped feeling sorry for everyone else and concentrated on feeling sorry for myself.

Three men took turns questioning me, though their faces began to blur into one. There was hardly any natural light in the place. I kept falling asleep in fits. They gave me coffee in the mornings that tasted suspicious and not nearly enough food to keep my head straight — stale bread, thin soup.

"What you did was a sin," said the uniformed man — whichever one it was. It didn't matter. They were the same person really, the same machine, saying exactly the same things, over and over. They pushed me back through time, to where they thought it had all started, then they pulled me forward, making me relive it in words. Then we'd go back again, forward again. I was a dirty piece of clothing going up and down the washboard and maybe soon I'd be spotless.

A week or so into the sessions, I was given a stack of books and told to read them — *Das Buch Isidor, The Myth of the Twentieth Century*, a collection of Hölderlin's poetry, *Mein Kampf*. All the compulsory books from school. The books that everyone else had pretended to read, books I actually had read because I was a good girl and did exactly as I was told. I read them again. I gobbled them up, actually. I was so grateful

241

to have something to do. And it was more educational the second time around, with my new eyes, the eyelashes properly grown back.

The sketches in *Das Buch Isidor* didn't seem funny anymore, and the romantic imagery in Hölderlin no longer filled me up. *The Myth of the Twentieth Century* was a big slog, just like it had been the first time, but *Mein Kampf*, that was useful.

People will more readily fall victim to the big lie than the small lie, since they themselves often tell small lies in little matters but would be ashamed to resort to large-scale falsehoods.

People who are good don't lie, I knew that.

But this was new—people who are good don't lie, except when they do.

I lied all the time. Of course I did. It was in me because I had been trained well. Subterfuge, denial, dishonesty . . . I excelled at them all. So when the uniformed man said to me at our next session, "What you did was a sin," I replied, "Yes."

There was joy beneath the surly mask of his face. I was sure there had been a wager on who would get me to admit to it first.

"It's not something that is in you," he went on.

"No," I said.

I wanted to know what this something was. What was this stuff that could not be rinsed out? What was it woven in there since I was very little, or maybe even before?

"These people are cunning and wily," said my interrogator, offering me a way out.

"Yes," I said, taking it, not knowing who "these people" were he was referring to.

"They lead you astray."

"Yes."

"So tell me, Fräulein Keller, of your duty . . ."

"To be faithful, to be pure, to be German."

"Good girl."

At the end of that session, I earned myself something — a bra, and one of the things from my confiscated belongings.

What I really wanted . . . Clementine's essay notes. I could see the edge of them, inside a clear plastic letter file, beneath the other documents on the desk between me and my interrogator, the loops and smudges of her passionate handwriting. I could still remember every word. I'd always had a good brain for that — lines in plays, shopping lists. I pictured how the words were laid out on the page and the picture stuck. That was why I always did well in the BDM task where we had to read instructions, eat the paper, then carry out the order.

But still I wanted to see those notes again. Touch them. They would have given me something — strength. Comfort, maybe.

But of course, I couldn't ask for that. I chose a warm sweater instead.

He told me that he lived in the Party-owned boarding halls on the road that climbed north from the main street. He'd said this when we were out on a date at the cinema.

One evening during the week of the press interviews, he had turned up unexpectedly on our doorstep telling my mother that he had tickets for a film and would Jessika care to join him. I thought that after the concert he might leave me alone. That he would be embarrassed by his conduct in that interview room, or that he would now view me as dangerous. But no.

"I'm too tired," I said. It was true. Wearing a hero's mask had been exhausting. But my mother pushed me to go.

"It's just what you need right now," said my father, joining the conversation in the hallway and having the final word.

I suspected Fisher had been instructed to take me, to draw me out further on how Clementine had come to do what she did. But if that was Fisher's mission, he did a poor job of it. He spent the entire film (another war movie where we pummel the Americans and the guy gets the girl) working his hand slowly up from my knee to a just-acceptable section of my thigh. His touch made me feel hot and eager yet repulsed all at the same time. As we stepped into the sharp outside air, I felt queasy from spending ninety minutes on the edge of something. That was when he gestured up the road, showing me where his halls were located. There was the suggestion that we could go there, continue the movement of his hand up my thigh. I told him it was getting late and he walked me home instead, just like Herr und Frau Keller would expect him to.

Heading to the halls in broad daylight, I was anxious about who might see me. But I realized as I crossed the main street in front of the Party building, it was silly to fuss about that. Everyone would notice me. EVERYONE. I was no longer just my father's daughter; I was the Reich's favorite daughter. There was nothing I could do about it, only exploit the benefits.

I prepared myself as I walked, built up my character, what I was going to say. It could all slip away so easily if I was made to wander through the corridors asking all those military men which room to go to. They'd know exactly what I was there for. Or they'd think they knew.

The stars were on my side, though. There was a bank of named buzzers nestling between the branches of the ivy that climbed, all lush and out of place, up the front wall. I found his name next to Dirk's. An electric fizz sounded through the building as I pressed. I straightened my hair, positioned myself, chin up, in the lens of the small camera beneath the buttons. I didn't get a greeting, though. There was just a loud click and another electric fizz with a different tone. I pushed my way in.

The hallway had a red patterned carpet and a white painted staircase. There was a telephone table and dark wooden cubbyholes for mail. It was silent and soulless. It stank of disinfectant and boys.

"Hello?" I called.

"Jess?"

The voice came from above. There he was, leaning over the banister, wearing a tight white T-shirt and baggy gray sweatpants, his hair falling forward, all shaggy and wild, not combed down neat like usual. You could almost smell the sleep, the bedclothes . . .

I made myself think of Herr Hoffman and how he had so easily turned Fisher into a puppy dog.

"You should have answered the door in person," I barked.

I snapped my head back, faced the blank space in front of me where I expected him to be. "Did you not see me, on the camera? Did you not see who it was calling?" I had been too meek at the cinema, too submissive. I was in charge. I was the Reich's favorite daughter.

But Fisher wasn't rolling over yet. "I didn't know it was you!" His voice was playful, teasing. "Come on up!"

I stayed staring forward.

I had never seen him without his uniform before, never seen his bare feet — which were pushing through the gaps in the banister, firm and brown and sinewy.

"Come on up!" he called again. I glanced his way. He beckoned me with an arm — an arm covered in that fine blond hair. Then his voice dropped, in line with what he was thinking. "I want to show you something."

I was thinking it too, of course. There was something in me, really in me, that liked it, that wanted it. It was a craving — for a touch that would send a charge through my brain. It got the better of me, made me forget what I was doing, who people really were. It stopped me being faithful and pure and German. It scared me. No one else is like you, I told myself. *Only men obey commands of the blood. Men and animals.*

"My father has sent me," I announced, cutting through the possibilities with a knife.

"Oh."

I heard his footsteps creak across the landing, then the quick *dum-de-dum* as he skipped down the stairs. He was in front of me then, smelling just like I thought he would.

"My father has asked me to collect the keys for the meeting hall," I said.

"Oh?" The shine of his eyes leveled into that metallic, drilled stare he used at the HJ and BDM meetings. He put his arms behind his back, stood a little straighter. Off-duty Fisher was slowly morphing into on-duty Fisher. He waited for me to say why I needed the keys. He expected the rest of my orders to include him.

"Well, aren't you going to get them, then, Herr Fisher?"

Herr Fisher. The address made him curl his lip into the beginnings of a smile; his eyes flashed. He thought it was a joke, a come-on. He studied my face for a moment. *Wait until my father hears about this!* I said over and over in my head, hoping the words came out in the tiny movements of my face. His smile disappeared. He stepped backward and, without another word, jogged upstairs. Moments later he was in front of me again, holding out the bunch of keys. I felt a surge of relief, a jolt of victory. I reached for them, and he snatched them away.

"Frau Gross has a set," he said. "For the Frauenschaft meetings. She only lives across the street from you."

I held his stare. I could have told him that she'd lost her set, or that she was away on holiday right now, but they were small lies. They would have unraveled as easily as a badly stitched hem the moment Fisher bumped into the old goat on the main street.

He was smiling again.

"There is to be a meeting," I said, in a whisper.

The smile cracked.

"A secret, off-radar meeting." I made him hear quote marks around "off-radar." These were not my words.

The smile faded completely.

"It is to be between my father and a representative of the American judiciary regarding the arrest of Amanda Levy . . ." I spoke fast and urgently so he had to lean in. I left gaps in the story for him to fill. That's how you do it. The other person must always join up the circle.

"No one," I said, pausing for emphasis, "is to know about this, or to jeopardize its security. Which is why this obscure location has been chosen."

He was nodding now, his mouth a little open.

This is your moment, I told him, and myself, without having to say it at all, *the moment you've been waiting for all your life—a great big crisis that you can stand on top of, hands on hips, and demonstrate your brilliance. Don't fuck it up this time.*

"Okay?" I said, feeling my head swim with the power.

He nodded, and handed over the keys.

One day the warden who collected me was different. Not old or gnarly or rough, but young, with a warmth and a light glowing from beneath her pale, freckly skin. She had tight brown curls pinned back from her temples like wings. I was thrilled just to be near her. Everything else in that place was so ugly.

We went on a longer route to my session, one that took us outside for a moment—OUTSIDE!—through a covered walkway between two of the site's buildings. The shock of the light hurt my eyes, even though it was nothing more than overcast. The blast of wind whistling through the gap in the buildings was amazing—delicious! I promised never to take the weather for granted ever again. I would dance in the rain, write poems about lightning.

And that wasn't even the best bit.

As we traveled between those two doors, I saw other girls— OTHER WOMEN!—in gray smocks and rubber clogs just like mine, standing in pairs and threes, talking to each other—*actually talking!*—not handcuffed. Some were upright and smoking, others bow-backed and coughing. There was a whine coming from a tinny speaker at the top of the fence. Music, I think.

Some of these women looked my way as I passed through the walkway, making me all of a sudden realize that I still existed. Because I had begun to wonder. I drank in gulps of the cold, fresh air like it was a glass of milk.

"What day is it?" I asked the warden as we pushed back through the double doors, forgetting the hierarchy of things in my excitement and speaking before I was spoken to.

"Sunday," she answered, not *Shut up, bitch* or *Watch your mouth*. This, teamed with my first, exhilarating footsteps in fresh air, made me believe this warden was kind, that the journey outside was her idea because she wanted me to see that I wasn't alone, that I was working hard and soon I would be free. Or at least freer. She was a good person. She had recognized the same in me. I decided to talk to her some more.

"Gosh, the wind travels sideways around here, doesn't it?" I exclaimed.

She said nothing. She had a hard little mouth, despite the freckles and the angel wings.

Then I said, "You're very clever," because I thought that a piece of kindness deserved a little bit of kindness in return. (Or a bit of flattery, depending on how you wanted to look at things.) "You're clever to know your way around, I mean. Because everything here looks the same to me."

Nothing again. I needed to ask a direct question if I wanted a response.

"So." I leaned my head toward her, nudging her shoulder with mine, just slightly, to show that we were friends now. "How long have you been working here?"

She stopped walking then. She took the hand that was

handcuffed to mine—her strong one, not the free one, so I had to be involved in the movement too, whether I liked it or not—and she struck me hard across the cheek.

"Shut up!" she said.

My yelp echoed against the white walls and the white floors. This was one person who understood the element of surprise.

"You disgust me," the freckly warden muttered, shuddering a little, shaking my words off her shoulders. "You really do."

She made us continue our walking. I clutched my face, but the pain was nothing compared to what I felt inside. I'd failed some kind of test, just when it seemed like I was getting somewhere. I had been stupid. But that's what desperation does to you, I think.

Once at the room, the freckly warden told the man in uniform what had happened, except it sounded like something that had happened between two other people. Two other people on some other planet. I didn't get my say.

I had doomed myself to go back to the beginning—again—and this time I was even less sure what I was being punished for. The something that they kept saying was inside me, or not inside me . . . It could have been anything. One of so many things.

I truly wondered, though, if it was my power to disgust.

You disgust me.

It was a terrifying thing for her to say, considering all the other things that went on in that place.

I made straight for the meeting hall, taking the shortcut back through the graveyard, crossing over the main street, then up toward the old cricket club.

I took the path carefully mown flat in the field, looking over my shoulder now and again to make sure no one had followed. All was quiet—only the sound of my feet on the grass, the rasp of stray barley stalks against my shoes. Everyone was at work or had gone back to school. There were only a few of us who were still in this limbo, waiting to head off. I would be gone in ten days' time.

Mum was slowly filling my trunk. It sat open-jawed on the floor of my bedroom. Each day she'd sneak in when I wasn't there to leave another new thing on my bed. Then she'd wait in the kitchen for me to run downstairs and gush my thanks. She wanted the reaction. Occasionally she'd come into my room while I was there, her face all serious, bowing down on one knee, her skirt and apron spilling, and she'd lay the next new object ceremoniously before me. A warm sweater for training, bed socks, a set of Berlin Girl Mystery Romances, new bright-yellow guards for my skates. She would crack her serious face only when

I laughed at this solemn act of hers. It distracted her from the fact that I was going away, I think, these offerings from the gods. Lilli would then provide even more distraction by throwing a momentous tantrum over every present—because she hadn't been given anything lately and it JUST WASN'T FAIR.

Mum couldn't afford to be getting everything brand-new. We had more money than most, but not so much to place ourselves too far above the workers; that would have been vulgar. It had never bothered me in the past, getting stuff secondhand. Angelika Baker had always been a snob about it, never quite understanding that extravagance was an ugly vanity while frugality showed a dedication to the future of the Fatherland. But these secondhand things bothered me now. I spread the warm sweater out across my bed. Cashmere, the label said. I leaned over to sniff it—nice, but "other." It made me uneasy. Where had it come from? Who had it come from? Where was the girl who'd once owned it?

I let myself into the meeting hall and flicked the switches that made the fluorescents clink and flicker awake. I crossed the room repeating a small, comforting lie to myself (well, a big one, perhaps) that I really wasn't doing anything wrong. I wasn't trespassing. This had been my territory for the last eleven years—sewing and singing and hammering and reciting. Why shouldn't I come here when I needed the place most? I'd be back here tonight with the few others who were left. I'd give a wink to Fisher at the right moment, just to keep the story going.

The meetings weren't about us older girls anymore. We were only there to pass on what we knew to the little ones who'd moved up into our time slot. They looked young in a way I don't think we ever did. They seemed silly and soft. I didn't care about them. It was a terrible thing to admit, but it was true. We had been taught to defend our own Mädelschaft to the death. We'd been filed as sharp as we could ever get on that, and I WOULD have defended them to the death — even Ruby Heigl and Angelika Baker. But the small ones? They didn't seem like my sisters. I remember the outgoing girls who spoke down to us last year; they felt it too. You could tell. Indifference. There were some limits to our unity.

But there I was, in the silence of the hall that afternoon, doing exactly what they'd trained me to do — defend one of my sisters to the death. They only had themselves to blame.

I picked through Fisher's keys, looking for the one that opened the cupboard. Then once inside, I pulled out my favorite machine — the pale-blue manual with the least temperamental ribbon. I set it down on one of the tables that was pushed up against the side of the room, lifted a chair off the stack. I'd brought my own paper in my bag and threaded a sheet into the roller.

I sat there, looking at the empty page for the longest time, scared to start. Above me hung that week's inspirational poster. IT IS NOT MERELY ENOUGH TO SAY: I BELIEVE. RATHER ONE MUST SWEAR: I WILL FIGHT.

I pushed down shift-lock, took a deep breath.

THIS IS CLEMENTINE AMELIA HART

I bashed those keys like I was clattering through a Beethoven piano sonata at the Royal Albert Hall. I threw the carriage back, hit the line spacer several times to create the right amount of room. I took the photograph from the front pocket of my bag and held it against the paper, checking that the gap I'd left was sufficient.

There she was.

My friend.

She looked neater and more composed than she ever did in real life. We had traded ID pictures last year, snipping off the bottom image from our strips. She was wearing her BDM uniform—because the photos were for new membership cards. That was why she was giving that face to the camera— half-snarling, certainly defiant.

And then it hit me, like a cannonball to the gut—she was gone. She was gone. How had I let Herr Hoffman separate me from her, let the news crews twist history? How had I carried on skating, eating, sleeping, going to the BDM meetings? How could I have celebrated my eighteenth birthday in the garden with my family wearing a stupid paper hat when she was gone? I'd been in a dream, a self-induced coma. I felt a shame that I had never felt before.

The only consolation—she was so alive in my head now I could barely contain her. I could still see her that last day in the garden, the way the sunlight made her look like a goddess. Immortal. *The time is out of joint. O cursèd spite, that ever I was born to set it right.* I put her picture down, wiped away my tears.

THIS IS THE GIRL WHO SET HERSELF ON FIRE AT THE JAY ACKER CONCERT IN TRAFALGAR SQUARE.

255

I typed.

THE AMANDA LEVY STORY IS A BIG LIE.

CLEMENTINE AMELIA HART IS A
~~GERMAN CITIZEN~~ BRITISH CITIZEN
WHO BELIEVES IN FREEDOM.

The crossing-out was wrong. I was sure that the place Clementine had come from before was Berlin, her father's hometown. Her German language was always so much slicker than mine — that head start she'd had when she was little, the immersion. But Clementine would have liked the crossing-out, the ambiguity of it. It didn't matter who we were, where we were from — we were all prisoners.

THEY TOOK AWAY HER PLACE AT MUSIC
COLLEGE. THEY TOOK AWAY HER MOTHER'S
JOB. THEY TOOK AWAY HER FATHER. THEY
WERE GOING TO CUT HER OPEN AND STOP
HER FROM HAVING CHILDREN.

CLEMENTINE AMELIA HART DID WHAT SHE
DID BECAUSE SHE WAS DESPERATE.

AND BECAUSE SHE WANTS YOU TO BE FREE.

There were gaps in the story. People would add in their own knowledge, their own suspicions, all the secrets and shame that they kept squirreled away. Just like I had. That was what would really start this revolution—getting people to think for themselves. I hit the line space lever.

DEUTSCHLAND ERWACHE!

Her words. I hit the line space lever some more. Then:

FOR MURDER, THOUGH IT HAVE NO TONGUE, WILL SPEAK WITH MOST MIRACULOUS ORGAN.

Hamlet. My words.

I sat back in the chair.

I had done something that I believed in. Not something I had been instructed to do, but something that came from within me. It felt good. It felt like being good.

Then came a voice: "What are you doing here?"

They pulled it out of me, tipped me upside down, and clapped me on the back to make sure I was empty. Then they set about filling me up again.

"Do you know why we didn't cut off your hair?" my interrogator asked at the end of my last session. On that brief walk I was given outside, weeks back, I'd seen girls with hair shorn tight against their heads and others with long braids. Like much of what went on in there, I thought it was all random.

"We don't do it to the clever girls," he told me. "The girls with excellent heritage."

I nodded. My hair grew very fast at home. Mum would trim it regularly. Here it had grown hardly at all.

"We knew we could re-educate you. And quickly. Quicker than it would take for your hair to grow back."

I was supposed to be thankful, but I was nothing but angry— that they thought they had me all sussed out, right from the start.

It was not only my hair that had stopped growing there, but my nails too. Everything had slowed—my breath, my pulse. I was becoming stiller, a tortoise. I stayed in my shell most of the time.

"We've had a few hiccups, haven't we, Fräulein Keller?" He grinned. "But your mind is clean now. I will personally vouch for that." He signed the piece of paper in front of him with a flourish. My skin felt tight over my jaw. It would have hurt to say thank you, so I didn't.

The freckly warden collected me. But she was a different person now. She wasn't pretty, not viewed from the inside of my shell. Perhaps the place had turned her ugly. We collected my few belongings from the single cell—my toothbrush, spoon, cup, dish, the warm sweater—and she took me on my first long walk outside in two months. It was freezing, but I didn't care. The light, the blue, the feeling of the wind pushing my smock between my legs, the birdsong clear, not muffled—I had jumped into a lake after the longest, hottest day.

"This way."

We turned the corner of a long, thin building. Ahead, a group of women moved rubble from one end of the fenced parade grounds to the other. Wardens stood watching. German shepherd dogs panted clouds into the air.

"You will learn to become useful again," the uniformed man had said. "And to do that, you must get back in touch with the land, with work."

Useful to whom? He didn't say. I was useful to no one. I could barely put one foot in front of the other. We came to a door.

"We're putting you in with the politicals," the freckly warden said, each word a grudging gift. "Count yourself lucky." She hooked a finger under the black triangle on my chest and tore it off in a swift yank. "Don't let them see you with that." She shoved a flimsy red triangle into my palm instead. "If they did, they'd eat you alive."

The breast of my smock was ripped and flapping, my loose gray bra on show.

The freckly warden punched me in the back, her knuckle meeting bone. I thought of Fisher's gentle touch loosening my spine as he kissed me behind the curtains of the meeting hall. Just a different kind of force — no better. The room was warm and muggy, and silent as soon as I came in. Heads turned and lifted from their beds.

"Baumann!" the freckly warden barked.

A tall woman in a gray smock stepped forward. "Yes, Fräulein."

"She's all yours," muttered the freckly warden, and I was handed over.

I leaped out of my seat, put myself between the typewriter and the door, my backside on the keys. I thought I had locked myself in. WHY HAD I NOT LOCKED MYSELF IN? My heart was climbing out of my throat. I looked up.

GG—standing in the spill of light. Dirty riding trousers, untucked shirt, tall black boots. It could have been worse; it could have been one million times worse.

"You have to go!" I spluttered. "Go away!"

"What?" She grinned.

"I'm serious, GG. Go! Pretend you never saw me."

"What *are* you doing? Sneaking around in here in the daytime, Secret Agent Keller . . ."

She closed the door behind her and headed my way.

"I'm serious, GG." My voice climbed an octave. "You're going to get me in trouble, or I'm going to get you in trouble."

Killed, I wanted to say. *You're going to get us killed.*

She ignored me, came right up close. I pressed myself back against the typewriter and the table. Her eyes were red, as if she'd been crying. But GG never cried, so that couldn't have been it.

"Come on, Jess," she said, all quiet and low. "We're going to be hundreds of miles away from each other in a few days' time. No one is worried about . . ." She didn't finish. She took a great big stuttering breath and buried her face in her hands.

There was a weird silence. Then an even weirder snort from behind her fingers.

It took me a few moments to realize. GG was crying. GG. Crying.

I wanted to move forward and comfort her, put my arms around her, but I couldn't. MUSTN'T. I kept my hands pinned to the frame of the typewriter behind me.

"Sorry," she said, coming up for air. "I've just had to say good-bye to Sassy. Mum and Dad have sold her because I'm going away and . . ."

She buried her face in her hands again.

"When do you leave?" I felt like a monster, just watching her sob.

She lifted her head. "Thursday. You?"

"Next week."

She nodded.

We stood there for a moment in the quiet of the hall, watching dust motes fall from the skylights.

"It'll be good there," she sighed. She was talking about the stables, not skate camp; reassuring herself, not me. Her chest started hiccupping from the tears.

"More horses," I offered brightly. "New ones that you might like better."

She scrunched up her face to show how little I understood.

"Sorry," I said.

She closed the gap between us and peeled one of my hands off the typewriter. "It's okay," she said, playing with the ends of my fingers. "Bit like me saying you'll find another Clementine at skate camp."

She met my eyes. I was speechless. That she had said her name, more than anything. No one had since the concert. Only Herr Hoffman, only to condemn her.

"Are you okay?" she asked.

I nodded. I thought about asking her the same thing back. *Are you okay? That all along I loved someone else?*

"Do you know what's happened to her?" asked GG.

I shook my head. I started to cry. I let myself ask—GG was in all sorts of trouble now anyway, just being in this meeting hall with me. "I couldn't see," I said. "Afterward. Did you see?"

"I saw them carry her offstage but . . ." She stopped; she shrugged. Then her arms came around me. I let her pull my head into the crook of her neck—figs, brown sugar, mixed with a little bit of horse.

"I miss her so much," I said, tasting my tears and her skin.

"I know you do."

What I wouldn't have given for someone to have done this on the day of the concert. In that blacked-out car that took us home, couldn't my father have held me then? No one would have seen. My mother could have squeezed me tight when I came into the house, all sooty and stained. Or would that have been an admission? Of something . . .

"I just want her back," I sobbed.

"Me too."

She let me cry, then she gently pulled my head away from

263

her neck so she could kiss me full on the mouth. A kiss of life. I kissed her back, hard and urgent. This was all I had wanted, someone to be truthful.

GG went over to the door and locked it. We took ourselves behind the curtained section at the back of the hall and made a bed of the PE mats. I was grasping at love, I realize, and I knew GG might be the very last of it.

The tall woman with the cheekbones stepped forward. If not for her gray smock and rubber clogs she would have looked like one of the girls in Clementine's magazine. Angular, underfed.

"Clara Baumann. Block senior," she announced. Her newscaster English made me stand up straighter. The rest of the women in the room started creeping—cats toward a bird.

"Name?"

I gave her absolutely all of it. "Jessika Davina Keller."

It wasn't what she was expecting. Her hard jaw dropped. "Sorry?"

"Jessika Davina Keller," I repeated.

The cats slunk nearer.

Clara twisted her neck to look at me with one questioning eye. I thought she was gearing up to slap me, but no, she started laughing.

"You're kidding me! You're *kidding me!*" She spun around to call to another of the cats. "Bells! Bells! Come here, look at this."

A short, stout woman elbowed forward and came to stand alongside Clara, making her seem even taller, giraffe-like.

"Daniel Keller's daughter!" Clara announced.

They knew me.

How could they know me?

Bells narrowed her eyes, the grooves in her forehead rivaling those of a toast rack. "Can't be." Her voice was like gravel. "We would have had word of this." She folded her arms.

The pair stared, Clara's face wavering between amazement and suspicion, Bells's face unimpressed.

Clara coughed; she sharpened her vowels. "Right. Tell us what happened on August thirteenth." She laid it down as a challenge.

I didn't know what to say. If I had been in one of those whitewashed rooms with a tape recorder whirring, I'd have understood which version of events to give. If I had been standing in front of a smiling peppermint lady . . . But what did these women want?

The cats were shoulder to shoulder now, bringing with them the sour smell of unwashed hair.

"There was a concert," I began, "in Trafalgar Square, and . . ."

"Oh, for goodness' sake!" Bells cried out—her words came as if raked through a cheese grater. "She would know all of this even if it wasn't her."

"Who was your neighbor on Lincoln Drive, then?" Clara chimed in.

My mouth opened and shut uselessly, like a fish on dry land.

She knew where I lived.

How could she know where I lived?

"See!" cried Bells. "She don't know nothing. She's nothing but a liar."

266

"No," I said. "I'm not a liar!" Not in that moment. "The Hart family!" I blurted. "The Hart family were my neighbors!"

Clara gasped. Bells narrowed her eyes. The cats shuffled closer.

"First names," prompted Clara.

"Jocelyn . . ." I began.

A little cry of *oh gosh* . . .

" . . . Um . . . Simon . . ."

. . . a few laughs of joy . . .

" . . . And Clementine Amelia Hart."

Delighted squeals from them all.

"Still . . ." muttered Bells. "But she's still . . ."

"No, she's not," said Clara. "Not if she's in here."

But Bells wasn't giving up. "It looks nothing like her! The Nazi's daughter had meat on her bones!"

Clara took hold of my chin, lifted my face to the light. "I can see it, can't you? Her father. Look at the nose, the eyes."

I twisted free of her grip. I was nothing like him.

"Tell us what happened on August thirteenth," Clara said again.

"There was a concert," I said. "In Trafalgar Square, and . . ."

"Shhh!" Clara spat to the whispering cats behind her.

"And . . ." I said.

"Go on . . ." she said.

A terrorist made an attempt on our young people's lives.

"I can't," I said. I looked over my shoulder. Had the freckly warden really left? Did I imagine that? Had she heard everything? Would she be reporting back? "I just want to . . ."

They moved as one, wordlessly, and created a cocoon around me.

"They can't hear you," Clara whispered. Her breath was sweet but stale, her lips a firm and definite line. "You can tell us the truth."

I could feel the warmth of them. They bent their heads in. They all wanted it. They wanted me to say it, even though they had heard it already. To them, this was good news, proof that the fight goes on.

WE SHALL NEVER SURRENDER!!!

WE SHALL NEVER SURRENDER!!!

WE SHALL NEVER SURRENDER!!!

"Clementine Amelia Hart tried to start a revolution," I said. All around me, teeth, smiles.

"And what did you do?" Clara asked, a tear trickling down her sharp, gray cheek.

"I put out the fire."

The women held their breath.

"But only because," I said, "I wanted to save my friend."

The cocoon fell in on me, so many arms wrapped tightly around my vanishing body, even the reluctant arms of Bells.

We stayed curled up into each other.

I wished that I'd had a moment like that with Clementine, a quiet and gentle moment that I knew for sure was the last. I wanted to go back, say a proper good-bye.

"It's terrible what happened," GG said, her mouth close to my ear. "I can't stop thinking about it. Whatever made her . . ."

"I understand, I think." I traced a finger across GG's chest, joining one scattered freckle to the next.

Ever since I'd learned to talk, I'd learned to be careful about what I said and who I said it to. Even a good friend could betray you. So this was self-destruction.

"There were too many reasons . . ." I told her. I pictured my typed list:

THEY TOOK AWAY HER PLACE AT MUSIC COLLEGE. THEY TOOK AWAY HER MOTHER'S JOB, THEY TOOK AWAY HER FATHER. THEY WERE GOING TO CUT HER OPEN AND STOP HER FROM HAVING CHILDREN.

The list snapped me back to reality. GG must never hear Clementine's reasons coming from my mouth. She must not see the paper. Had she seen it already? I leaped up.

"Where are you going?" she asked.

"I have to . . ." I found my bra and fastened it in place, gathered together my hair that smelled of rubber from the PE mats beneath us, pulling it into a neat-enough bun. "I just have to . . ." That sting of disgust at myself again, for my desires. I was wicked. I let it pull me off track, away from the most important thing I would ever do. There was something wrong with me. All the risks I would take and the risks I was willing to ignore. I slipped on my underpants, bundled the rest of my clothes together, and walked out from behind the curtains.

"What happened to her parents?" GG called after me.

I dropped my clothes by the typewriter and ripped the typed sheet from the roller, slipping it carefully into my bag.

"I don't know," I called back.

"Are they dead?" She was out from behind the curtains, still naked, holding her jodhpurs, shirt, and underwear against her chest. The blond triangle of hair between her legs made me think of fish scales, of mermaids.

"I think so." My voice came out as a whisper. "They don't do all of them in the square, or on the lamppost." There had been a man on the main street earlier when I passed through, quite young, the flies just getting word that he was there. I STOLE FROM PARTY PREMISES AND SOLD THE SPOILS FOR MY OWN PROFIT, his sign read. "They do some of them quietly," I told GG. I had listened through the door one evening when Dad

270

had Fräulein Krause over for urgent business. I'd heard him dictate the word *guillotine*.

"I'm not quite sure why they waited so long," I went on. "They could have avoided so much trouble for themselves if they'd just taken the Hart family away when they first discovered that . . . If they'd just done it, I mean, just gotten on with it, then . . ."

What was I saying?

WHAT WAS I SAYING?

"No," I spluttered. "I didn't mean . . . I didn't mean . . ."

Defending the Harts would get me killed. Condemning them meant I was an animal.

GG's mouth was open.

"I have to go." I couldn't look at her anymore. I couldn't have her look at me anymore.

I lifted up the typewriter, the sharp metal edges pushing into my arms and bare belly, and started toward the cupboard.

A loud crash stopped me in my path—the sound of a bunch of keys falling to the floor. The bolt was turning in the meeting hall door. The door was opening. Fisher's keys sang as they slid across the floorboards in the door's path. I backed away from whoever might be coming in. GG, not caring that she was naked, stepped forward to get a better view.

Fräulein Eberhardt. Her piled-up hair, like a squashed plum pudding, came around the door.

"G-girls?" she stammered, her mouth then forming a perfect O.

And in my panic, I dropped my favorite typewriter, shattering it to pieces at my feet.

The sirens meant something to me now. They meant get up, get washed, get fed, even before the day had begun. The second siren meant go and stand in the "playground," be inspected, be counted.

Roll call could go on for hours. If anyone got dizzy and keeled over, Clara picked them up and smacked their cheeks, but only after being given the nod by our Frau Aufseherin — our boulder-like prison officer that Clara alone, not Bells, got away with calling by the unexplained nickname "Boogie." It was usually Nellie that crumpled to her knees. She was the oldest woman in Red Block — eighty-seven, toothless, and bent as a spoon. She refused all offers to be propped up once she was conscious again. One of these mornings, I knew we'd be carrying her lifeless body to roll call and have them strike her off the list.

In my first lineup I spotted the woman with the chins who had made me sign away my things. I thought she had been staff, but no, she was a prisoner like me. Although not exactly like me. She was standing in the green-triangle section — the criminals. ("The hard bastards," according to Bells. "They make

the best kapos. They get a kick from ruling over their own.")
The woman with the chins was wearing a lovely striped scarf.
My lovely striped scarf. It took all I had not to yell across and
unmask her as a thief, but Bells had warned me never to mess
with a Green, not if I was at all attached to my pretty face.

Lineup done, we walked the two miles of country lanes to
the factory, men honking and jeering as they passed in their
trucks, driving fast through the puddles and soaking us to our
underwear. We sewed all day until our fingers bled and our
eyes refused to focus, breaking only for a lunch of watery soup
and a hunk of bread.

I sat next to Clara. I was her trophy — a sign that the cause
was living strong.

"The Reich's favorite daughter!" she'd exclaim — quietly,
of course — between slurps of the diarrhea soup, shaking her
head, smiling her smile. "The Reich's favorite daughter! And
here she is!"

"How do you know I was called that?"

There was no television in the place, no radio, no magazines.

"Oh, we get all the information we need," she said with a
wink.

The Reds' letters were usually edited, literally, with sections
snipped out. The ladies would hold them up in the dorm, cry
"For fuck's sake!" then stick their tongues through the holes.
They got parcels too — photos and chocolates, gloves and
socks, nice-smelling toiletries, a jar of jam. The Reds were the
best fed and the best dressed in the playground. The criminal
Greens and the girls from the whore block had nothing on
us, even if one of them had pinched my lovely scarf. The

only other women who measured up were the small, proud group on the far side of the tarmac. Good skin. Nice coats. None of them had lost their hair. Sonderhäftlinge was what Bells called them. *Special prisoners.*

"Special how?" I'd asked. But she'd shrugged, embarrassed, and told me she didn't know.

"You'll start getting parcels soon, don't you worry," Bells said one lunchtime at the factory. She'd finished organizing the Table Girls who distributed the bread. She cocked a leg over the bench opposite me and sat down. "They've probably been holding back all the stuff you were sent in solitary," Bells went on, talking with her mouth full. "It'll be like Christmas Eve when . . ." She trailed off—because Clara was widening her eyes and shaking her head. They exchanged a look of understanding. Bells dropped her gaze into her empty bowl.

Silence. Zwischenraum.

"Where's my stuff?" I asked, politely first.

Thieves, they were all thieves!

"Well," said Clara, speaking like an adult would to a difficult child, "firstly, we don't like to think of it like that, as 'my stuff.' We share. You got a scraping of marmalade from Gitta's jar. All of us took a chocolate candy from that tray of Emma's. The shampoo is always pooled, and . . ."

"Where are my letters?" I cut in. I felt hot—nothing to do with the soup, because that had arrived at the table barely lukewarm.

"Calm down," hissed Clara. "Don't attract attention."

"I want my letters," I hissed back.

Clara and Bells exchanged guilty glances.

274

"What have you done with them?"

I wanted a picture of my family to pin on the wall like the others. I wanted to know what Ruby and Angelika and stupid Frau Gross were doing. I wanted Mum to send a tin of her lemon biscuits—experience the comforting taste again. Did Clara and Bells think I wouldn't have shared? Was Daniel Keller's daughter not to be trusted? At home or here, would I never be trusted?

"There aren't any," said Clara.

"What?" I said.

"No one has sent you anything."

"Oh, come on!" I didn't want to cry. The cotton dust made our cheeks sore and our throats dry. Salty tears would only make it worse.

"I checked." Her voice was soft. She took my hand under the table and squeezed. "The first night you were here. I do it for all the girls. I go to Boogie and I chase down their things . . . But there was nothing, Jess. I'm sorry."

"The trunk of stuff I came with . . ."

"Gone."

"But . . ."

"You lose your things. That's how it goes." She took a breath of decision. "Unless you're classified as a Sonderhäftling; then you live like a queen."

"Special how?"

Bells was squirming now, hearing this question for the second time.

"Well, you might be considered a special inmate," explained Clara, "if, for example, you have a high-ranking relative."

"But I have a . . ."

Clara was shaking her head. I was so upset I started speaking German. "Aber ich habe einen . . ."

"No, you don't." She gripped my hand a little tighter. "Not anymore."

"We've been with the horses," GG told Fräulein Eberhardt, her eyes stretched wide with panic. "We were muddy and smelly and thought we'd come here to change our clothes." Her voice was trying to keep pace with her pulse, tripping over itself in the rush.

Fräulein Eberhardt looked us up and down — GG's ruffled hair and naked body, me with my messy bun, wearing only my underwear.

"And the typewriter?" All eyes went to the pieces of it on the floor.

"We were messing around," I said. We had to confess to something, or Fräulein Eberhardt would have sniffed out the truth. "We're really sorry," I told her.

"Yes," said GG. "It's just that I'm going away this week and it's making us all feel a bit . . ."

"Giddy?" offered Fräulein Eberhardt. A word that was preferable to so many others.

In the days that followed, I waited for the explosion. I waited for Mother to lecture me while we washed the dishes. I braced myself for another trip to Dr. Hardy. I expected Dad to throw something hard against something breakable. It would get back to them eventually, somehow. Fisher could mention the keys to Dad (I had shoved his set back through the boarding hall mailbox folded up in a piece of paper with his name on it; I had no nerve left to hand them back in person), or Frau Gross would be at our door, brimming over with a wicked little story that she'd heard. I'd told Fräulein Eberhardt that the bunch of keys had come from Frau Gross, you see, not wanting to lead her back to Fisher. But that was a foolish thing to do, opening up that well-greased channel for rumors to slip back to our house.

Or Fräulein Eberhardt could have simply come and told my parents herself, knocked on our door and asked for money to replace the broken typewriter. But would she? Would she actually dare?

I slid my typed poster between the pages of a copy of *Das Deutche Mädel* on my bookcase, and I waited to see if I still had the guts for the next important step.

It may have been our last good-bye, but that wasn't the last time I saw GG. The morning she was to leave for the West Country she turned up at the ice rink to watch me skate. She must have sneaked in by the fire exit and found her place high up in the stands. Ingrid spotted her straightaway, always very aware of who might be watching or listening in. But when she started to yell up at GG, ask her what she was doing there, I grabbed her sleeve and shook my head. I mouthed the words *It's okay*, and reluctantly, Ingrid agreed to carry on.

We were to attempt the triple axel that morning—without the pole harness.

We—even though it would be me all alone when it came to leaping from the ice.

Of course, it had all been for Ingrid. It was important to her that I execute the jump successfully, just once, before I left for skate camp. That way, she could tell everyone that she had taught me all I knew. Who she would tell, I really didn't know—maybe just herself—but even so, I wanted that for her. It would be my parting gift.

Ingrid set the music running, Bruckner's *Fantasie*, and I skated figure eights waiting for the section that demanded the jump. The piano became louder, more earnest, and I picked up the routine, Ingrid shouting last-minute nervous instructions through the mist of the ice. "Remember, you need to stay lower than you think, get a good grip on takeoff." And I felt strangely cool and detached from it all as I skated backward, made that twist forward, struck, and—one, two, three—landed. As if it was nothing.

Ingrid exploded with excitement. I glanced up at GG, thinking she would be the same, but there was no reaction from the stands. Perhaps she didn't want to draw attention to herself, or perhaps to the inexpert eye it was just a jump like any other.

"You did it!" Ingrid shrieked, skating over, joyfully clattering into me. "You did it! You did it!" She grabbed my hand, waving it around as if I were the victor of a fight. "You are going to do such great things!" She was crying tears of real happiness. "This is just the start for you, Fräulein Keller!"

I felt so warm in her excited presence, triumphant as she hugged me.

But it was time to leave Ingrid. I loved her for her rebel's heart, but I didn't want to begin to hate her for being scared to act upon it. I told her that I really couldn't have done it without her, any of it, and I promised, solemnly, to do everything I could in the future to make her proud. Because that was the truth, and because I had learned that it was important to say things to people while they were still there in front of you, not regret the unsaid later, when they were gone.

When I finished my session, GG wasn't there. I walked around the banks of lockers—the guards on my skates making my stride long and loping—thinking I might find her. But her bus would have been leaving early. The day at the meeting hall really had been our good-bye.

I was alone now.

I pushed my key into the slot of my locker, feeling very grown up all of a sudden, the realization that I was on the cusp of something settling firmly on my shoulders—and then I froze.

NESTBESCHMUTZER.

On the locker door, in front of my nose, scrawled in big, black marker pen was the word NESTBESCHMUTZER. It hadn't been there when I'd put in my things, I was sure of it. How would I have missed it? I looked around. No one. I could hear voices echoing back from the rink—Dani and her coach. GG would never have written a thing like that, nor Ingrid. And anyway, Ingrid had been with me the whole time. To suspect Dani was too far-fetched. We were rivals, but in a quiet way, our weapon of choice being total indifference, even if she had gotten word that I'd beaten her to pulling off a triple.

NESTBESCHMUTZER.

I was scared to open my locker door, in case I found something else inside, something deserving of a Nestbeschmutzer — somebody who dirties their own nest, somebody who shits on their own people. I swung back the door with my eyes closed and when I opened them again — nothing. Or rather, my things — exactly as I had left them, utterly terrifying in their ordinariness.

I'd been cut loose and I was drifting. Who was I, who would I be, without them? I remembered Dad taking the training wheels off my bike for the first time when I was seven and pushing me off, down the wide, empty pavement of Lincoln Drive, my mind squealing on a loop: *now what now what now what . . .*

I searched for the good.

Morning lineups became an opportunity to see a beautiful sunrise, evening lineups a chance to watch the Suffolk trees turn to silhouettes against the pink. Those exhausting walks to the textile factory could be transformed by a glimpse of a woodpecker or the tune of a Singvogel. In the dusk, deer might leap across our path, making us stop and gasp. We saved lumps of inedible gristle in the pouches of our cheeks at lunchtime and spat them into the hems of the SS uniforms before sewing them up.

I got a new family.

One rainy evening a girl called Ute killed herself. She'd smuggled a pair of fabric scissors out of the factory in the lining of her smock and used them to cut her own throat. We mourned her, of course, with a small, quiet ceremony in the dorm. Candles and tears and illicit prayers. But also we tried to be thankful. We were thankful that Ute had found some peace, that she had carried out her awful act in the shower block where it was easy for us to clean up—because that was our job, just like it was our job to pull actual lumps of shit from the drains when the sewers backed up. We were thankful for Ute's things, which Clara doled out among us, gifting me with my first pair of gloves. And I was also thankful for the space Ute left in one of the dorm's "families." Her grieving "Schwester" Nina chose me to be her new sister.

Nina—with her long, shaggy hair the color of sand, her eyebrows as big as slugs. Like many of the women, she was in there for some petty remark. A neighbor had reported her for naming her pigs after the Führer and two of our Reich ministers.

"It was meant to be affectionate. I fucking love those pigs."

Now she was locked up, all her affection gone. For our leaders, that is. She still talked longingly of the pigs, more than her human family.

Our "Mutti," Kika, slept in the bunk above us with Ann, an aunt of sorts. We checked each other's hair for lice, like a concentrated bunch of baboons; we protected each other's stash of bread and bed socks; we kept each other warm. Because it did get cold. I thought about how I had stamped my feet on the pavement during the rounds for last year's Winterhilfswerk. That had been nothing compared to the razor-sharp coldness of sleeping in that dorm.

We spooned one another in bed, Nina and me.

"I might kill myself too one of these days," she'd say after lights-out, her voice clicky and nasal in the dark. "I'm going to run at that fence. I'll die in a shower of sparks."

"Amazing."

"It'll be electric!"

We snickered. This wasn't a gloomy conversation. The idea that there could be an end to things, an end that might somehow be in our control, was soothing.

"Or I might steal a pair of scissors too, but I'd use them to cut strips from a blanket."

"Then what?"

"I'd make a noose. I'd swing, of course!"

We were quiet. Sharing the silent image of Nina peacefully swaying a meter above the ground.

"Where do you think you go?" I asked Nina. "Afterward."

"Oh, they put you in one of those incinerators around the back of the toilet block," she said. "Then they mail you back to your family in a little cardboard box." She wriggled farther under the covers, taking me with her.

"No," I said, "I mean, where do you go, the thing inside your body."

"What thing?" She buried her face in my hair. "There is no thing."

"A soul?" It sounded like a polite request. "Don't you think that something must live on?"

I could feel her shaking her head, her chin rubbing against the base of my skull. "No, this is it, Jess." She tightened her arms and legs around me and squeezed. "You have to do it all here, right now. It's the only chance you get."

I listened at doors.

They started having hushed little arguments. And Mum took to drinking. Not much, just a gin and tonic in the evening, but it was quite a development considering she was all set to have another baby once I'd flown the nest. Something had to be badly wrong for Mum to throw purity out the window.

I was convinced it was all about me, the bickering. They were deciding what sentence to dish out—for the keys, for the typewriter, for GG. But when no punishment materialized, I told myself I was paranoid. My time as a national hero had led me to believe, mistakenly, that I was the center of everything. The graffiti at the ice rink—that was just a coincidence and not the harshest of words. VERRÄTER would have done the job better. *TRAITOR.* My parents' spatting, meanwhile, was down to their wobbly marriage. Mum's plan to have another baby was a fantasy. She was too old. I had seriously started to doubt then whether she had even given birth to Lilli. A memory of my mother fat and pregnant just wouldn't come to the surface. Dad, of course, still had a lot to offer.

So I left them to it. I moved on.

I volunteered to walk with Lilli to school, which might have raised suspicions if that bus weren't taking to me to skate camp in three days' time. We were all allowing ourselves to be a little more sentimental—like the families on the television dramas who stroke each other's hair in broad daylight and tip their heads to the side in love and admiration. And actually, I did feel sad about leaving Lilli, and my parents.

"You know it's not your job to look after the new neighbors," I told my little sister as we headed along the shortcut toward the stream and the ditches. I'd slipped on Wolf's leash and brought him with me. Moral support. His claws skittered against the pavement beside us, his furry back bouncing reassuringly.

"What do you mean?" Lilli asked.

Yes, what did I mean? Because I did want her to look after them, just like I had tried to look after Clementine. But I also knew that was too much responsibility for an eleven-year-old.

"I mean, you don't have to play with them if you don't want to. If you really don't like them."

"I don't ever play with anyone I don't like," Lilli replied smartly. And I could hear my old arrogance in her voice, the sense of position and entitlement you got from being in our family.

"Good for you," I replied. And I think I meant it. I envied her, that she could feel so sure of herself.

I dropped Lilli at her classroom, promising to meet her there at the end of the day, and took the fork in the path leading to the main office, tying Wolf to the school sign. He curled up straightaway, grateful for the rest.

At the desk, I rang the little bell and Fräulein Gruber's stockinged legs *snip-snipped* her over to the window of reinforced glass. Her long, neat nails slid it open. I couldn't shake the idea that Herr Hart's sleeping bag should be there underneath her desk.

"Fräulein Keller, how lovely to see you!" She adjusted the position of her glasses on her nose as if focusing binoculars. "Not off to skate camp yet?"

I shook my head. "Three days' time."

"Well, we're all so looking forward to seeing you on television in the National Championships." She beamed, I grinned back, and we stayed like this until our smiles wore out.

"So what can I do for you?" she offered.

"Well, I've written a newsletter," I announced, pulling it from my bag and sliding it across the counter for inspection. "It's for everyone in our old Mädelschaft, a bit of information on what everyone is up to now."

A bit premature, isn't it, Fräulein Keller? she should have said. *Some of you have only been gone a day or two.* But Fräulein Gruber wasn't someone to be bothering with original thought. Not in the presence of the Reich's favorite daughter.

"Oh, how lovely!" She picked up the newsletter and held it at a distance, as if it were a piece of art to be put on the wall and admired, not something to be read. This was probably for the best, as most of it was made up.

"So," I told her, "I need the key to the photocopy room."

The rest of the day, I wandered, scared to head home with my bulging bag, all those copies of Clementine's face. I went up to the main street and had a cup of tea in the H Place, shivering at one of the outside tables because Wolf was too whiny to leave alone. My mother had been nudging me to organize some kind of meeting with Fisher where I could lay down the case for us to remain a couple throughout my time at skate camp. I momentarily considered heading to his lodgings to do this, if only for a more awful distraction from the awful thing I'd just done. But I knew I couldn't go there with my bag stuffed with posters. I wouldn't be able to do anything with any real focus until they were out of my hands. But I had to wait, until the last minute. Do it, get on the bus to skate camp, get out of there. That was the plan.

I busied myself buying small going-away gifts for Mum and Lilli in Fascinations, then I went in search of something to give to Dad, picking up title after title in the bookshop but not finding anything right.

Then after struggling to fill the time, I managed to leave a whole five minutes late to meet Lilli. This became ten minutes when a strange woman grabbed me by the arm on the street and asked directions to the train station, ignoring all of my claims that I was in a mad hurry. Three times I ran through the very basic instructions before she would let me go. I sprinted the last stretch to Lilli's playground, Wolf struggling to match my pace. I arrived hot faced and sweaty as the last of the kids trailed away with their satchels and paintings of sunsets. I went up to the door of Lilli's classroom just as Fräulein Kling was shutting the door.

"Oh, she's gone," she said, not taking her hand off the handle or looking me in the eye.

"Are you sure?" I asked. "We'd arranged to walk home together."

"Quite sure. She left with a man, I think," said Fräulein Kling. Then quickly: "Though I couldn't possibly say for sure." She closed the door and flicked the latch. *A man!*

"Wait!" I banged on the glass, but Fräulein Kling had left the classroom, pretending not to hear.

Guilt hit me hard and immediately. Crazy with panic, I went to every set of swings near the school, yelled her name across the fields, Wolf joining in with sorrowful howls. I would find her, I told myself, no one need know, all would be fine. That thought danced menacingly with the belief that I would certainly discover her mutilated body in the woods. I worked my way back to the main street, Wolf limping now, on his last legs. Lilli wouldn't have left with a man she didn't know, I was convinced. She understood the rules of stranger danger. Fräulein Kling was mistaken. She must have sneaked off alone, to get me a going-away present in town. But she wasn't there; I checked at Fascinations, everywhere! Nothing. The little daisy-chain bracelet I'd bought for her suddenly felt heavy in my bag—heavy with tragedy.

I was going to have to go home, raise the alarm. I started running, past the Party building, past the florist, up toward the turn for County Roads Estate . . . And then, there she was. She was stepping out of the back of a large, black car. I ran to her as she waved her driver away.

"Where have you been?!" I shrieked.

"For a milk shake," she said. The most obvious thing in the world.

"With who?"

"That man."

"Did he hurt you?"

I worked my hands down her hair, face, arms, checking for damage. Wolf licked at her ankle.

"No, of course not." Again, the way she was talking, I was the stupid one. "He was actually quite nice."

She took my hand and started walking us back in the direction of our home. I was the kid sister now and she was the grown-up.

We walked past the lamppost. And we both stared, because today it was a girl. I recognized her. She was just a couple of years older than me. From the rough end of town. The sign around her neck read VERRÄTER. Just that. VERRÄTER. We were to fill in the rest, with our own guilt, our own shame.

"What was his name?" I asked Lilli, my voice trembling. "This man."

"He didn't say."

"Oh," I said. I looked back over my shoulder at the girl, her hands tied behind her back, her head to one side like she was waiting for the answer to a question.

Then my little sister said, "But he knew your name."

"He did?" A ball of something hot rose into my throat.

"Yes," Lilli said, so pleased with herself. "He said you're called Jessika and really you ought to be more careful."

We didn't always talk about death. Sometimes we talked about love.

"Do you like girls more, or boys?" Nina was pinching my feet between her thighs to warm them. In return, I rubbed her hands, careful to feel in the pitch-black for the newest of her blisters and not press too hard upon them. "In the real world, I mean."

"Well, it's not like there's much choice in here," I snorted, because I wasn't sure how to answer honestly.

"I like boys most," she told me.

"Right," I said.

"Well, I did before I came in. Not so sure how I'll feel when I get out."

"Can you change, then?" I asked. We swapped hands and feet. She shoved her steel-cold toes between my legs. I could feel the indent in her calf from the dog bite she'd gotten that week, the wiry stitches resting against my thigh.

"I dunno." She went quiet for a while. "They send men into the whores' block sometimes. Men from other camps, the ones who have sex with other men. It's supposed to make them normal again."

Nina pinched each one of my fingers in turn, forcing the blood back into them.

"Does it work?" I asked.

"How should I know?" She placed my hands together on the mattress, making a pillow of them for her warm cheek. "Can't stamp out the gays, can you? They just keep getting born right under their noses." She laughed at this. This was funny. "I wouldn't let them know you like girls, though," she said, serious again. "Not in that way."

"I never said I liked girls," I replied, "in that way."

I wished it weren't dark and that I could see her eyes.

Nina went on. "Clara says if a guard gets word, they send you off to a room with a soldier to . . . you know . . . get put right again."

"That's not true." I knew that wasn't true. I felt bad for cutting her down, though. It wasn't like I still believed that only Commie bastards did it, Commie bastards who kidnapped nice German girls.

"Besides," I whispered, "all the women in here are at it. So how could they possibly . . ." They were—you could hear them, in the night.

"It's only because of this place." Nina rolled over, pushing the curve of her back into my chest. I put my arms around her. "You've got to get your affection somehow."

I listened to her breath getting slower and deeper. Usually I fell asleep quickly, no matter what terrible things had happened that day. My brain was only too happy to switch off.

Today's horror—having the new Frau Aufseherin, the one standing in for Boogie, a woman made of a different metal, come into the dorm and demand to know which one of us was going to beat Stephi for falling asleep at her workbench. My "Mutti," Kika, had been the first to shoot her hand into the air. There were plenty of volunteers—maybe that was what upset me most.

"Someone has to do it," Kika argued. "It may as well be me."

She would be given cigarettes and extra bread as payment. Being part of her family, I would profit.

So off she went with Stephi, who returned half-dead, her clothes drenched in blood. She'd had to remove her underwear and be strapped down while Kika whipped her ass until the skin was gone. Lesson learned—Stephi wouldn't be falling asleep again for days.

And I couldn't sleep.

I thought of Clementine, about how when her family got to the United States at the end of their mythical escape they would have undergone a process of "de-Nazification." Clementine said it didn't matter if they were revolutionaries or not; they would be detained and questioned and counseled until the Americans were absolutely sure they held no sympathies whatsoever with the ideals of the Greater German Reich.

"What ideals?" I had asked her.

She gave me a long list. I didn't recognize any of them as beliefs that belonged to me. I didn't realize I had any ideals.

But now I saw.

Exactly the same thing was going on in here. We were being detained, questioned, counseled, with some hard labor and harsh punishments thrown in for kicks. And then, in the end, though the intention was entirely different, the result was exactly the same. De-Nazification. All my sympathies, gone.

293

Oh god oh god oh god . . .

I ran through the house, unlocked the back door, burst out into the garden.

There wasn't any time. There wasn't nearly enough time.

"Where are you going?" Lilli squealed after me.

"Nowhere!" I shouted back. "Don't follow me! If you do, I will kill you!"

I tripped over myself to get to the trees, to the swing, to the stream, my heavy bag slamming against my kidneys. Wolf came with me, full of some kind of second wind, all deer leaps and skipping. To him this was some kind of game. It wasn't. That girl on the lamppost had been for me, sacrificed just for me.

I stopped at the swing, the earth kicking and wheeling beneath me, my head spinning like I'd fallen from a badly executed spin. I would have toppled down the bank if it weren't for Wolf yipping at my feet, keeping me there, present, ready to act. I dropped my bag to the ground, fell to my knees, and I started to dig, using fingers, pulling at the soft dirt. Wolf joined in, his front paws pedaling at the hole. We kept going. Panting, both of us. When the space was big enough, I opened up my satchel, pulled out the stack of posters, and dropped them in, Clementine's face looking back at me, that sneer. Wolf's eyes peered up at me, all wet and eager.

Oh god oh god oh god . . . It wasn't going to work! It was never going to work! Wolf would dig them back up the first chance he got. I needed something else. I needed fire. I ran back to the house, Wolf still with me, springing at my heels. I slammed into the kitchen. Lilli was at the table, drinking juice she'd poured for herself. There was a pool of it on the table all around her cup.

"Urgh!" she cried, gulping down her mouthful. "You're all messy!"

I yanked open the junk drawer and grabbed the box of matches. Wolf was turning in crazy, muddy-footed circles in the kitchen, woofing out a *now what now what now what*.

"Where are you going?" Lilli whined as I flew outside again. "Why can't I come?"

We bolted the length of the garden, Wolf and me, and when we got to our hole in the ground, there it was—our next game. *Oh god oh god oh god* . . . Wolf spotted it quicker than me. He was off. Playing catch. The breeze had lifted the top sheets of posters and was casting a trail of them down the bank and into the water. Off they went, some of them becoming little rafts, heading downstream.

Into the water we went. In to save my skin. Not bothering to take my shoes off first. I didn't care. I wanted to live, I realized. I wanted to protest, I wanted to have my say, but also I really, truly wanted to live.

* * *

Mum's first words when she got back from her Frauenschaft meeting: "Oh, for goodness' sake, Jess, look at my floor!" I was standing by the washing machine, stripping away my soaking, filthy clothes. Wolf was at my feet, dripping, wearing a tea towel. Lilli loitered behind my mother in the doorway.

"And she's been playing with matches," she piped up.

"The fuck I've been!" I spat back.

My mother gasped. I put my hand over my mouth.

I never said words like that in front of her. Ever.

"I mean, I'm sorry, I'm sorry," I gabbled. I'd known that there was no chance I'd get cleaned up before she returned. I had prepared my lie. "It's just that Wolf fell in the stream and I had to go in and get him and I was really scared because I thought that he was drowning and . . ." I was crying. This was perfect. I couldn't have rehearsed it any better. Wolf looked up at my mother with a pitiful face, slipping expertly into his role.

"Just get upstairs," my mother muttered. She was shedding her coat and cardigan, ready to tackle the mess. I slunk past her wearing just my underwear.

"Not you!" my mother bellowed, snagging Wolf by the collar before he could follow me onto the hallway carpet.

I showered quickly, still doing everything to the beat of my racing heart. I raided my skate-camp trunk for clothes. I'd been carefully not wearing anything I might want to take with me, but I had nothing left. They'd have washing machines where I was going, I told myself, I needn't worry.

I didn't bother to dry my hair. I got back to work. I shoved a chair up against the door to stop Lilli wandering in, and lifted down my stack of magazines from the shelf above the desk. I pulled out the birthday celebration edition of *Das Deutsche Mädel*. I hadn't hidden it exactly, because what better hiding place than in a stack of other completely harmless magazines. I flicked it open. I'd pulled out the wrong one — the genuine one. I tossed that aside and went through the spines looking for Clementine's version.

Not there.

I spread them out across the floor, looking for the cover — the Faith and Beauty girls spelling out WIR GEHÖREN DIR.

Not there.

I went back to the edition I'd thrown aside, flicked through it again, expecting it to suddenly transform into the illegal version. No.

Not there.

Where was it? WHERE WAS IT?

Then I thought — Lilli. It had to be. She had been in here, stealing my things. I was all set to storm across the hall and create a tornado in her room when another thought arrived . . .

No, I told myself. *No, no, no, no, no.*

I crawled over the carpet to the loose piece of baseboard, slipped my finger down the gap.

Not there.

Clementine's notes. Gone.

Oh god! I climbed to my feet, backed up against the door, and clattered against the chair, forgetting it was there.

"You okay?" This was Mum's voice.

"FINE!"

Could I tell for sure? Would there be a clue? They must have left a trace, surely. I searched for it, no desire on this earth to find it. But there it was, on my windowsill. My skating trophies. They were neatly arranged, evenly spaced. That was okay, but I always organized them according to which win I was most pleased with, left to right, ascending order. Two trophies had switched places.

I couldn't breathe.

Everyone in this house knew my trophy system. We had discussed the merits of each victory at length. Only a stranger would have made that silly error. Not my parents. It couldn't have been my parents. The men must have come while we were all out. Acting without my father's permission. Or the women. Maybe they send women to do the searching. Who knew? No one. That was the point.

I couldn't leave my room. I couldn't look my mum or dad in the eye. With one glance they would just know. I was no longer the Reich's favorite daughter. I'd dropped the role. I hadn't kept up my side of the bargain. I was not good.

I sat on the floor by the door. Didn't shift. I pictured the magazine and the essay notes sitting on a desk somewhere. A wet poster hanging up, drip-drying—because we hadn't gotten all of them, Wolf and me. I'd waded as far as I dared without getting pulled under by the current. I ripped the soles of my shoes on the rocky bed in the process. Wolf swam merrily, the ripples breaking over his face, freed by the buoyancy of the water from his irritating limp. The wet posters I collected, I rubbed into pieces at the stream edge until they were nothing but pulp that washed away. The dry ones I burned. I tried to picture the path of the stream—where those runaway posters might wash up. I imagined a group of faceless people standing around that evidence on their desk, speaking in murmurs, deciding my fate. Would it be a public one, where they sold tickets for the viewing gallery with Kaffee und Kuchen, where Ruby Heigl could strike up a verse of "Eine Flamme Ward Gegeben" just so she could, eternally, in my last moments, make it all about her? Or would I get a lamppost, a one-word sign? Or maybe something private?

I stayed curled up and waited for the doorbell, for the men to come. Or the women. To take me away. And my family for harboring me.

And during all of this, despite my regret, still my admiration for Clementine swelled, that she had faced all this and more, every day, without cowering in the corner of her bedroom. I was no revolutionary. What was I thinking? I was a failure, a coward. I was a traitor.

Sundays were our day of rest. We washed our underwear and swept the dorm. We walked up and down outside, trying to catch a ray of sun.

In the late afternoon, we did a show for one another, performing poems and stories we knew by heart. Clara would read aloud her letters home to her husband before she sent them — brilliant, sparkling things. She captured our days in a way none of us could ever have managed. The sight of two silvery airplanes in the sky sent her musing on how far we'd come as a human race but how far we still had to go.

Nina had a lovely singing voice, all sad and lilty like a bird falling from the sky. She performed old English folk songs about bonny lads and cuckoos, songs that began with someone going a-walking or a-courting. Bells told rude jokes and did impressions, her favorite being a loving rendition of Marlene Dietrich all full of phlegm, warbling out "Leben ohne Liebe kannst du nicht." *You can't live without love.* Bells also impersonated the guards, including Boogie. They would often sit in and watch, the guards, laughing the loudest, yet still it felt dangerous. Could there be a Sunday coming when Boogie wouldn't find it funny anymore?

"What can you do?" Clara asked one weekend while our show was under way. I always sang along and cheered and cried, but the things that I had memorized as a child had no place in Red Block. I thought once about doing that speech from *Hamlet*, the one where he exclaims to Rosencrantz and Guildenstern, *What a piece of work is a man!* But I was scared that Boogie would report back when she heard me declare, *Man delights not me.*

"I can ice skate," I told her.

Clara clapped her hands in delight and was straight up on her feet, up on the bench. "Listen, ladies, listen!"

Bells's sing-along (a dirty version of "Es Klopft Mein Herz Bum-Bum" that involved bending over and slapping her backside) came to a stumbling end.

"Listen!" Clara was flapping her bony arms like a hopeful flightless bird. "Jessika can ice skate!"

The room fell into a chorus of oohs and aahs.

"You kept that one quiet," honked Bells. They had known so much about me when I first arrived, I assumed they knew this too. After being good, wasn't it my most defining feature?

The women pushed and shoved, maneuvering me into the middle of the room, onto the circle stage we'd created on the dormitory floor.

I started to laugh. "But I can't do it for you now. Not without skates, not without ice."

"Of course you can," Clara called. "Just pretend; slide around in your socks or something."

I shook my head. I wasn't going to do that. That would be silly.

"What music do you need, Jess?" Nina asked, hopping from one foot to the other at the prospect of seeing something new. There was a reassurance in watching the ladies repeat the same acts over and over, but, yes, we also got bored. "Shall we hum, Jess?" asked Nina. "What do we know?" She began conferring breathlessly with the women beside her on the benches. The idea of music seemed to slice through my reluctance.

"Do you know Bruckner's *Fantasie?*"

"Ummm." Nina looked around her. "Well . . ."

"Yes. We. Do." This was Boogie. She placed her hands on her extensive thighs and hoisted herself to standing. With a smug and satisfied grin, she pulled the belt of her skirt up and over her belly and swaggered off toward the door of the dorm, the chain of her keys clanking against her hip. "While I'm gone," she called after herself, "open up all the windows."

We looked to Clara to see if we should do as we were told. It was only a degree or two above zero outside. Clara shrugged and began flinging open the casements.

"It'll be freezing," someone cried.

"It'll be like a fuckin' ice rink," Bells cackled.

As we sat waiting, shivering, for Boogie to return, it started, through the loudspeakers outside. She'd made us open up the windows so we could hear. Bruckner's *Fantasie.* Those low notes at the start. Boogie was back in our doorway, looking terribly pleased with herself. All faces turned to me in the middle of the rink. The high, hopeful notes arrived . . . and I opened like a flower.

I slid and I jumped and I spun. It was stupid and ridiculous, but sort of wonderful all at the same time. The women oohed and aahed as I moved in sweeping movements across the floor. They shuffled the benches back and back, widening the rink as I went.

When it was time for the camel spin, I felt the same nerves that I did on the ice. Never a hard move by any measure but the one that always let me down. I got some purchase on the floorboards and flicked my body around for a spin or two, then held myself in position, imagining the rest of the revolutions. I showed them my heart. Then I set off again, skipping backward in preparatory circles. It was time at last to make Ingrid proud. To show an audience all that she had taught me. I turned forward, struck the floor with the edge of my foot, and I leaped. I'm sure it was only a turn and a half in reality, but oh goodness, it felt as good as a triple. The women were on their feet, throwing gloves and socks, pretending they were flowers.

I stood there in the center of the rink with my eyes closed, listening to the applauding and cheering and whistling, my muscles burning, not feeling like my own anymore. My ankles and knees would never be strong enough to do it again on actual ice. The realization cut through me like a blade. I hoped I would eventually find some meaning in it all, like Clara had with her silver airplanes, because right then I felt so irredeemably sad. I had promised Ingrid that I would always skate. That I would always be free. But that was my last dance.

All those futures that would never be.

I took my bow.

They didn't come. The men, the women, whoever took my magazine, Clem's notes.

Mum called up brightly at 6 p.m. that it was time for tea and I crept downstairs, slowly, cautiously, expecting fire and brimstone. Instead I found that my wet and muddy clothes had been washed and hung up, and the only person acting weird was me.

I stayed on my guard; of course I did.

"Relax, Jessie," my father repeated on a loop, thinking I was coiled tight about going away. "You'll do us proud, I know it."

On the Wednesday, the day before I left, my favorite meal was on the table. Roast chicken. There was a cake too, with the words VIEL GLÜCK! in piped cream and a little plastic figure skating across the icing. I looked into my parents' eyes, just to check, just to make sure that this wasn't to be a last supper of a different kind, but they were genuine and smiling and kind. Dad spoke soppily of all the things I'd done as a kid, seeming to forget Fisher's stiff presence across the table. He talked about the first time I'd put on skates and glided across that rink as if I'd been born with blades for feet. Mum told Dad to stop because he was making her cry, then urged him to tell another story, and another, and another. Lilli was in classic form, arguing pedantically about every vegetable that passed her lips, claiming all the while that she wasn't hungry, then demanding extra portions of pudding. It was how I'd always imagined it would be when I left. I would miss them so much, all their faults. At that table, I regretted everything I'd ever done to cross my parents, to disappoint them, all the things they knew and all the things they didn't.

The next morning, Lilli sat on top of my trunk so Mum could close the clasps, while I was forced to have a conversation on the phone with Katrin at athletics camp. ("Good luck, yeah," she said, unbothered. "Thanks," I replied with utter nonchalance. We honored the truth of our relationship.) Dad carried my hulking trunk down the stairs and to the end of the driveway. We waited for the bus to come. I was dressed in my BDM best, the knot in my necktie tight and straight, my Party pin shiny and centered on my pocket. I didn't care one bit that I'd have to make small talk with Dani Hannah all the way there. I was just so thrilled that the day had come. I was blessed, I decided on that warm September day, to have been given a talent so clear and obvious that I could carve a whole life from it. Disappear into it. Forget everything else. I was blessed to have been given a second chance to have that life, after what I did. I would have to steer a whole new path, and once I was away from home I would be able to decide how to do that.

Here it was, a beginning . . .

The large, black car pulled up, and the driver got out to put my trunk in the boot. I was too busy with good-byes to ask where the bus was, where Dani was. Fisher gave me a stiff peck on the cheek before stepping aside for me to have my last moments with my family. Mum hung a purse of money around my neck and sobbed as she held me tight. Dad kissed my head. Lilli threw her arms up and around my waist, and Wolf stood on his hind legs, trying to be part of the hug.

As I was driven away, my father stood very upright and solid chested on the pavement. He didn't wave. He had his arm around Mum, who had tears spilling down her cheeks and a tissue balled up in her hand. Lilli had already made her way into the front garden of the empty house next door and was picking the last of the summer daisies, Wolf sniffing at her fingers, hoping for food.

"Ich liebe euch," I said to my family as the car took me away from Lincoln Drive, though they wouldn't have heard me or even seen my lips move through that blacked-out glass.

And I meant it, when I said it. I really did.

Ask me now if I love them. Go on, ask me.

Because despite everything, I'd have to say that I do.

drei

AUGUST 2014

One day, a cat started coming into our kitchen.

It was white with a fat, black tail and splotches of tortoiseshell across its back. For a stray, it was remarkably sturdy, but there are plenty of mice to be had on the farms around here. I could tell it was old, from its fur, from its soft belly hanging low. It had a rolling gait, one paw put right in front of the other as if walking on an invisible tightrope — one that it might fall off any minute.

"Guten Tag!" I said as it wound itself through the gap in our door.

Meow! it replied, loud and demanding, mimicking the patterns of my speech.

"How are you?" I asked.

Me-meow!

I went over and lifted up its tail — it was definitely a girl.

It continued to visit every day, so I gave her some ham scraps and a saucer of milk. But she only sniffed and took a quick lick. She seemed interested in the idea of food but not the actuality.

When Jan saw the cat he said he would have to take a spade to it.

"It can barely walk," he said. "There's something wrong with it."

"It seems happy enough," I said.

"Happy enough for what?" he asked.

"I dunno." I shrugged. "Life?"

It's amazing what you can get away with when you're only talking about a cat.

Jan and I married in March, just when the buds were starting to show on the lilac trees. He's not so bad, Jan, and I could have done worse. I like him enough (that word again, *enough*) and I think I might get to like him more. He's kind and gentle and not so arrogant that I can't open my mouth and have an opinion every now and again. Some of the girls at Elmdene got sent off with some real chest-beating bears, let me tell you.

Jan looks exactly like the big, blond boys in the pictures in our biology books from school — all chest muscles, pumping arms, and strong thighs, striding through the long grass in running shorts with their eyes on the horizon. Angels, gods, paragons of animals. It's sort of disgusting if you think about it. So I try not to.

I enjoy the touch of him, though. I suppose I've never really had much of a problem with that.

We sat through hours of brain-bogglingly embarrassing lectures on sex at Elmdene. Women, unlike men, are always capable of intercourse. Women should keep themselves attractive or must hold themselves responsible for the rise in male homosexuality. That kind of thing. It only left me wondering how happy I might have been if I had lived in a world where I could have settled down with GG. Or Clementine.

What a piece of work is a man.

I wore one of the white dresses they kept in the cupboard for the ceremonies. They tried to make it seem sacred and special and mystical. There were flowers, a shrine, and pledges to the Fatherland. It reminded me of that day in April when I was ten years old, being sworn into the Jungmädelschaft:

I promise
In the Hitler Youth
To do my duty
At all times
In love and loyalty
To help the Führer
So help me god.

Back then, when I was ten, it had felt like the biggest deal, such a huge responsibility, but the marriage ceremony? Deep down, we girls all knew (or at least I did and really not that deep down at all) that these marriages were just a formality. They weren't going to let us out of Elmdene unless we did it. So we did.

Now I'm Davina Gunn. They thought it best that I ditch the first name too. Just in case. A proper fresh start. It sounds like a movie star, I think — Davina Gunn. Too much of a name for someone who works a vegetable patch, mucks out chickens, and feeds a few pigs.

Babies will be the next job, I guess.

We spent much of our days at Elmdene in the nursery helping

bathe the babies, feed them, change their diapers. Once they'd been with us awhile and we knew that they were healthy, they were handed over to waiting couples. Nice families. When I did my first handover, I got a bit upset and was taken into Matron's office for a talking-to.

I had been thinking about Lilli as I shifted that warm weight in its blanket into the arms of a new mother. The truth finally came and choked me. Lilli had never been ours. I was sure of it. She had arrived fully formed one day, with her blond hair and her blue eyes, looking absolutely nothing like Katrin or me. Of course I didn't tell Matron this.

So many things fell into relief at Elmdene, and at the most unexpected moments. During one of our lengthy evening talks by the fire in the drawing room, Frau Catchpole had us discussing Himmler's diaries. All of a sudden, I remembered that I had, for years, read and memorized parts of Clementine's diary whenever I was at her house and she was out of the room. The memory of it came to me so fresh and vivid, yet I'd not let myself recall it until then.

In one entry, back when we were still very young, she'd written about the robot costume Mother had made for me for the Jungmädel summer costume competition. I had a cardboard box on my head and another around my middle, cardboard tubes on my arms and legs. Any exposed skin was sprayed silver. I had won first prize. Of course.

Or rather, her mum won first prize, Clem had written. *Jess could barely move, couldn't dance around or enjoy any of the food or drink. She got told off for sweating because it made the paint run. I feel so sorry for Jess and how her parents use her as a weapon in their ugly war.*

I burst into tears, right there in the drawing room, in front of everyone.

"Whatever's the matter?" Frau Catchpole had asked, forcing me to pretend that some passage of Herr Himmler's memoir was so perfectly phrased that it had made me emotional.

To Matron, after I had gotten upset about handing over a baby, I said, "It will never happen again." I told her that I had gotten too attached to that particular child — a boy the nurses had called Sebastian — and that was why I had quivered, gone dizzy, and refused to let him go. This wasn't exactly a lie. I couldn't even begin to imagine how those other girls felt, the valuable girls who were sent to Elmdene because they had gotten themselves into trouble with valuable boys. If Fisher had had his way that evening in the meeting hall . . .

They arrived at Elmdene, those girls, all saucer eyed and full and fat, only to leave empty-handed, expected to go home and act like none of it had ever happened. Or go back to their correction camp and get back to work, fielding all the "Jerry Bag" name-calling because they'd dared to sleep with a member of the male staff to get an extra bit of bread.

They made me feel lucky. At least I didn't have to go back anywhere and pretend.

I have a new life.

And it makes me see how my old life was chaotic and noisy, everything jerky and unexpected. The calm isn't as terrifying as I'd thought. I sit with it — this quiet filled with birdsong and barking and the distant sound of tractors. Sometimes there are the voices of cows and sheep, whatever is let out to roam in the field next to ours. I let that quiet in. I don't get out-of-body experiences anymore. I don't feel the need to sing or march or recite anything to keep the feelings at bay.

I am Good Jessika and Bad. All of it is in me. But I am whole. And I am here.

Still, I let myself go backward and forward in time occasionally and think about what might have been. If I had gone to skate camp, would I be competing for my country now? I find it hard to picture — me doing something so beautiful in the name of the Reich. To pull off a triple you need a strong belief, and without Ingrid there, I'm not sure who I would have been doing it for. Ingrid, I know, will be training some new little six-year-old now who skates like she was born with blades for feet. I think about Fisher and guess that Ruby Heigl probably swerved into his lane as soon as I left. I imagine how our marriage might have been, a lifetime of sideways glances, double-crossing, and doubt. I think about Lilli and what story my parents might have told her to explain where I am. I think about what story my parents told themselves.

My story? I run through it in my head all the time. Sometimes I pretend I am in a meeting room much like the one at the grand hotel in Trafalgar Square — carpeted, air-conditioned, air-freshened — except this one is in America. I am being detained, interrogated, and counseled. I try to work out what my ideals and beliefs really are. It feels like being thrust into Red Block all over again, that moment of not knowing which version of the truth to tell. What I feel and what I should feel get mixed up. Sometimes I tell my story as if I am back in one of those whitewashed rooms at Highpoint with the three faceless men and the tape recorder whirring. I slip into old ways of thinking as easily as I slip into my German tongue. I try desperately to get myself off the hook, only to realize that I have incriminated myself all over again.

But usually I imagine myself telling my story to you. A girl much like me, a woman ready for life to begin—except that you have spent your life reading those magazines of Clementine's, wearing your trousers too tight and listening to boys sing about love. *It's all nothing,* I imagine you thinking. *It's all so easy that I don't really have to think at all.*

When this gets too exhausting, I read. I disappear into other people's worlds. When we took over the farm, the house was completely derelict. It was our job to bring it back into shape. I found a box of old books in the loft.

"Maybe some of them are illegal," Jan suggested.

"Maybe," I said with a smile. "I won't tell if you don't."

I'm working my way through *The Rime of the Ancient Mariner* at the moment.

And the coming wind did roar more loud
And the sails did sigh like sedge.

Perhaps the real reason I do not complain or kick against my situation is that I see this time as penance. And there is penance more to do.

And I am happy to do it.

Ready.

Deutschland erwache!

The cat sleeps in the kitchen now. I found an old crate for her and put a folded towel inside. She snores, because she is fat and because there is almost certainly something wrong with her nasal passages as well as her legs. She grumbles in her dreams in a way that reminds me of Wolf and makes me homesick. He is my weak spot.

The snoring is another thing that makes Jan want to fetch his spade.

"I like the sound," I tell him.

"She rattles like she's faulty," he says.

"So what?"

Jan puts his hands on his hips, watching her sleep, twisting his mouth as he tries to work out this puzzle.

"She might have kittens," he says.

"Won't that be nice," I reply.

The cat is my first victory. Softly, softly catchee monkey.

When I left Red Block, with hugs and kisses and messages for loved ones, Clara had great expectations for me. She liked to use the image of a forest fire. That was how protest and defiance spread—fast, from one tree to the next. Clementine got her idea from Egypt, Clara said; they were all doing it there. Just one person at first, then another, then another. So who in the Greater German Reich, in England, would be next?

I told her, "I'm not sure that Clementine did the right thing."

"How can you say that?" Clara gasped.

"Because what good is she now?" I said. "Locked up . . . Or worse."

Clara exhausted all her contacts trying to find out what happened to the Hart family. We never got anything conclusive. Sometimes I am grateful for this. If she's not certainly dead, then she must always stay alive. Though in the camp I so often thought to myself, *Death must be so much nicer than here.*

"She got her message out, didn't she?" Clara snapped back at me. "She ruffled some feathers."

But we both knew there was no revolution back in August. Not really. Only inside of me.

"The strongest rebellion is to stay alive," I told her. "That way you can change things, have your say. Outnumber them."

In our biology textbooks at school, there was this repeated phrase alongside those images of the "right" kind of families and the "wrong" kind:

Deutschland must live, even if we die!

The same went for us, I told Clara, if we ever wanted to have our voices heard.

After celebrating Christmas in Red Block, singing "O Tannenbaum" though we had no tree with lovely branches to sing it to, I believed they would take me away from the camp to be executed. The inspirational poster on the wall of the factory cafeteria toward the end read: BEFORE THE EARTH TAKES YOU BACK, HAVE YOU MADE IT FRUITFUL? I hadn't. For most of my life, I'd been part of the problem, not the solution. On the table, a prisoner who had eaten there long before me had etched into the wood: THEY'LL SHOOT YOU ANYWAY.

So I couldn't have been more surprised when they dropped

me off at Elmdene, a stately rectory in the countryside with large wood-paneled rooms, crisp white sheets, decent food, and flower-filled gardens. I'd been washed clean of my sins, I'd learned the meaning of hard work, and now I was to be taught to be civilized again.

I got proper Faith and Beauty classes after all. Eat your heart out, Angelika Baker. I became an expert in hairstyles and all those lovely dances. Cooking too, weaving, darning, flower arranging—skills that have been almost completely useless while I've been living with Jan.

I spend my days in wellies, in the company of sows, hoping that Nina is back with her piggy family somewhere. I imagine GG in the same getup as me, wellies and overalls, only in the more glamorous company of horses. Of course I also imagine that she may not have made it to Gloucestershire, that her bus was also replaced by a large black car. But I don't let myself dwell on that too much because I will never know the answer, just like I don't let myself stare when Edith Bauer at the cottage down the way chats and laughs with her mother at their front gate. I will never have that either.

In weaker moments, I doubt that the signature on the order to lock me up was genuine, and I believe that my family is still out there waiting for me to return. In stronger moments, when I can be honest with myself, I know it can't be true. And more than that, I cannot see myself slotting back into my old position.

I am not what I was.

So I continue to build this new life. I have no real foundations, no clear structural plans. I'm laying bricks on top of riddles and secrets—the ones that belonged to my parents and their parents before them and their parents before them. I'm laying bricks on ghosts. It's not the easiest task, but I'll make it stand up if it's the last thing I do. I have an image of how it's going to look, at least.

Of course, in recounting all this to you I have told you a lie. Or rather I have left out something that you might consider to be crucial.

I did get to use the lovely dances with Jan. Once. We were driven out to the market town near Elmdene at the beginning of the year for a local festival with lights and food stalls and music. The Elmdene leaders thought it would be a good chance for us to get to know our prospective husbands. We ate giant pretzels and sipped spiced wine to keep back the cold, and then danced in the square following the shouts of the caller. "Allemande left! Weave the circle! Bow to your partner and blow him a kiss!"

They had also installed an outdoor ice rink as part of the festivities. This was just beyond exciting to most of the girls. And the men — though they tried not to show it. I didn't join in. I stood at the edge and watched as the girls tried swirling to the lilting breaths of the prelude from *La Traviata* while also avoiding the daredevil knee-sliding of little boys threatening to poleax them at every turn. I used to think that the only place I could ever be free was on the ice. Now I believe otherwise.

Jan refused to skate too, thinking he must keep me company. He held my hands to keep them warm. This was when I realized he had potential, that there was something in him, really in him, and that I could make him see it too in time. This is what Clementine must have thought when she first met me. I hope.

Or in that moment when I did the "wrong thing" and kissed her. *Oh my darling, oh my darling, oh my darling Clementine.*

She was the princess, I was the frog.

Thou art lost and gone forever, dreadful sorry, Clementine.

My turn.

I have the name of the village in Cornwall memorized, and the name of the cottage too. It is in me — as if I once slipped the paper it was written on into my mouth, chewed it up, and swallowed. Clementine knew I read her diary, she must have. Why else would she have put it in there?

One day Jan and I will go and visit, not because I think we should escape but because I want to convince the people who go there to stay. *What will we achieve if we all run away to America?* I will tell them. *What will change if we do not take arms against this sea of troubles?* I will make them see that the Reich cannot control our desires, which makes it a fight worth fighting. A fight we are likely to win. It will be difficult, I know, but I am trained well. For now, I must keep my head down like Ingrid while slowly delivering knocks and taps, like I learned from my mother. Then, when the moment is right, with a fire in my belly and in my heart, slow and steady . . . REVOLUTION, ARSCHLÖCHER.

"I used to know a girl who was good at ice skating," I told Jan that evening as we watched the others slide and stumble. We had been asked not to talk about our pasts, but that didn't seem fair. These boys were taking us on with assurances that our heritage was good and that our sins had been erased, but with no actual information on what any of us had done. I felt I owed him something, even if they were exactly like us, being forced to marry to atone for the terrible things they had done before.

"Really?" said Jan, pulling my hands up to his mouth and blowing warmth into both of our gloves. I think he could see that there was something in me as well. A truth, maybe; the one that can only belong to you. "How good was she?" he asked. "Your friend?"

"Oh, she was really good," I told him. "She was really, really good."

Glossary of German
Words and Phrases

aber	but/however
aber ich habe einen . . .	but I have a . . .
alle in die zugeteilten Räume! Sofort!	go to your designated room! Now!
an einen Ort, von dem ich nicht zurück kommen kann	somewhere I can't come back from
antworte mir!	answer me!
Arschlöcher	assholes
aufstehen!	get up!
Ausgewählte Reden	Selected Speeches
Ausgewählte Reden aus der Geschichte	Selected Speeches from History
Bund	league/association (as in Bund Deutscher Mädel—the League of German Girls)
dann	then
Das Buch Isidor	a collection of anti-Semitic sketches by Mjölnir and Goebbels, 1928

Das Deutsche Mädel	*The German Lassie* (monthly magazine for Hitler Youth girls)
das Dritte Reich	the Third Reich
das ist lecker	that is delicious
deutsch/deutsche/ deutscher/deutsches/ deutschen	German
deutsches Mädchen	German girl
Deutschland: Damals und Heute	*Germany: Then and Today*
dieser gute deutsche Mann	this good German man
drei	three
"Eine Flamme Ward Gegeben"	"A Flame Was Given" (song)
eins	one
Endsieg	final victory
Entschuldigung	sorry
er ist ein guter Mann	he is a good man
erzähl mir von deinem Vater	tell me about your father
erzähl mir von dem Ort, an dem du vorher gewohnt hast	tell me about the place where you used to live, before

erzähl mir was von letzten Wohnort	tell me about the last place you lived
"Es Klopft Mein Herz Bum-Bum"	"It Knocks My Heart, Boom-Boom" (German war-era song)
es tut mir leid	I'm sorry
es war bestimmt nicht so schön wie hier, oder?	I bet it wasn't as nice as here, was it?
Familie, Kinder, Haus	family, children, home
Frau/Fräulein	Mrs./Miss
Frau Aufseherin	Madame Overseer/Matron
Frauenschaft	Women's Association
Frauen Warte	*Women's Observer* (Nazi women's magazine)
Fritten	fries
Führer	leader
für dich, für uns beide	for you, for us both
Götterdämmerung	the title of an 1876 opera by Richard Wagner, meaning "the twilight of the gods (a disastrous end)"
grüß dich	hi (literally: greeting you)
guten Tag	hello (literally: good day)
Hakenkreuz	hooked cross (swastika)
Hausfrau	housewife

Herr	Mr.
Herzchen	darling (literally: little heart)
ich hab dich lieb/ ich liebe dich	I love you (The first is a fond, platonic expression, literally: I have love for you. The second is stronger.)
Ich, Jessika Davina Keller, dulde keine Terrorakte gegen das Großdeutsche Reich!	I, Jessika Davina Keller, cannot condone acts of terrorism against the Greater German Nation!
ich kann mich kaum erinnern	I can hardly remember
ich liebe euch	I love you (plural — to more than one person)
ja, gut	yes, fine
Jungmädel	Hitler Youth group for girls ages 10–14
Jungmädelschaft	fellowship of young girls
Jungvolk	Hitler Youth group for boys ages 10–14
Kaffee und Kuchen	coffee and cake
Kameradschaft	fellowship of boys
kaputt	broken
"Kein Schöner Land in Dieser Zeit"	"No More Beautiful Land in This Time" (song)

"Leben ohne Liebe kannst du nicht"	"You Can't Live Without Love" (song)
Leberwurst	liverwurst, a sausage made from pigs' or calves' livers
Mädchen	girl
Mädelschaft	fellowship of girls
Mädel von Heute, Mütter von Morgen	*Girls of Today, Mothers of Tomorrow*
mein kleiner süßer Singvogel	my little sweet songbird
Mischmasch	mishmash, hodgepodge, or concoction
Mutti	mommy
Nationalsozialistische Deutsche Arbeiterpartei	National Socialist German Worker's Party (Nazis)
nein, überhaupt nicht so schön wie hier	no, nowhere near as nice as here
Nestbeschmutzer	nest defiler, a whistleblower, or a traitor
Oma	grandma
"O Tannenbaum"	"O Christmas Tree" (song)
Papi	daddy
Reich	nation/empire
sag es	say it
salutier, Schlampe	salute, slut

Schätzchen	darling/dear (literally: little treasure)
Schutzpolizei	security police (uniformed police)
Schutzstaffel	the SS Nazi protection force
Schweinehund	pig dog
Schwester	sister
Seelöwe	sea lion
sing fröhlich, du Hure	sing gladly, whore
sing, Schlampe	sing, slut/bitch
Singvogel	songbird
Sonderhäftling(e)	special inmate(s)
Sonnenwendfeier	summer solstice celebrations
Sonnenwendfeuer	summer solstice fire
Staatsfeind	enemy of the state
Sturmbannführer	Major
"Tanz Rüber, Tanz Nüber"	"Dance Hither, Dance Thither" (song)
Uropa	great-grandpa
Untermenschen	subhumans
Unterscharführer	Junior Squad Leader
Vater	father

verdammt	dammit
Verräter	traitor
viel Glück	good luck
was sagste, Fritz, sollen wir eins für den Führer machen?	whaddya say, Fritz, shall we have one for the Führer?
Wehrmacht	armed forces of the Third Reich
willkommen	welcome
Winterhilfswerk	an annual aid program (literally: Winter Help Work)
wir brauchen ihn. Wir brauchen das.	we need him. We need this.
wir gehören dir	we belong to you
wohin?	where to?
wohin gehst du?	where are you going?
zeig mir dein Herz	show me your heart
zeig mir deine Liebe	show me your love
Zimtschnecken	cinnamon buns (literally: cinnamon snails)
zwei	two
ZweiKinder System	Two-Child System
Zwischenraum	literally: between space

Historical Notes on *The Big Lie*

"This is science fiction, but it is science fiction in
terms of what is here now."

—William S. Burroughs talking about The Nova Trilogy

Okay, so *The Big Lie* isn't, strictly speaking, "science fiction" but it does take place in an unreal world of my creation. I prefer the term "alt-history" or Margaret Atwood's description for this kind of book—"speculative fiction." *The Big Lie* is me taking a guess at what might have happened.

I returned to my copy of Margaret Atwood's *The Handmaid's Tale*—which I first gobbled up as a teenager—when I was asked to write a note for the back of *The Big Lie*. In the back of Margaret Atwood's book you'll find "Historical Notes on *The Handmaid's Tale*" where she imagines a Cambridge professor speaking in the year 2195, giving his opinion on the long-dead oppressive regime described in her story.

This fictional professor explains how none of the cruelty in Gilead was new or original; it had all gone on before somewhere on Earth. He then backs this up with real examples from the reader's world.

This is when you come to see the power of science fiction (or speculative fiction or alt-history or whatever you want to call it)—at its heart, it's not really fiction. It's a patchwork of the terrible things humans do to other humans, all the time, every day, in our very real world.

So it was with *The Big Lie*. There was very little that I had to make up. My fiction just grew from the facts.

The Bund Deutscher Mädel was a genuine organization in Nazi Germany that instilled a fanatical love for the Führer and the Fatherland among its teenage female recruits. Women were encouraged to be strong and pure as the nation's future baby makers, and for a period young couples took marriage examinations to ensure they were healthy enough to make a good match.

Mädel von Heute, Mütter von Morgen was a real book that taught young girls about being a woman, *Das Deutsche Mädel* was a genuine companion magazine for members of the BDM, and those posters on the walls of the meeting hall were produced weekly by the Nazi Party's Central Propaganda Office. When Jessika describes exercises in her school biology textbook, she is describing the real pages of *Leitfaden Der Biologie 1*, which instructed students on what would happen to society if "quality" people didn't do their duty and have more than two children. And all the songs Jessika sings in *The Big Lie* can be found in Nazi music books. When Jessika's mother tries to give her daughter a warning as they wash dishes, she alludes to *The Poisonous Mushroom*, a children's storybook designed to instill a fear of Jewish people. Jess and Lilli's puppet show, *Trust No Fox on the Green Heath and No Jew on His Oath*, is from another such storybook.

But it wasn't just the Nazis who were writing. Their detractors, predominantly Communists, produced *Tarnschriften* (camouflaged publications) that on the outside looked like innocent pamphlets on housekeeping and shampoo but inside criticized Hitler's regime. Here came the inspiration for Clementine's smuggled magazines.

Jessika's experiences at Highpoint are based on accounts that I heard and read from women who were held at Ravensbrück concentration camp. The babies at Elmdene developed from stories of Aryan children stolen from their Eastern European parents to be brought up in "good" Nazi families. Disabled children, like George Hart, were euthanized under Nazi racial hygiene rules, while women (and men) suffered forced sterilizations for "health" reasons, both physical and mental.

Even the small details came from a place of truth. Clara's letter about silver airplanes is a paraphrase of a beautiful piece of writing by a political prisoner in Ravensbrück to her husband, words that I just could not shake from my head. Also etched into my mind was a piece of graffiti etched onto the wall of a death camp — *They'll shoot you anyway.*

So perhaps all I did was create a terrible jigsaw puzzle rather than write a book. But if that is what I did, it is certainly not a jigsaw puzzle of the past.

The main leaping-off point for this book was my seven-year-old son asking at the dinner table, "What would have happened if the Nazis had won World War II?" Although a stable of books have tried to answer this question (mainly written for adults, I might add, mainly written by men), I only decided to add my own thoughts to this collection after Justin Bieber visited Anne Frank's house in Amsterdam and wrote in the visitors' book: "*Anne was a great girl. Hopefully she would have been a Belieber.*"

Social media was awash with fury about this remark. But I liked what he'd written. Maybe Anne would have been a Belieber. Why must we put her in a musty box labeled "the past"? Read Anne Frank's diary and you'll find a fun, rebellious girl who liked music and boys and talking smart.

It is a seduction to think of the past as another place where they do things differently (to paraphrase L. P. Hartley). It lets us off the hook too easily. If the Nazis rose up now, we tell ourselves, we would never have been hypnotized. We are nothing like those people from history. Which leads me neatly back to that William S. Burroughs quote . . .

The Big Lie is science fiction written in terms of what is happening right now.

Across the world, young gay people are still sent to priests, psychiatrists, and needle-wielding doctors to "correct" their sexuality. At least seventy-eight countries have laws against same-sex relationships, and in five of these countries you can face the death penalty if convicted.

In Kiev in 2012, a topless Femen protestor took a chain saw to a giant wooden crucifix because she was furious at the sentencing of the Pussy Riot protestors, who dared to express their opinion about their leaders and the church. On release from prison, Pussy Riot's Maria Alyokhina and Nadezhda Tolokonnikova spoke of the gynecological examinations they had suffered while incarcerated and how they had to sift feces from the drains before they could take a shower.

In 2010, a young man named Mohamed Bouazizi, who worked as a street vendor in Sidi Bouzid in Tunisia, had his goods confiscated by the authorities. No longer willing to tolerate continual harassment from the police, and desperate for the return of his produce and equipment, Bouazizi set himself on fire outside the governor's office — and triggered a revolution.

In the U.K., where I live, the front pages of the newspapers choose a different group of immigrants each week to blame for unemployment, crime, and problems within the health service. Only a few years ago the British National Party managed to hold two seats in the European Parliament and get a voice on *BBC Question Time*, a party which, in an echo of Jess's schoolbook, says on its website: *Given current demographic trends, we, the indigenous British people, will become an ethnic minority in our own country well within sixty years—and most likely sooner.*

British children are separated by the schools they go to—though money is the great divider here, not the shape of their foreheads—and the children who attend the small percentage of private schools will go on to occupy a disproportionately large number of the positions of power. And while society may not demand that women stay fit and pure for childbirth, if a high-profile woman should leave the house without makeup or if she gains some weight, that woman is then shamed in the national press. (The illegal magazine that Jessika pores over in the book is real, a recent issue of a popular title.)

The Western Allies like to think of themselves, historically, as the great liberators of the Jewish concentration camps. Yet in May 1943, while World War II was in its final years, a Jewish Polish socialist named Szmul Zygielbojm killed himself in London. *By my death*, his final letter read, *I wish to give expression to my most profound protest against the inaction in which the world watches and permits the destruction of the Jewish people.* On the day I sat down to write this, I listened to accounts on the radio of Jewish people in London, who live in fear of violent anti-Semitic attacks every day.

Perhaps what finally convinced me to write this book was a conversation I had with my five-year-old after a gymnastics class. "If you fall to the bottom of the foam pit," he told me, "you end up in China."

Just like Jessika in the book, I laughed. And just like Lilli, he was cross that I didn't believe him.

It made me realize how readily we accept the things adults tell us, no matter how big the lie. We might be told these things directly, for fun (Santa Claus, anyone?), but we also receive a drip-feed of snobbery, sexism, and racism from society as we grow up. *Slowly, slowly catchee monkey.* Often these lies stay with us and they feel like truths. *I must behave this way because I am a woman. I must not trust this group of people because they are bad. We are a democracy and our leaders do everything in our best interests.*

So when Jessika says at the start of the book that people like us challenge everything just because we can—is she right? Or do we think in the way she describes at the end of the book—*It's all so easy, I don't really have to think at all?*

I'm not suggesting you set fire to yourself in the market square. Absolutely not. Please don't. You are much more effective while you are alive. I'm saying revolution starts by asking, *Is this right?* And if it isn't, trying to do something about it.

Julie Mayhew
United Kingdom
2015

Acknowledgments

Lots of people helped me write this book.

I spent a great deal of time at the Wiener Library and am incredibly grateful for their extensive archive of Nazi-era literature. I want to extend particular thanks to Kat Hübschmann for her expertise on the experiences of young women living under Hitler. I am indebted to all the historians whose nonfiction works provided sparks for this novel. If you would like to read more on the themes in *The Big Lie*, a list of some suggested titles follows.

In 2014, I was lucky to be at the Southbank Centre to hear Horst von Wächter and Niklas Frank, now in their seventies, talk about their high-ranking Nazi fathers. While Niklas denounces his father, Horst still believes that his father was somehow a good man. Their honest discussion of their paternal relationships helped me shape Jessika's psyche and her connection with her father.

Thanks to all the coaches and skaters at Planet Ice Hemel Hempstead who helped me, probably without realizing. If you want to learn any of Jessika's basic moves, Robert Burgerman's videos at ice-burg.co.uk are a great resource.

The German language in this book sounds colloquial and genuine because of guidance from Claire Brooks and native speaker Kat Sellner. As well as pruning my dialogue, Kat was incredibly generous in sharing her experiences of being a young person in Germany now, growing up under the long shadow of World War II. Tausend Dank, Kat.

Lee Simpson taught me the difference between the World Wide Web and the Internet, several times, with diagrams. Though it was never necessary to explicitly explain it in the book, it was important to me that Simon and Clementine Hart's manipulation of communications hangs together in the background. The only reason that it does is because of Lee and his patient technical explanations of DDoS, VPN, etc.

Thank you firefighter Guy Pedliman for teaching me how to, well, fight a fire. And to my husband, for lending me his degree in history, political thought, and philosophy. You can have it back now, Thom. I hope I haven't scuffed the corners too much.

A raised power-to-the-people fist to Hot Key Books, who are certainly publishing's rebels. Thanks in particular to Emily Thomas for championing the book, Matilda Johnson for her passionate editing, Jenny Jacoby for her keen eye, and to Jet Purdie for tirelessly tracking down our cover girl in the U.K. edition. In the U.S., I give my thank-yous to Nicole Raymond, Katie Cunningham, and the Candlewick team.

My agent, Louise "Marvelously Nitty-Gritty" Lamont, has stoked the fire in the belly of this story every step of the way, and has always had Jessika and Clementine's backs.

Want to Know More?

For further information about life under Nazism, I can recommend the following. A few of these are hard to get from bookshops and libraries—try secondhand book websites.

Binet, Laurent. *HHhH*. New York: Vintage, 2013.
Seemingly a novel about a real-life plot to assassinate the chief of the SS, but really it's a story about an author's struggle to tell the truth. Do all accounts of history contain lies?

Crew, David F., ed. *Nazism and German Society 1933–1945*. New York: Routledge, 1994.
Includes several revealing essays on women's lives in Nazi Germany, and explores how some people resisted the Nazis and others complied.

de Gaulle Anthonioz, Geneviève. *God Remained Outside: An Echo of Ravensbrück*. Translated by Margaret Crosland. London: Souvenir, 1999.
A personal account from Charles de Gaulle's niece, who was sent to Ravensbrück.

Frank, Anne. *The Diary of a Young Girl*. New York: Penguin, 2007.
Whether she would have been a Belieber or not, Anne was a wonderful writer, bringing to life the joys as well as the terrors of being young and Jewish during World War II.

Funder, Anna. *Stasiland*. London: Granta, 2011.
This is actually about the former East Germany rather than
Nazism, but Anna Funder's book is useful if you want to
understand more about how states try to control their people.

Heineman, Elizabeth D. *What Difference Does a Husband Make?*
Women and Marital Status in Nazi and Post-War Germany.
Berkeley: University of California Press, 1999.
Particularly good for researching the Nazis' attitudes about
marriage—and their management of it.

Hirschmann, Maria Anne. *Hansi: The Girl Who Loved the*
Swastika. Eastbourne, England: Kingsway, 1973.
An unusual autobiography from a former BDM member.
When Hansi discards her Nazi thinking, she replaces it with
the evangelical belief that God speaks to her.

Humbert, Agnès. *Résistance: A Woman's Journal of Struggle and*
Defiance in Occupied France. New York: Bloomsbury, 2008.
A stunning memoir by art historian Agnes Humbert, who
was put in prison for her part in the French Resistance and
forced to work in appalling conditions in factories in Eastern
Europe.

Knopp, Guido. *Hitler's Children*. Translated by Angus McGeoch.
Stroud, England: Sutton, 2002.
Exposes how seductive the Hitler Youth and Bund Deutscher
Mädel were to young people in Nazi Germany.

Lower, Wendy. *Hitler's Furies: German Women in the Nazi Killing Fields*. London: Chatto & Windus, 2003.

An abundance of evidence demonstrating that women were not always innocent bystanders in Hitler's regime.

Maschmann, Melita. *Account Rendered: A Dossier on My Former Self*. Lexington, MA: Plunkett Lake Press, 2013.

Melita, who was in the BDM, writes this book as a letter to her former Jewish school friend, trying to explain why she betrayed her during the war.

Morrison, Jack G. *Ravensbrück: Everyday Life in a Women's Concentration Camp 1939–45*. Princeton, NJ: Markus Wiener, 2000.

A comprehensive resource for understanding the day-to-day horrors, and mundanities, of life in the women's camp.

Overy, R. J. *The Battle of Britain: Myth and Reality*. New York: Penguin, 2010.

This book gives some insight into the never-realized Operation Seelöwe (the Nazis' plan to invade Britain) and is useful for understanding the cracks in the Allies' campaign that were fortunately not exploited.

Schoppman, Claudia. *Days of Masquerade: Life Stories of Lesbians During the Third Reich*. Translated by Allison Brown. New York: Columbia University Press, 1996.

Vibrant and heartbreaking firsthand accounts from women forced to hide their sexuality in Nazi Germany.

Sereny, Gitta. *Into That Darkness: From Mercy Killing to Mass Murder.* London: Pimlico, 1995.

Truly startling book in which the author attempts to understand how a charming family man came to be the commandant of Treblinka death camp by spending time with him in the prison where he is serving time for his war crimes.

Sommer-Lefkovits, Elizabeth. *Are You Here in This Hell Too? Memories of Troubled Times 1944–1945.* London: Menard, 1995.

A stark memoir by a woman who was deported to Ravensbrück and then Bergen-Belsen, and survived.

Online Resources, Films, and Organizations

Rachel Jane Anderson. "Lieder, Totalitarianism, and the Bund Deutscher Mädel: Girls' Political Coercion Through Song." McGill University, Canada, 2002.
http://digitool.library.mcgill.ca/dtl_publish/8/29493.html
An online research paper examining the power of the songs in Wir Mädel singen!, *the Bund Deutscher Mädel's official music book.*

Arts Emergency — www.arts-emergency.org
This action group works toward making arts and humanities careers accessible to all young people, and runs a national alternative to the old-boy network that aims to create privilege for people without privilege.

Calvin College — http://research.calvin.edu/
This website has a large archive of Nazi propaganda, including those weekly NSDAP posters referenced by Jessika in the book.

United States Holocaust Memorial Museum — www.ushmm.org
A comprehensive resource on the Holocaust, but also a good place to go for more on the treatment of LGBTQ people by the Nazis.

We Are Legion: The Story of the Hacktivists. Luminant, 2012.
For an insight into hacking and organized online protest, this is a great documentary.